Silken Chains

Sophie took her hand away from Abbie's breast and reverted to shelling the peas, her eyes on her work.

'Are you alright?' she said matter-of-factly.

'I think so,' Abbie said faintly. 'But I don't know what's happening to me.'

'Are you wet?'

She nodded. Now that the feelings were starting to subside, she knew how marvellous they had been, though while they were happening, they had frightened her as if she was going into the dark and unknown.

'Well, you've got all the right responses, Miss Abbie, so there's nothing to fear when the time comes. And that's how you'll need to be for a man to pleasure you,' Sophie said with satisfaction.

For G.

Silken Chains
Jodi Nicol

BLACK LACE

Black Lace books contain sexual fantasies.
In real life, always practise safe sex.

This edition published in 2003 by
Black Lace
Thames Wharf Studios
Rainville Road
London W6 9HA

Originally published 1997

Printed and bound by Mackays of Chatham PLC

ISBN 0 352 33143 7

Chapter One

Abigail Richmond's parents had frequently been
heard to comment that their daughter had been
born curious, and her insatiable thirst for knowledge
had found her in plenty of trouble in her tender years,
since well-brought-up young Victorian girls were not
supposed to question things, but to accept demurely
whatever fate dicated for them.

But feminine as she was, Abigail had also been born
with a strong-willed nature, and the kind of quick-
thinking mind that was more usually attributed to a
man. She had rejected any idea of fate acting on her
behalf, when fate had cruelly killed both her parents in
a freak boating accident and she was despatched to the
care of an elderly uncle.

It was a situation that suited neither of them, and
severely restricted the untamed spirit that was yearning
to be set free. Living in the sterile environment of a man
who found her presence a nuisance and an irritation,
with only a dreary tutor for company most days, was
certainly never going to endear her uncle to Abigail.

For that reason she spent more and more time in the
lively kitchen atmosphere below stairs, rather than in

1

the stuffy above-stairs chambers in The Grange. In any case, to Abbie, gossip with the free-and-easy kitchen-maids was far more enlightening than any tutorial lessons. Kitchen maids knew all about a side of life about which she dearly wanted to learn.

By now Abigail was a nubile young woman of almost eighteen, ripe and ready for love, and more than irritated by the fact that these low-bred girls apparently found it so easy to lift their skirts and take a tumble, whatever that entailed, with any boy who asked them, while she was still confined to the boring schoolroom and music and drawing lessons. She especially envied Sophie, who was the same age as herself, but vastly more experienced.

'You'll have me shot if your uncle was to know what you wanted me to tell you, Miss Abbie,' Sophie giggled. 'Besides, I'm not sure I ought to be saying these things to you. There's time enough for you to learn about the wicked ways of young gentlemen.'

Abigail exclaimed impatiently. 'I'm not talking about young gentlemen,' she persisted. 'Your Tom doesn't come into that class, does he?'

Sophie's eyes gleamed, seeing that sudden heightening of the young lady's cheeks, and the way her breasts rose and fell inside the bodice of her pretty dress. Lord, but she was turning into a real beauty, Sophie thought, with that glorious blonde hair that caught the light in a sheen of silver strands, and those clear blue eyes that went a deeper and more lustrous shade whenever Sophie tantalised her with hints of what went on after dark in Tom's hay loft.

And that mouth, that soft, full, inviting mouth – Sophie didn't envy much of the high, stiff-necked life of those upstairs, but she really envied the young mistress that pouting, voluptuous mouth. Tom would envy it too, if he could see it right now, all dewy and half-

2

parted, and just the right size to capture a throbbing part of him between those neat little teeth –

Sophie grinned, remembering last night, and thankful that she always kept Tom well away from The Grange and a glimpse of the luscious Miss Abigail Richmond. But she knew a farm-hand like Tom wouldn't be welcomed here. He was too coarse, too brawny, and too outspoken in his likes and dislikes.

'Suck it, girl,' he'd said hoarsely, when she'd sunk her own misshapen teeth into his huge erection. 'Go on. Do it as hard as you like. You won't hurt me –'

She thought it more likely that she might hurt herself if the thing got stuck in her gizzard, but she enjoyed it so much she always resisted telling him that much. Besides, she was hardly going to complain at the size of it when she opened her legs and he thrust it vigorously inside her until she felt near to splitting with the pleasure it gave her.

'Are you going to tell me things today, or not?' the impatient Miss Abigail Richmond said now. They were in the secluded kitchen garden where the kitchen-maid was gathering peas for the evening meal.

'What things?' Sophie teased her.

'You know! What it's like being with a man – and I don't just mean walking in the garden with him, so don't fob me off any longer. You've got to tell me, Sophie – or I might just tell my uncle where you sneak off to every night.'

'You little bitch! You'd do that and all, wouldn't you?' the girl said indignantly.

Abbie immediately backed down. If she once told her puritan Uncle Brindley what she knew, Sophie would be dismissed at once. And she didn't want that. She was fond of Sophie, and she quickly put her hand on the maid's arm.

'No, I wouldn't. It was a silly thing to say, and you

know how I'm always saying silly things without thinking. Forgive me, Sophie.'

'Yes, well, we all know you speak before your brain has time to start working. All right then, let's go into the shrubbery, and I'll give you a lesson your strait-laced tutor ain't up to.'

Abbie followed the girl, her heart pounding. Until now, Sophie had never actually said what *really* happened between her and her Tom. It was always suggestive remarks and *double entendres* that got Abbie more and more frustrated at trying to guess the finer details. Because of her uncle's strict and rigid ways, there were no relevant books in the house to tell her anything.

She was as ignorant of both the pleasures and mechanics of sexual matters as it was possible to be, and only the developing longings of her own body told her there was far more to be learned in the world than could ever be found in the schoolroom.

And it was making her angry and frustrated to think that this simple girl knew all about it, and she didn't. What was the good of so-called education if you didn't even know the most fundamental things about a man and a woman?

The two young women sat down on one of the shrubbery benches, well hidden from the old house, and Sophie began shelling peas into her bowl. It was all very well having agreed to tell the young lady what she wanted to know. But where to begin? she was thinking, so as not to frighten little Miss Innocent half to death, or to push her the other way, straight into some rogue's arms?

'Tell me, Sophie,' Abbie commanded. 'Tell me everything you and Tom do in the hay loft, from start to finish. I promise I shan't be shocked.'

Oh no? But the gleam returned to Sophie's eyes. If the

4

little fool wanted to know it all, then she could have it all.

'Well, the first thing we do is kiss and cuddle, see, to get us in the right mood – not that we're ever *not* in the right mood, if you get my meaning.'

'Not really –'

'Gawd Almighty, were you born yesterday or something? The minute I see Tom I'm in the mood, and when I'm not with him I think of him all the time, so I'm fair to dripping by the time we get together.'

Abbie looked totally blank, and Sophie sighed. This was obviously going to need more explanation than teaching a kitten to lap milk.

'Down here.' She thrust her hand on top of her Mound of Venus over her starched kitchen apron. 'When you're badly wanting a man it gets the juices flowin', see? And seeing as how that's where he'll be puttin' his thing, the wetter you are the better it fits.' And God help us, she was a poet now.

'What thing?'

Sophie stared at her. 'Ain't I been telling you for weeks now that Tom and me get things together?'

'Yes, but I wasn't sure what you meant, and I didn't like to ask, but now it's eating me up with curiosity.'

Sophie took pity on her, seeing the mixture of emotions in her face. And who better to teach her than an expert in the art, which was what she considered herself to be – with Tom's help, of course.

'Well then. When we've done a bit of ordinary kissing, we go on to French kissing,' she said, deciding she'd better recite the whole procedure like a well-trained teacher. 'And before you ask, it's when we both open our mouths and he teases me with his tongue, and I tease him with mine, licking and nipping. And then Tom pushes his tongue into my mouth, jabbing it in and out as if he's already down there.'

She pressed her crotch again, already feeling the hot

pulsing that sometimes had her up half the night giving herself frantic relief with her fingers when dreams of Tom became too erotically powerful to resist.

'You don't mean he puts his tongue – down there?' Abbie said, following the movement, and Sophie jerked her thoughts back to the tale she was telling.

'We'll get to that later,' she said quickly. 'You wanted to know it all, bit by bit, didn't you? So let me get on with it.

'Next, he undoes my bodice. I daresay you ain't never had your jollies exposed to the cool night air, have you, sweetness? It gives you a feeling I can't rightly explain, and when his mouth closes over each rosebud and he tugs at 'em and makes 'em all damp, I could scream at the pleasure of it.'

She swallowed as the pulsing in her crotch became stronger, but she tried to ignore it. This wasn't the time to go in a corner and relieve herself, with Cook waiting for the bloody peas, and the young lady gaping at her with flushed cheeks and open mouth, and clearly agog to hear more.

And without warning, Sophie found herself enjoying the telling. She'd never related it to anyone before, nor wanted to. But with such a willing listener, such an attentive pupil, it was almost as stimulating as lying beneath Tom's thrusting thighs.

'He tugs at your nipples with his lips?' Abbie recited, trying to imagine how that must feel.

'And his teeth, to give 'em a little bite now and then. And then he sucks 'em, and that starts the aching below even more. The sucking is the best part, Miss Abbie, and they come up like organ-stops and go a dark red colour.'

Abbie could see the evidence of Sophie's dreaming in the way her nipples had suddenly strained against the brown kitchen dress. She had never noticed them before, but now she couldn't take her eyes off them. And as if

6

Sophie wanted to accentuate her words, she cupped one of her heavy breasts in her hand, and circled the protruding nipple with her finger.

'See? Just thinking about it can do it,' she said.

'I think I must be deformed then,' Abbie said, amazed at the ease with which the other girl's nipple had erupted into life. 'Mine are just flat and pink.'

'That's because you ain't been stimulated yet,' Sophie said. 'Once you've had a man, it'll be different. Here, I'll show you, if you'll excuse the liberty. I know I ain't a man, but it's the touching that counts, and you want to practise it on yourself when you go to bed.'

Before Abbie knew what she was about to do, the maid had reached forward and squeezed Abbie's full breast. Both of them gasped: Sophie with the unexpected feel of its softness, and Abbie with the shock of realising how much she liked it. And then Sophie was searching for and finding the unused nipple with her blunt fingers, and circling it with slow, sensuous movements. And within seconds, it was budding into life, just as Sophie said it would.

Abbie was flushed with joy. She wasn't deformed after all. She would be able to respond to a man when the time came. If she could respond to Sophie, then she could surely respond to the man who would initiate her into the rites of loving.

As the circling went on, she became aware that both of them were breathing more heavily, and Abbie suddenly felt a shooting sensation in her groin, followed by a spreading, gathering sense of exquisite pleasure, as if something more powerful than herself was dictating the pulsing rhythms of her body. Her eyes dilated, and she gave an involuntary long, shuddering moan.

Sophie took her hand away from Abbie's breast and reverted to shelling the peas, her eyes on her work.

'Are you all right?' she said matter-of-factly.

7

'I think so,' Abbie said faintly. 'But I don't know what's happening to me.'

'Are you wet?'

She nodded. Now that the feelings were starting to subside, she knew how marvellous they had been, though while they were happening, they had frightened her as if she was going into the dark and unknown.

'Well, you've got all the right responses, Miss Abbie, so there's nothing to fear when the time comes. And that's how you'll need to be for a man to screw you,' Sophie said with satisfaction.

'I don't know what you mean.'

Sophie grinned. 'Then for Gawd's sake don't ask that starchy tutor of yours, or he'll die of shock. You can call it what you like – making love, or connection, or fornicating, or setting the cheese to the mouse-trap. It's still screwing, but it's usually only the likes of us low-life who use that word for it.'

'Then perhaps I had better not,' Abbie said.

'I think it would be best,' Sophie said dryly. 'So where did we get to?'

'Tom had your bodice open and he was biting your nipples,' Abbie prompted, finding the whole idea of it more exciting by the minute. Even saying the words made her tingle very pleasantly. There seemed to be a heat in her very veins that had never been there before, and she didn't dislike the feeling at all.

'Oh yes. Well, then we get our clothes off. In fact, by then, we're usually tearin' 'em off –'

'What – all of them?' Abbie said, staring.

'Of course, all of them, dummy – oh, beggin' your pardon, Miss Abbie. But how the devil d'you think he – we – oh Gawd – you're such an innocent, and it'll shock you –'

'No it won't. It's all right, really it is. Please don't stop now, Sophie.'

She was so excited at wanting to hear more now, that

8

she didn't care what Sophie thought of her or called her. She freely admitted that in the practicalities of sexual matters she was a complete ignoramus. But she wouldn't mind wagering that all the kitchen staff, and the gardeners, and even Uncle Brindley himself, since he'd been married for a short time, knew all about this screwing. The sheer knowledge of it put them all into a sort of exclusive club, and one to which she felt perfectly entitled to belong.

'Oh, all right then. Well, Tom always spreads a blanket in the hay loft, so the straw won't dig into us,' Sophie said, suddenly so dreamy with remembering that it almost transformed her plain face. 'Once we're both naked we start fondling one another. As he's done my jollies by then, he usually starts at my toes and works his way up, and I start at his chest and work my way down. He's got a lovely hairy chest and it's fun to try and work up his flat little rosebuds.'

She sighed, glancing at the other girl, and Abbie struggled to come to terms with the quick conversion from dreaminess to practicality in the girl's voice.

'I suppose you didn't even know men had nipples?'

'Of course I did. I remember seeing one of the young gardeners stripped to the waist on a very hot day in the summer, before my uncle shouted at him to make himself decent or he'd be out on his ear,' Abbie said.

'So did you see the gardener's chest then?'

Abbie had. And she'd seen the sinewy muscles in his back and chest and the hardness of his arms. And in the remembering, she also remembered that strange shooting sensation that had trickled through her at the time, only to trickle away just as quickly when her uncle started shouting at the young man.

'I didn't see him for very long,' she said. 'But I remember thinking he must have been in the sun a long time, because his skin was as bronzed as mahogany, and his chest was covered in curly dark hair –' she swallowed, registering that the memory had remained with her more than she had realised.

Sophie laughed now. 'Oh, Miss Abbie, I begin to think your uncle needs to get you married off quickly, before you explode with unfulfilled lust.'

Abbie started. She wasn't finding out all these things with the object of being married off to some dry old suitor her uncle might find for her. She just wanted the knowledge.

'I'm not getting married for years and years yet,' she said crossly.

'Oh no? That's not the gossip going around the kitchen and stables. You'll be eighteen in a month, and they say your uncle's already got a couple of old lechers lined up who are more than willing to hand over a handsome dowry in exchange for a young bride.'

Abbie gasped. It was one thing to learn of the goings-on of a kitchen-maid with a boy of her own age. It was something quite different to imagine having to do these things with one of her uncle's contemporaries with their fumbling fingers and wrinkled, senile bodies, and their rasping, evil-smelling breaths. But she didn't doubt what Sophie said for a minute. The lower orders always knew what went on with their betters, almost before they knew it themselves.

'They'd have to drag me to the altar first,' she said angrily. 'I'm not marrying anybody until I'm good and ready.'

'You won't have a choice,' Sophie retorted. 'If you don't do as your uncle says, he'll turn you out. Once you're eighteen he can wash his hands of you. Everybody knows that.'

Abbie licked her dry lips. 'If that's what he's planning for me, then I might as well run away before he gets the chance –'

'Oh, Miss Abbie, you wouldn't, would you?' Sophie said in a fluster now. 'Where would you go?'

She shrugged helplessly. There was nowhere she could go. They didn't socialise, since her uncle was something of a recluse and The Grange was an isolated estate in deepest Sussex that had no near neighbours. Besides, she had only said it on the spur of the moment in a spirit of bravado. She didn't even want to have to think about it. And today there were more interesting things to talk about.

'Nowhere. I was just musing. Go on telling me about you and Tom.'

But Sophie had gone off the boil. The peas were shelled, and Cook would be ready with a scolding for her if she didn't take them back to the kitchen soon. She stood up, smoothing down her skirts over her ample hips.

'I'll tell you another time. I reckon you've learned enough to be going on with, anyway.'

It wasn't nearly enough to satisfy Abbie. It was only enough to make her want to know more. She wanted to know more about the mysteries of sex. To know it all.

She had always been able to ferret out the things she needed to know by artless persuasion or downright cajoling, and few people could refuse her when she turned on the charm from those startlingly huge blue eyes.

But the one thing she didn't want to know about was the plans her uncle had in store for her, not if they involved an arranged marriage with a suitor of his choice. It would merely be exchanging one prison for another. And the older she got, the more she realised how truly she was imprisoned in this staid environment with a man she loathed.

Other young women her age lived in London and went to parties and dances and concerts, and even rubbed shoulders with royalty. For years, the Queen and Prince Albert used to be seen walking out with their large family of children in Hyde Park.

There were fashionable establishments in the towns where clothes were made out of silks and satins that felt sensuous to the touch, instead of the serviceable cottons and lawns the approved dressmaker was ordered to make up for the countrified Miss Abbie Richmond.

She was feeling more frustrated than even she had realised. Frustrated with her lot, with this place, and with life passing her by, which was a shocking admission from a young lady on the brink of becoming eighteen. But when that day came, she knew Sophie's shrewd comments would be realised. Her uncle's obligations towards her would be finished. She would either be obliged to marry whomever he suggested, or he would turn her out to fend for herself. Since they had only ever tolerated one another, she was under no illusions that if she did not obey him, he would do exactly that.

But she refused to let the worry of it fester away at her. The late summer day was very hot, and her clothes felt sticky against her skin. And at the far end of the estate the lure of the secluded stream, overhung with cool trailing willows, was calling to her. She went to the stables to mount her mare, ostensibly to take a ride around the estate, and headed straight for the copse where the winding stream was hidden from view.

From past experience, she knew no one ever came here but herself. She doubted if anyone else really remembered it, or knew of its existence. But it was the perfect place to take off her dress and shoes and underpinnings, and wade into the stream in her stays and drawers, even if she did have to wait for ages afterwards while they dried before she could ride back to the house. But the sun was so warm, and she could lie on the grass and spend the time dreaming.

Once she had tethered her mare, Abbie undressed

quickly. She always had a towel hidden in the stables to bring with her, to dry her body and her long, silvery hair. Her uncle would be outraged if he knew what she was doing, but she revelled in this one small act of defiance that was always so pleasurable to her.

She folded her clothes on the ground and stepped cautiously into the barely sun-warmed water, shivering a little at the shock of it on her bare skin, but glorying in the blissful softness on her toes, her ankles, and then, as she sank deeper into it, feeling it caress her thighs and finally her entire body as she embraced the water, splashing and cavorting in the only sense of freedom she knew.

'I must be mad to feel the way I do,' she said aloud a while later, coming up spluttering as the droplets of water ran down her face and neck. 'I'm not a prisoner, am I?'

'I don't know, me darlin',' said a voice close by. 'Are you?'

The shock of hearing another voice sent her rigid. The fact that it was a male voice made her dive down beneath the water again, so that her hair streamed out on its surface like rippling, shimmering silk. Her whole body shook with alarm. The trees dappled the strong sunlight, dazzling her eyes so that she couldn't see the owner of the voice yet, nor guess the age of the intruder. But intruder he was, and the realisation made her smother her fear and call out angrily.

'Whoever you are, you're on Richmond land, and I'll thank you to leave immediately.'

'And deny meself the pleasure of seeing a silver goddess in the flesh? And such delectable flesh too,' he added with a leer in his voice.

Abbie knew how vulnerable she was. Nobody knew she was here, and nobody came to this place except herself – and now this man.

'You could at least show yourself,' she snapped.

'If that's an invitation to join you, I accept,' he said, and before she could say it wasn't what she meant at all, he had stepped out of the shadows of the willows and was grinning down at her, clearly enjoying her crimson embarrassment.

'You wouldn't dare,' she spluttered, and the fact that he was tall and reasonably good-looking was over-shadowed by noting his rough clothing and his brawny, unshaven appearance. He was clearly no gentleman, neither by his presence here and disallowing her her dignity, nor by the lecherous way he was appraising her now.

He didn't answer. He merely kicked off his shoes, relieved himself of his breeches and shirt, and stepped into the stream in his under-drawers. Abbie gasped, because the audacity of the man was just as startling as the huge bulge inside the soft fabric of the garment, and she wished frantically that Sophie had told her more about this male thing that the maid seemed to find so erotic, and of which Abbie had no knowledge at all.

'Don't look so scared. I'm not going to hurt you, me darlin',' the man said, and now that she listened to him properly, she recognised a similar accent to one of the stable-lads. This one was an Irish tinker, no doubt, she thought scornfully, or a gypsy, passing through – and where there was one, there might be more. She felt renewed fear.

'I'm not scared,' she lied. 'But my guardian will be here soon, and you had better make yourself scarce before then, or he'll set the dogs on you.'

The man laughed, moving nearer to her through the water, and Abbie could see those small, flat nipples of which Sophie had spoken so lovingly.

'Your guardian is old, and there are no dogs in the house. I've watched you for long enough to know that.'

'You've watched me?' she gasped. 'Not – not here?'

'To be sure I have, and enjoyed the sight, mavourneen.'

Her mind whirled sickly. How often had he watched her luxuriating in her private stream, thinking herself unobserved? How often had he watched her lying on the grass in her stays and drawers, her long legs bare to the sun? And how often had he watched her drying the intimate parts of her body that no one but herself had ever seen?

'This is an outrage, and I'll have you horse-whipped for it!' she snapped.

And then she stumbled and foundered, losing her footing and splashing down beneath the water. As she came up gasping, the man was beside her, hauling her to the surface, his arms closing around her, his body so tight against hers that she could feel every sinew of it.

She could feel his chest flattening her breasts, and she could feel that huge lump probing into her. She felt threatened and vulnerable, praying it was only because he held her so tightly that she could feel its rock hardness, and that he truly intended her no harm. But she was so very aware of that piercing presence that her mouth dried. She couldn't even speak, let alone scream. And surely it moved against her. Surely she wasn't imagining that the thing had a life of its own and was throbbing ever so slightly against her.

The man looked down at her with an amused smile on his lips, and she knew he was fully aware of her reaction.

'You see what effect a sweet young virgin like yourself has on a lusty man like meself, don't you?'

'I'm not – I don't –'

Whatever she was trying to say had no effect on him. He merely laughed louder and didn't relinquish his hold on her at all. And although the thing was still probing at her, she thanked God that she still had on her stays and drawers. But they were clinging to her flesh

15

now – and then his gaze lowered. To her horror, Abbie saw that in the struggle her breasts had become freed from the upper part of her stays, and her nipples were erect and fully exposed to view.

'Well now, what have we here?' her captor said softly.

He ran his tongue around his mouth in a way that she couldn't mistake, especially after Sophie's revelations earlier in the day.

'If you touch me I'll scream,' Abbie said shrilly. 'I'll have you put behind bars –'

'Don't fret yourself, girlie, I've no intention of defilin' you, and I'm about to move on from these woods tonight, so you can have the place to yourself again.'

'You've been staying here?' she said stupidly. He had been living on his wits, and watching her.

'That I have. And before I go I'll have one sweet kiss from those luscious lips,' he said, as arrogantly as if it was his right.

He bent towards her and pulled back her hair with his free hand while his mouth fastened over hers in a savage kiss, forcing her lips apart and foraging inside them with the tip of his tongue, and then simulating the act of which she wasn't yet aware, but which sent shudders of mixed revulsion and tingling eroticism surging through her body.

The man raised his head for a second, hearing her sharpened breathing.

'Sweet Jesus, but the man who deflowers you has a rare treat in store,' he said hoarsely. 'All that ice – and all that fire.'

Then, as if unable to resist the impulse, he was cupping her breasts in his hands and licking each nipple in turn, and Abbie seemed powerless to stop him. Her legs were turning to water, and the surging, shooting sensations were filling her groin and making her groan. The normally small, round nipples were engorged with blood and standing proud now, and her head was thrown back in unconsciously wanton abandonment.

'Jesus, but I never saw such fine honey-pots for a man to suck,' the man muttered. 'And if the law wasn't after me I'd be tempted to stay a while longer. Or better still, take you with me. But I'm thinkin' you'd be more of a hindrance, since I'd surely to God be wantin' to fornicate with you at every opportunity.'

He seemed to be talking more to himself now, grandly elaborating on his wishes with all the blarney of the Irishman, and Abbie was only vaguely registering what he was saying. He suddenly let her go, and as she sank back into the soft water, she heard him blundering about the copse, and then there was nothing but silence surrounding her once more.

She was still stunned by the swiftness of the encounter, and she lay back in the caressing water for a while longer, trying to forget it had ever happened. Her eyes were tightly closed, as if she was reluctant to open them and admit, even to the trees and the sky, that she had just had her first sexual experience with a stranger.

And, wicked or not, that it had been more stimulating, exciting, and seductively awakening, than she had ever imagined it could be in her wildest dreams.

Chapter Two

*A*bbie knew the exact time when Sophie would be in the kitchen garden again the next day. One of the maid's duties was to collect the fresh produce for the household meals, and it was always a useful time for the two of them to talk without interruption or prying eyes.

The moment Sophie saw Abbie she paused in her task. Her eyes narrowed, and she put down the trug containing the cut lettuces and cabbages and the tiny ripe tomatoes that were Brindley Richmond's favourites.

'Something's different about you today,' Sophie said at once in a knowing, daring voice. 'Has my lady been playing games with herself and practising like I suggested?'

'Of course not!' Abbie said, feeling the colour rise in her cheeks, but certainly not prepared to confide in the maid about the Irishman. There were some things a lady didn't do, and she ignored the incongruity that she had begged Sophie to tell her her most intimate secrets.

'Well, something's put that sparkle in your eyes, miss, or perhaps you've just been letting your thoughts turn into fantasies.'

She spoke even more daringly. She must have known she could be in real trouble if she was overheard speaking so freely to the young lady of the house. Fortunately Abbie herself never took too much exception to her manner.

But nothing on earth was going to make Abbie confide in Sophie about the man at the stream. Such people stayed awhile and then moved on, and she was sure she would never see him again. He might even have been just a fantasy. In the clear light of day she wondered if the encounter had really happened at all, or if he was merely someone she had conjured up out of her own vivid imagination to prove that her growing sensuality wasn't a complete fabrication.

'Well?' Sophie prompted, seeing the dreamy look in Abbie's blue eyes.

'Oh, for heaven's sake! I just want you to continue with the story, ninny,' Abigail said impatiently. 'And if I look more excited than usual, it's all your fault for letting me hear about such deliciously wicked goings-on between you and Tom.'

She knew she was being deliberately provocative now. She was letting Sophie know that she wasn't at all averse to being a kind of listening voyeur on their most intimate moments. Sophie described it all so graphically that Abbie could almost see it all happpening in front of her; could almost feel the man's hands roaming, lingering, exploring her body; could almost taste the texture of his skin and smell the musky odour of his masculinity.

'We'd best go into the shrubbery again, then,' Sophie said with another knowing grin, as Abbie's throat constricted in a gulping swallow. 'I don't want you expiring with lust for all to see.'

It hardly painted a very feminine picture of her, Abbie thought, mildly affronted. But as far as she knew, there were no rules that said a woman couldn't feel just as much lust as a man, even if they never showed it. It was an intriguing thought.

Abbie had certainly felt lust yesterday. Felt it and wanted it and ached for it, and in the privacy of her own room last night, she had intimately explored her own body for the first time.

She had been tentative at first, and then more and more searching. And she had discovered an erotic pleasure in watching herself in her mirror as she fondled and teased her breasts into peaking, awakening arousal.

Then she had let her hands slide down over her firm young flesh until they reached her thighs, opening them wide and brushing her fingers against the curling mass of silky hair at her crotch. She had parted the silvery triangle, carefully fingering her body's tingling folds and crevices and slippery warmth. And in doing so, she had found a small pea-shaped knub that had responded magically to her touch when she pressed her fingers over it.

In fact, the more she rubbed it, the more pleasurable it felt, until she was gasping with unexpected, sensual delight. And all the while she was watching her own erotic, abandoned reflection in the mirror and feeling no shame, only that hot, burning pleasure. On and on she had rubbed, arching her back, breathing so fast, so deliciously fast – and then had come that rush of pulsating sweetness between her legs that had made her groan aloud with the sheer, exquisite release of tension.

And she was wet, so wet. And she instantly recalled Sophie's words, that this wetness was what made a woman so ready for a man. She had almost crawled down under the bedcovers then, drowsy with the aftermath of pleasure, and reminding herself to ask Sophie about the small, pea-shaped thing that could produce such powerful feelings.

* * *

20

The memories and images were still as powerful in her head now. They were tightening her groin as she and Sophie settled down in the shrubbery on the same wooden bench as before.

'So did you have good dreams last night?' Sophie said, with the easy chatter of the kitchen-maid.

Abbie flushed, hoping this was no more than an artless question, and that the girl couldn't see right inside her head. She still wondered if she had dreamed all that had happened in the past twenty-four hours – the encounter with the stranger, and doing those lovely, private things to herself. She was relieved to realise this morning that she wasn't marked by the devil for her wickedness and nor was she hurt or sore, despite her frantic rubbing.

But she still couldn't be sure of anything about yesterday. The entire day and evening seemed to have been one long, dreaming voyage of discovery into sexual awareness, and she was no longer sure where dreams and reality merged.

'I probably did,' she murmured in answer to Sophie's question. 'But if I did, I don't remember any of it.'

Sophie grinned, as if doubting what Abbie was saying. From her own experience she must have recognised the effects of sexual activity the morning after, whether it involved a partner or was done privately. Since Sophie knew there were no likely men in Abbie's acquaintance, she must have guessed that she had been playing and experimenting with her body and was learning fast.

'So where did we get to in the hay loft, my lady?'

'You and Tom were fondling each other's bodies. He was going upwards starting at your toes, and you were going downwards, starting at his chest.'

She stopped abruptly, and now her cheeks were really on fire. How *could* she talk so freely about such things! And to a kitchen-maid too. But ever since yesterday, she seemed to have lost so many of her inhibitions, and Sophie was openly chuckling at her now.

'My, my, we are coming out of the closet, aren't we? I wonder if you pay such close attention to the lessons your stuffy old tutor gives you.'

Abbie jumped to her feet, her hands clenched.

'If you're just going to mock me, I shan't bother listening to you any more –'

'I meant no such thing, miss, and I'm sorry if it seemed that way,' Sophie said quickly. 'I'm really admiring, honest to God I am. Some young ladies never change their prissy ways until the day they die, but I knew from the outset that you were different from the rest. You're not satisfied with what you've got, and you'll go on searching until you find what it is you really want.'

'Good heavens, you're quite a little philosopher, aren't you, Sophie?' Abbie said, but secretly quite pleased at this assessment of her character.

'I don't know about that, miss, but I recognise spirit when I see it, and you've got plenty.'

'All right,' Abbie said, her annoyance subsiding. 'So go on with the telling.'

'Well,' Sophie said, with a sidelong glance, 'when we've done a bit of proddin' and funnin' we usually like to play sixty-nines for a while.'

Abbie held up her hand for an explanation. 'You'll have to stop there. What's all this proddin' and funnin? And what on earth is playing sixty-nines?'

Sophie grinned. 'If you know anything about your own body, you'll know about the little man in the boat,' she said. 'Or maybe you won't. Anyway, it's right here, a little knob-shaped thing, see?'

As she pressed her own groin, Abbie kept her face as blank as possible, but the redness in her cheeks and the darkening in her eyes betrayed her. She knew very well what Sophie was talking about.

'It gets me all worked up when he rubs it and makes the sides of me thing swell up and push out,' Sophie continued with growing enthusiasm. 'Tom likes that. He says it tells him when I'm ready for the next step.'

She didn't pause now, her pale eyes dilating and gazing into space. Abbie realised she might as well not be there at all, for Sophie was off somewhere in her own imagination, and she didn't dare to interrupt.

'He puts his finger inside me then, and pushes it in and out until he makes me squirm. Meanwhile, I'm playing with his thing and gettin' it up to size.'

The questions brimmed on Abbie's lips, but she still didn't dare ask, and there was so much more to learn.

'Then we do the sixty-nine, which means I lie head to feet over him, takin' his cock in me mouth and givin' it a good old suck. And I'm over his face so he can tongue me at the same time. Sometimes we do it the other way round, but either way, I tell you, Miss Abbie, until you've played the game of sixty-nine, you ain't lived!'

Her face came slowly into Abbie's focus again, and the two of them realised how hard they were breathing. The maid gave a throaty laugh.

'Gawd, I'm comin' faster'n if Tom was inside me now. See what just thinkin' about it does for you?'

'Yes,' Abbie almost croaked, keeping her knees pressed tightly together, and thankful for the ankle-length skirts and petticoats that decorum dictated. They were always so hot in the summer weather, but they conveniently hid the fact that she was wriggling beneath them now, and feeling as if she was almost flooding with her own juices at these revelations.

'Go on then. Or is that the end of it?' she said hoarsely, seeing Sophie crouch on the bench for a few minutes as if trying to relieve herself of some deep ache.

Her own lower regions were throbbing so hard she thought she would die from it, but it was such a lovely feeling, she knew she couldn't bear to die now and miss a second of it. It was lovely, *lovely* .

'Course not,' Sophie said, as hoarse as Abbie now. 'Then we screw.'

There was that word again. That presumably forbidden word that had such a dark thrill to it, but which Abbie knew she musn't ever use in this particular context, except privately and in her head, where nobody else could get to it.

'Tell me about that,' Abbie said, still hoarse, still twisting her damp hands together on her lap, and feeling as wrung out as if she had been galloping her mare for miles across the Sussex Downs.

'That's the best part,' Sophie said. 'By the time we get around to it, Tom's as hard as iron and I'm as wet as washday. I lie on me back and he puts his thing inside me, and pumps me as hard as he can go till I can hardly bear it no longer. Then he shoots me.'

'What?'

Sophie laughed, rubbing her hands on her apron to rid them of their tackiness.

'Not literally, of course. He ain't got no gun nor nothin' – except for his big wet weapon,' she said, sniggering at her own graphic turn of phrase. 'But we have to be careful to see that we don't risk any little offshoots.'

Abbie waited, knowing the explanation would come. There was so much to discover, far more than she had ever suspected. It was like learning a foreign language – not that Sophie would know anything about that. But just when you thought you knew it all, there was always more.

'It's how you make babies, see, in case you was wonderin'. If he shoots his spunk in me, there's a risk that we'll make one. So he takes his thing out of me at the last minute when he knows he's near to comin', and lays it on me belly and shoots it there. I like that. It's as

24

hot as mustard, and it feels as good as if it's still inside me. Then if I ain't come, he finishes me off with his finger.'

Abbie opened her mouth to ask exactly what that meant, but they both heard Cook calling impatiently for that slut of a kitchen-maid to bring the vegetables inside, and the opportunity was gone. But by now, she was beginning to work it out for herself.

That lovely feeling – the one she'd felt last night when she'd found what Sophie called the little man in the boat, and the feeling she'd had just now when Sophie was describing it all to her – that shooting, wonderful, mind-exploding feeling, that was coming. And it was what a man and a woman had to do to make the loving complete.

When she was alone, Abbie spent a good few minutes catching her breath, then she got up and walked unsteadily through the shrubbery and around the gardens, thinking she had learned more in these last two days than in all her almost-eighteen years. She was excited and restless, and scared too.

Scared because this thing that Sophie had spoken of – this big, wet weapon that sounded so formidable – was still an unknown quantity to her. And the only real evidence she had of its existence was down at her stream when a stranger had pulled her close and half-seduced her.

Her breath caught in her throat again, vividly recalling the audacity of the oaf, and forcing herself to remember who she was. She was the niece and ward of a gentleman, brought up to strict Victorian values and gentility, if not love. And it was beneath her dignity to admit that she had become sexually excited by a near-naked rogue of an Irishman.

As she wandered about the grounds of the estate, ruminating on the changing images that surged relentlessly through her head, she caught sight of the young gardener she had seen before, stripped to the waist and incurring her uncle's wrath. He wasn't stripped now, but his shirt was stretched tight across his chest, the sleeves rolled up to the elbows, and it wasn't hard to notice the virile muscles inside it. He bent over his task, dead-heading the summer roses, and his buttocks strained against his coarse working breeches.

As he caught sight of her shadow as it fell across the rose bushes, he straightened up. He turned to smile at her, and she was aware of how generous his mouth was, and how white and unbroken his teeth.

'Were you wanting me for something, Miss Abigail?' he asked, touching an imaginary cap as he did so.

'No – no, thank you, Sam. I was just thinking how sweet-scented the roses are this year.'

'They are that. As sweet-scented as a lady's boudoir, I daresay,' he said cheekily.

Abbie gave a small laugh. Apart from Sophie, she rarely spent time bantering with the household or the outdoor staff, since her Uncle Brindley frowned on such frivolity. But then, he frowned on all the natural instincts of a young girl, preferring to keep her in virtual chains until he could decently get rid of her in marriage to a man of his choosing.

She turned away abruptly now, drawing in her breath, and then she heard the gardener calling after her uneasily.

'I ain't offended you, have I, Miss Abigail? I meant no harm by my remark, and if you was to complain to your uncle he'd have me horse-whipped for impertinence –'

He stopped speaking, and Abbie felt a swift pity for him, and anger at her tyrant of an uncle. Even a virile and powerfully-built youth like this one could feel cowed by Brindley Richmond's narrow ways. So what hope was there for her? She turned back to the gardener, and without thinking, put her hand on his arm.

'I'd never say anything to him, Sam. His world is a stuffier one than that of our generation, so have no fears.'

She smiled into his eyes as she spoke, meaning nothing more than a kindly reassurance, but she suddenly recognised a boldness there that she had never seen before. Dear Lord, surely he wasn't taking her unexpected familiarity as an invitation for him to take liberties with her!

'What I mean is,' she added haughtily, her voice several degrees cooler, 'I wouldn't want to get any servant into trouble, so please just get back to your work, and forget that I ever spoke to you.'

He looked at her steadily for a moment, and then he shrugged and went back to his work, snapping off the heads of the dead roses with more ferocity than before. And as she hurriedly continued her walk, Abbie thought she heard him mutter something beneath his breath.

'So she's nothin' but a little cock-teaser, just like all the rest. I might have known it.'

Abbie couldn't be sure she'd heard aright, and in any case, she didn't rightly understand what he meant. She dismissed it from her mind, breathing more easily as the summer breezes lifted the silken weight of her naturally wavy hair that she didn't yet wear pinned up, being under the age of eighteen.

She gave a sudden heavy sigh. So many things were destined to change when she reached that special age. And none of them were the changes she most desired.

What *did* she desire? she asked herself as she lay full-length on the sloping grass of the enclosed lawns. She tried not to squint at the sun – that would produce fine wrinkles around her eyes and make the housekeeper – her self-appointed protector – scold her for lack of attention to her complexion.

She certainly didn't want to be married – at least, not yet. One day, of course – it was every young lady's destiny to be loved and cherished by her husband. But not yet, and not until she made her own choice. She hardly felt she had lived yet, certainly not in the way Sophie lived, so free and easy, and sneaking out to be with her boy whenever she felt like it. Was that what she wanted? Abbie asked herself. To have clandestine meetings in a hay loft with a lover?

It wasn't a lady's role, but there was a darker, wanton part of her that defied all the soft, normal trappings of a lady's life and yearned for more, so much more. There was nothing of the tomboy about her, but she sometimes thought ruefully that she was probably a throwback to more ancient times, when lady pirates roamed the high seas, taking their pleasures as wildly and flamboyantly as any man.

And now she knew all about sexual pleasures, or at least as much as Sophie had told her. She knew the theory as well as she had learned the theory of the pianoforte, weeks before she had been allowed to play and run her fingers over the keys to feel their sensual smoothness and the way they responded to her touch.

She drew in her breath, knowing she was thinking of something other than the inanimate piano keys. And knowing, too, that all the theory in the world meant nothing unless you could put all you had learnt into practice.

A shiver of excitement ran through her. She had discovered some of that last night, finding her fulfillment in such an unexpected way. But it took a man and a woman to find the ultimate pleasure. Two sides of the same coin, fitting together so closely that they were one and the same person. The very thought of it was both stimulating and seductively erotic.

And now that Sophie had told her all that she had begged to know, it seemed as if she could think of nothing else, Abbie reflected, her emotions suddenly switching to something approaching anger. For what use was any of it, when all she could do at night was lie in her own bed and play games with herself? And it would be even more frustrating to spend her time imagining the scene between those two in the hay loft, which probably wouldn't be all that difficult now.

She sat up, her arms around her knees, knowing she was just as restless as ever. Now that she knew it all, there wasn't a single, productive thing she could do about it. Not unless she had a man of her own. But she didn't know any men of her own class, and it was hardly something you invited a stranger to do. She quickly shied away from the thought of enlisting someone like the young gardener, who would doubtless boast of his conquest for everyone to hear.

'I've been sent to find you, Miss Abigail.'

She started at the sound of the disapproving voice, and turned quickly to find the starchy housekeeper bearing down on her. Miss Phipps, with her black dresses and her concave chest, and her narrow eyes that seemed to find fault with everything about Abbie. Even more so since the girl had developed a voluptuous womanly shape that Miss Phipps privately thought was a sheer invitation to the sins of the flesh. The sooner the girl was married off and out of temptation's way the better, in her opinion.

Abbie sighed, knowing only too well how the God-fearing woman saw her. She knew her Bible as well as Miss Phipps, though perhaps not as intimately, since the Good Book seemed to be the housekeeper's only companion. And she knew that in Miss Phipps's eyes she had the shape and allure of a harlot. If she had her way she would undoubtedly hack off all Abbie's glorious silvery hair, considering it the invitation of a temptress.

In defiance now, she tossed her hair back over her shoulders and leaned back on her elbows, knowing how such a pose would incense the woman. She ran her tongue around her lips, wishing she dared paint them with some of her powder paints as she sometimes did in secret, just to annoy her more.

'Who wants me?' she said unnecessarily, for it could only be her uncle. But she was in no hurry to do the housekeeper's bidding, and the woman should know her place.

'Your uncle, of course, miss. He wants to speak with you on a serious matter,' she snapped.

Abbie's heart jolted, all her bravado slipping fast. There could only be one reason for this meeting. Normally, he was just as pleased for her to keep out of his way as she was to avoid him. But Sophie's gossip about him finding an elderly suitor for her the minute she reached her eighteenth birthday, quickly alerted her.

She stood up, pushing past the housekeeper and just managing to resist running to the house to confront her uncle. Young ladies didn't run, and they kept cool and serene at all costs, she reminded herself blindly.

Her uncle was waiting for her in the study, and he turned with barely a smile creasing his lips as he saw her. Despite her outward calm, she was seething underneath, and her breasts rose and fell, accentuating her slender waist and all her femininity. But she couldn't prevent her warm, full mouth trembling, as much with anger as with fear, and she realised, from the appraising look Brindley gave her, that he had noticed her passion, no doubt with approval on behalf of his friend.

Abbie put her hands on his desk. She had read somewhere that confronting the enemy meant putting him at a disadvantage, and she intended to do just that. She tried not to betray her fear as her eyes flashed at him.

'I've been told you want to marry me off, uncle. And it won't do!'

'What's this?' His anger was roused instantly. 'If

someone's been talking out of turn, I'll have the hide off them. And how dare you defy me, girl?'

'I dare, because I won't be tied to some old man just so you can be rid of me,' Abbie said, but her voice was tight with desperation, knowing he held all the strings, and she was no more than a puppet in his hands.

'We'll see about that,' her uncle snapped. 'You'll present yourself decently at dinner this evening, and you'll speak when you're spoken to. Lord Eustace is coming to dinner and wants to inspect you.'

Like goods on a market stall! she raged. She was no more than that to him, to be sold off to the highest bidder. And she remembered this Lord Eustace, with his rheumy eyes and slack mouth. The thought of him slobbering over her in the marriage bed was as hideous as being bedded by a dog.

She shuddered visibly, wishing her imagination hadn't taken such a vivid turn recently, and her normally delicate complexion whitened even more at the thought.

'May I go now?' she said tightly.

He glowered at the chit who stood there, still openly defying him.

'Get to your room, bathe and powder yourself, and present yourself as decently as you know how. Wear something dark and unprovoking. We don't want Eustace to have a heart spasm at the mere sight of you.'

'If you think that, does he know what he's letting himself in for then, contemplating marriage at his age? He's hardly going to last long, is he?' Abbie retorted daringly, and then she fled before he could come around the desk and box her ears for such bold talk.

She slammed the door of her bedroom and went into her little adjoining sitting-room to gather her breath. The very idea of Lord Eustace groping her made her sick. The thought of him wanting to do the things Sophie had told her about, the fondling, the tonguing, and then the screwing that seemed to bring such licentious pleasure – she shuddered as though she had a serious affliction, and knew she had to do something to prevent it. To prevent him even wanting her. But what?

The Grange wasn't a modern house, but to his credit, Brindley Richmond had installed several bathrooms in it for himself and his niece, and another for the household staff. Typically, he had informed them insultingly that it was not so much for their comfort as the need for them to keep themselves clean at all times and not infest the house with their fleas and vermin.

But Abbie was more than ready to strip off her clothes now and wallow in soft warm water while she contemplated her future. The maids had already prepared the bath-tub, and she could either send for one of them to assist her, or step into it and attend to herself.

Abbie decided she wanted no one else's company at this moment. She left her clothes where they fell and slid into the caressingly warm water. The sensuous pleasure of it helped to relax her fraught nerves from the meeting with her uncle. Her favourite bath salts had softened the water, and the bubbles ran enticingly over her skin when she trickled the washcloth over her breasts. She looked down at them lovingly, aware of her own body as she had never been before.

What would I think of them if I were a man? she wondered, trying to see herself through a lover's eyes. And yes, her breasts were beautiful, she thought objectively. Large and full and white, with those little rosebud tips that could proudly spring into life like obedient soldiers on command.

She smiled, remembering. She palmed each breast gently, feeling the sensual weight of them and fingering each nipple as she lay back in the bath-tub, until they became pert and swollen. Her eyes were half-closed in ecstasy, until the chiming of a clock somewhere in the house reminded her that she shouldn't dawdle.

A short while later, wrapped in a bath-robe, she consulted her wall closet to decide what to wear. Something dark and unprovoking, her uncle had said. Abbie scowled. If Lord Eustace wanted a young bride, then he should expect to see someone gay and frivolous, not something inclining to the dried-up looks of a Miss Phipps.

She felt a sudden sense of mischief. Her uncle would be furious, but since she no longer cared what he thought of her, why not?

There was a deep red dress in her closet that she had only worn once, since it had been decreed that the neckline was too low for decency. And she had loved it so much, begging the dressmaker to make it up for her, despite knowing her uncle's reaction. She had been forbidden to wear it again, and in a fit of pique she had cut the neckline even lower, and only worn it in the seclusion of her bedroom.

Abbie fingered the heavy watered silk now, remembering how it made her feel like a princess when she wore it. It would infuriate her uncle if she dared to appear in it tonight, especially if she braided her hair so that it rippled in silken waves when it was released, and was coaxed into tendrils about her face, which he considered to be a temptation to a man's baser instincts.

An hour later she stared at the vision in her mirror. She looked like a wanton, she thought, with joyful satisfaction. A temptress – and yet the vision wasn't quite complete. The neckline of the dress was now so low that it revealed the upper part of her breasts, with a tantalising glimpse of nipple whenever she moved.

But her skin was as pale as alabaster, and her mouth, normally so red, seemed to have lost some of its brightness compared with the hot colour of the dress. She thought for a moment, her heart starting to beat faster.

33

And then she reached for the powder paints that were a part of every young lady's pastimes. She had sometimes brushed a hint of the carmine hue on her cheeks as well as her mouth, hoping that no one would notice, and she had loved the way it highlighted her cheek-bones and accentuated the contours of her heart-shaped face.

She coloured her cheeks now, and then she pressed the powder on to her lips, biting them gently together to imprint the colour there. Even she was startled by the effect, and on an impulse she dashed a flicker of blue over her eyelids, just to see how it looked. It was dazzling. Flushed with pleasure at the sight of herself, her gaze dropped lower, to where the small darker circle of flesh surrounded her nipples.

Without thinking what she was about, she pressed her powder pad inside her dress to daub the circles, and then the nipples themselves. She stood back to examine her handiwork, breathing heavily and excitedly as she gaped at the vision in the mirror. She looked like a whore.

After the smallest tap on her door, it suddenly opened, and the housekeeper entered without any invitation, as she had been in the habit of doing since Abbie was a child. The shock on her outraged face threatened to explode into a fit of apoplexy at the sight in front of her.

'What evil is this, miss?' she gasped, as soon as she could speak. 'Have you completely lost your sense of decency? You'll rid yourself of that devil's colour this instant, and wash that – that harlot's muck off your face, and – and –'

Her eyes went lower, to take in the protruding nipples and carmine flesh. Her thin mouth dropped open, and she staggered back against the door. If Miss Phipps had been of the Catholic faith, Abbie guessed that by now she'd be crossing herself against such blatant wickedness as this.

She lifted her chin, her eyes blazing, but knowing she

had to make a stand now, however scared she felt. And she *was* scared. If this was one reaction to her mood of defiance, Lord knew what else she might expect.

'Get out,' she screamed. 'And don't come in here again without my permission. I'll see that a bolt is put on this door immediately, and you will learn to respect a young lady's privacy, do you hear?'

She had never spoken to a servant that way in her life before. But she was doing so many things she had never done in her life before, and her voice and manner must have had the desired effect because the woman backed out of the room, muttering beneath her breath but clearly accepting and knowing her place.

Chapter Three

*A*fter the housekeeper left her room in such a huff, Abbie knew she couldn't go through with her plan to confront her uncle and Lord Eustace dressed like a whore. She found herself admitting that she did at least owe her uncle something for his years of feeding and housing her, however restrictive it had been. Without his guardianship, she would probably have been put into service in some other gentleman's house, and probably fared a good deal worse.

So she reluctantly removed the deep red dress, feeling more ridiculous now at seeing how the tops of her breasts were only half-covered in the carmine powder. She scrubbed at them until they were tender, but the powder paint was surprisingly stubborn and wouldn't disappear altogether. It was no better when she dealt with her face, and she felt a frisson of alarm at the remnants of colour remaining on her mouth and cheeks and eyelids.

Hurriedly she applied creams and lotions, and at last there was only a hint left of the stain. It made her look comely, but not over-provocative. She scraped her hair back behind her ears, though she couldn't completely

36

brush out the obliging kinks made by the braids. Finally she donned a deep navy-blue dress with a white fichu neckline and demure cuffs. She looked the epitome of the dreary young woman about to be sold off to the highest bidder as little more than a chattel. She sighed, going downstairs with a heavy heart when she heard the pre-dinner gong sounding from the hall below.

Her uncle and his elderly friend were in the drawing-room drinking *apéritifs*. Brindley looked her over with hard eyes, but to her relief he made no comment on her appearance.

'You'll have seen my niece on your previous visits, Eustace,' he said shortly. 'And no doubt you'd like to ask her some pertinent questions.'

Good Lord, Abbie thought indignantly. It was sounding even more like a cattle market than she had supposed. And as the senile lord looked her over and began the probing questions that were more like statements, he annoyed her intensely.

'You'll be of good child-bearing stock, of course. I need an heir, and age is catching up with me.'

Abbie could see that well enough. There was a trail of dribble at the sides of his mouth, and his hands betrayed a constant tremor. She could barely suppress a shudder when she thought of those hands touching her and fondling her and opening her – and even worse, what would the rest of him be like? She had a sudden horrific picture of a red, wrinkled thing, that could surely be nothing like the throbbing pressure of the stranger in the stream, or the firm, hard buttocks of the gardener who had looked at her with such hot eyes. But if Lord Eustace was so senile, was it possible for him even to perform the act to produce the child he desired?

Abbie gulped, seeing that he was waiting for her to speak. She felt as though the walls were closing in on her as she gave the expected response.

'It's not something any young lady can possibly know

in advance, my lord, but I'm sure I shall do my best to be a good wife to my husband,' she said ambiguously.

As looks of satisfaction passed between the two men, the words were screaming inside her. *But never to you, you horrible old man!*

'One sprog for the heir, and another for a spare, as royalty is always reputed to say,' Lord Eustace went on.

He chuckled as if he had made some brilliantly witty remark, and then he coughed violently and disgustingly until he was blue in the face. Abbie found herself hoping he'd expire there and then, and save them all the trouble of going any farther with this farce.

'I trust you're feeling better, sir,' she said politely from force of habit, once the paroxysm had subsided.

He leaned forward, his face puce now, and squeezed her hand. His skin was like damp parchment, and she had a job not to snatch her hand away as he made a gasping reply.

'Better for your concern, my dear. I can see we shall get along very well.'

As the evening progressed, the resolve became even stronger in Abbie's mind. She was trapped in this sterile house, and if she didn't break free, she would be trapped in a terrible marriage with a man old enough to be her grandfather. She couldn't bear it, and she wouldn't go through with it. If she had to steal away in the middle of the night and throw herself on the mercy of the first decent household that would take her in, so be it.

She listened to the two men making subtle plans for the marriage in a kind of fencing ritual. She was obviously going to have no say in it. But since she had no intention of going through with it either, she let herself appear modestly attentive, even while she seethed at realising there was going to be a handsome dowry paid for her. A bride-price. She was being sold off to the first bidder who came along just so her uncle could be rid of her and grow fat on the proceeds. The knowledge did absolutely nothing for her self-esteem.

But she also became calmer as vague plans began to take shape in her mind. She had the money her uncle habitually gave her for Christmas and birthday gifts and which she rarely had the opportunity to spend. She had always considered him too unimaginitive to choose more material gifts, and it had always seemed pointless to give money to a young woman who hardly left the estate. But she was thankful for it now. At least it meant she could buy food and lodgings until she merged into the anonymity of some faraway town or city.

A growing excitement began to take hold of her. Whatever the future held in store, it would be an adventure, the like of which she had never even dreamed about before. The entire world beyond the limits of the estate were practically unknown to her, which was a shocking and almost unbelievable state of affairs for a young woman to admit.

Dinner at The Grange was always served promptly at six o'clock in the evening. By seven-thirty, Lord Eustace was already belching and showing signs of fatigue, which would hardly endear him to a bride of any age, Abbie thought in disgust.

He left soon afterwards, saying he would be calling again soon, but that he normally liked to get his beauty sleep by nine o'clock, and giving Abbie a hideous wink as he did so, as if to imply that, when they were joined in what she could only think of as an unholy wedlock, she too would be expected to join him in the marital bed by nine o'clock. The prospect set her nerves on edge all over again, but she managed to smile dutifully as she bade him good night.

'You're very fragrant, my dear,' he whispered, in what she presumed to be a seductive aside. 'A gentleman always admires a lady who keeps herself fresh and dainty.'

And presumably one who doesn't daub herself with carmine powder paint so that she resembles a lightskirt, Abbie thought.

Once they were alone, her uncle spoke to her sharply.

'You conducted yourself well enough this evening, Abigail, but I do not approve of the frivolous attention to your hair. See to it that it's washed out before the morning.'

'Yes, uncle,' she said, keeping her eyes down so he wouldn't see how they flashed with hatred.

'I shall be in my study for the rest of the evening, so you may amuse yourself as you wish until bedtime,' he said, and left her without another word.

Abbie stared at the closed door. How would she amuse herself? she thought. By dressing and painting herself in a whore's colour? Or by lying on her bed and allowing the fantasies to begin, while she stroked and petted herself, imagining that it was a lover's hands that caressed her? At the thought a sudden thrill in her groin overcame the abhorrence she had been feeling all evening, because, no matter what they planned, she had discovered a new world now, and one that no one could take away from her.

But the atmosphere of the house was still stifling her, and she needed to get away from it to think, and to make plans, however vague and tenuous. Without bothering to go to her room to don her riding habit, she slipped out of the house, unseen by anyone, and went to the stables. There was no one there at this hour, and the stable-lads had long since gone to their quarters.

Abbie spoke softly to her mare, urging her to be steady as the animal became restless at being disturbed at such an unusual hour. She walked her to the block and mounted her, trotting her slowly until she was well away from the house before she let her have her head.

Then she rode like the wind out of the estate and over the Sussex Downs.

She wasn't running away yet. But she needed breathing space and time to think and plan her next move. She needed to clear her head, and to feel the rush of wind in her face and through her streaming hair that she had loosened so defiantly after her uncle's chastisement. This was the only real freedom she knew, and she badly needed it tonight.

She leaned low over the mare's neck, feeling the power and strength of the panting animal beneath her, and glorying in being a part of her. Her legs were spread wide over the mare's back, scorning the side-saddle she hated, and feeling a strange abandonment in riding like a man.

Without warning, Abbie realised she was straddling the mare in the same way Sophie had implied that Tom straddled *her*. She was so caught up in the sudden visual fantasy of it that she didn't see the jagged tree stump in front of her. She only registered the animal's squeal of fright at being unable to stop in time, and then the sickening sensation of flying through space as she was hurled over the mare's back and into oblivion.

She awoke very gradually to find herself lying on a strange bed. Vaguely she realised that it must still be evening, because the room was lit by many candles that glowed with a soft, pinkish-yellow light. The air was filled with a beautiful fragrance, a heady mixture of jasmine and roses alternating with the sharpness of lemons. She felt so lethargic she could barely open her eyes, and besides, she wasn't sure that she wanted to do so. Apart from a dull ache in her head she was filled with such a wonderful feeling of well-being that she was content to remain in this half-state for ever.

Perhaps she was dead and this was the transition period between this world and the next. If it was, she wished she could let the rest of the world know that death was nothing to fear, and that the aura surrounding her was part of the glory of moving into a different state of being.

Gradually Abbie became aware of shapes floating all around her. The images were clothed in pale gossamer garments that seemed to shimmer and catch the slightest breeze whenever their owners moved. Occasionally they bent over her, touching her, stroking her with featherlike fingers that felt cool and damp, and producing sensations of the utmost pleasure throughout her body.

When she forced her eyes to open a little more she could see that the shapes had faces. They were beautiful, honey-skinned faces, though they remained completely expressionless as the fingers of these visions caressingly massaged her naked body. And then the sudden realisation that she was naked shook her visibly.

She gave a small moan in her throat that was half-pleasure, half-terror. Dear God, what was happening to her? One of the shapes leaned over the bed on which she lay and gave her a faint smile, showing teeth that were very white against the honeyed skin.

'Where am I?' Abbie croaked from a dry throat. 'What are you doing to me?'

The girl didn't speak, and Abbie looked beyond her to where an older woman stood patiently, and then she spoke to her in fractured English.

'We prepare you, lady. You have been hurt for many days, but you will soon be ready for the Master.'

'What master?' Abbie said, frowning. 'What do you mean? Is he a tutor of some sort?'

She couldn't understand what the woman was talking about, and the thought that she had been here for many days was surely preposterous. But the dull ache in her head and the delicious lethargy that was still enveloping her was preventing her from arguing. All she wanted was to know where she was, and then she could drift back to sleep again.

'He is the Master,' the woman said, as if that was explanation enough. 'Now, lie still, so that you are not cut.'

Abbie felt a stab of alarm at her words. Her gaze was drawn downwards to where she realised much of the sweet scent was coming from. It was from herself. Her entire body glistened with the aromatic oils the young girls had been delicately massaging into her skin.

Even to her own eyes, she knew she was taking on the persona of a beautiful, shimmering statue. Her breasts were like golden globes in the soft candlelight, their tips standing out even more erotically as the massage continued. The girl's lips curved into a small smile again as she heard the soft moans escaping from Abbie's throat.

Dear God, but the feeling was breathtaking. She stretched her limbs without realising, and caught the flash of a silver blade as she did so. She caught her breath, about to let out a scream of terror, when the older woman paused and looked down at her, the blade in her hand.

'Please, lady, be still and you'll not be hurt,' the woman warned again.

Almost numb with fright, and having no idea what was to happen, Abbie gave a small nod that seemed to take all her strength. She was unable to speak, for fear had completely dried her throat now. And when she felt herself being parted, she thought for one terrifying moment that she was about to be mutilated. In the wake of her terror, the indignity of being exposed to all these eyes in this way was lost on her.

Then, while a second young girl held her legs apart, the older woman proceeded to slide the blade over the silvery triangle at her crotch, back and forth, gently and deliberately denuding her of all her silky hair covering.

She worked on first one side and then the other, and

all the while Abbie didn't know whether or not to let the sobs well up in her throat at this abomination and risk being nicked by the blade; or to admit to the sudden rushing feelings of pleasure that the movements and the act and the soft, oiled fingers were beginning to induce.

In the end she could deny it no longer. It was as if that part of her that was being so exquisitely manipulated was responding of its own accord, and she could do nothing to stop it. Finally, she was totally unable to resist the bursting, pulsing sensations that produced wetness and release. The older woman nodded with a pleased expression on her face.

'The Master will be much pleased that the lady reacts so well. Have no fear. The parts will soon return to normal, and you will be beautiful for the Master's inspection.'

She also inspected her handiwork as if she inspected a piece of embroidery, seeking out the tiniest flaw in the work, and was apparently satisfied. At her nod of approval, the girls gently closed Abbie's legs together and covered her lightly with a sheet. She didn't understand why she had been thus denuded, but she was suddenly too tired to ask. A glass was put to her parched lips and she was told to drink. She obeyed without question, and was then ordered to rest.

She slept almost immediately, and as she drifted deeper and deeper into the sleep that the soothing cordial induced, so the exotic dreams began. Aided by the aromatic oils and the flickering candlelight, and the seductive attentions to her body, by now Abbie was so ripe and ready for loving that there could be only one dream to control her mind completely.

In the dream she was dressed in diaphanous garments of white and gold, and her arms were a mass of golden bangles. Her fingers were heavy with jewels, and in her navel a ruby sparkled. As sensuously as if she was floating, she moved forward over a marbled floor in a large chamber whose walls were hung with costly Persian rugs. At the far end, awaiting her, a man sat on a kind of throne. Her dazed mind told her that this could only be the Master. She paused in her dream, awaiting instructions, and then she heard him speak.

'Come close so that I may see you more clearly,' he said in a cultured English voice.

She registered her surprise, because his skin was swarthy, his hair and eyes as black as night, and he had the total appearance of an eastern potentate, from the bejewelled turban on his head to the flowing robes he wore.

Abbie swallowed and glided forward. In some strangely bewildering way she was fully aware that this must still be her dream, because everything she did was so effortless. The Master said move, and she moved. He told her to stop in front of him, and she stopped. He clapped his hands and commanded her to dance, and she danced.

But she didn't know how to dance! Somewhere, or perhaps it was only in her head, she could hear music, such exotically sensual music that it made her want to sway to its seductive rhythyms, moving her arms and flexing her fingers and arching her body towards the man, wanting to please him; knowing that she must do so if she was to get the reward she craved.

The music quickened, and she moved faster, the floating garments swirling about her, while she felt the erotic pleasure of performing just for him. His eyes feasted on her, and she danced for him alone. He was her Master.

Just as quickly, the music stopped and, as if she knew exactly what was expected of her, she sank to the floor, her face hidden in the folds of the flimsy garment. Her heart pounded, her breasts rising and falling in antici-pation as she became aware that he was moving towards her now. His hand reached down to pull her to her feet, and to look directly into her eyes.

'You have pleased me,' he said calmly. 'You have earned your reward.'

Should she speak? Was it allowed? Abbie felt faint as he led her out of the dancing chamber and into a smaller, but no less opulent room, dominated by a huge bed on which there were black satin sheets.

A chandelier lit the room with a blaze of candlelight, in sharp contrast to the sconces in her own room, and the light was reflected in the mirrored ceiling and mirrored walls in a thousand pin-points of light. Everywhere she looked there were dozens of images of herself, and of him.

'Are you afraid?' he asked, as he led her to the bed.

'I don't think so,' she said, puzzled. 'Should I be?'

He gave a short laugh. 'Not of me, White Dove.'

She started. 'My name is – is –' she frowned, realising that for the moment she was unable to recall her own name.

'From now on you will be called White Dove,' the man stated. 'It appeals to me to name you as I see you.'

He led her towards the bed and lay down on the black satin sheets, while she stood awkwardly beside him, not knowing what was expected of her. But his words intrigued her enough to question them.

'Is that how you see me, sir? So colourless?'

He laughed. 'Not at all. The dove is the most loving and peaceful of birds, yet it has a will of its own, as I suspect that you do. And white is for purity, like your skin and your hair, and your virginity.'

He paused, while Abbie felt her face flame at the word.

'You do come to me unbroken, White Dove? If I have been mistaken in this belief, I fear I would have to throw you to my wolves.'

He smiled again as he spoke, and she had no idea

whether or not his wolves were real or if he spoke in metaphors. And although the charismatic smile widened his mouth and showed a human side to him, she detected a ruthless underlying hint of steel in his voice. He would show her no mercy if she was not a virgin.

'I have lain with no man, sir,' she murmured, her eyes lowered in modesty, but unable to disguise her indignation.

'Then you will lie with me now, and it will be my pleasure to initiate you in the art of love,' he said.

Without more ado he rose from the bed and removed the bejewelled turban from his head. His hair was very thick and he looked even more flamboyant without the foreign headgear, she thought faintly. Then he slowly unbuckled his robes and let them slide to the floor, and beneath them he was completely naked.

All the while his eyes never left her face, watching her expression and gauging her reaction to the bronzed, muscular torso and flat belly, and the swollen erection that was crowned at the base with more of that thick black hair.

Abbie felt her eyes flicker. He was magnificent, she thought, with a rush of excitement. A magnificent, predatory animal, intent on subjugating his female. Raping her – no, not that – If it was rape then the victim would have to struggle, to fight, to be afraid – and to her own surprise she was no longer physically afraid.

In any case, she thought, trying to hold on to her swimming senses, she would be more afraid of the consequences if she were to put up a struggle in this captive place.

She was becoming sexually excited beyond measure. She had never imagined her initiation would be anything like this. To have this beautiful man standing before her like a colossus, his legs slightly parted so that she was fully aware of the bulging scrotum hanging down between his legs, with all the promise of a vigorous lover.

How she knew these things and these words, she seemed incapable of questioning. She was still dreaming, and she had once been told that in dreams the mind drew on memories and imagination that were more sharply etched than reality.

'You may touch,' the Master said.

Tentatively, she put one finger on his erect phallus, and felt its slight throb as she did so. It was smooth to the touch, with a large, mushroom-shaped tip, and curiosity for this thing that held such life-blood made her examine it more closely. As she did so her hand automatically closed around it.

The man laughed thickly, and without any warning he pulled her head closer.

'You may also taste,' he said.

Despite the pleasure in his voice, Abbie was aware that it was an order, and she ran her tongue around her dry lips before delicately touching it to the smooth, bulbous tip. It tasted pleasant, and she guessed that it too had been anointed with sweet oil, and wondered fleetingly if the honey-skinned girls had attended to this task too.

'Take it in your mouth,' he commanded, as if unable to bear the tantalising flicker of her tongue against his hard flesh one moment longer. Closing her eyes, she did as she was told, finding it hot and hard against her teeth. She gave it the tiniest nip, and heard a groan wrenched out of him as his hands raked through her hair, almost dragging her to her feet and away from him.

'Enough!' he said, and her eyes flew open in fright.

'Have I offended you in some way?' she whispered.

'Far from it, but the time has come for me to inspect my White Dove and give her pleasure. You will disrobe now.'

She seemed unable to disobey anything he asked of

her, but the garments were strange ones, and her fingers fumbled with them. In the end, he became impatient and tore them from her, until she stood naked and trembling before him.

'You're truly beautiful, White Dove,' he said softly. 'You complement me very well.'

In the plethora of mirrors she caught sight of their two images, and thought swiftly that in the physical respect he was right. He was so dark and she was so fair – it was darkness and light, the devil and the angel. She watched their reflections as his hands passed lightly over her body. They still stood close together, as if he was in no hurry to take this virginity that was to be her gift to him.

He palmed her breasts, squeezing and pressing, his fingers slowly circling her nipples and bringing them to surging life. She knew at once how infinitely different was his touch from Sophie's, or her own questing fingers. There was no substitute for a man's technique with a woman. He had all the skill of the practised lover, and she groaned with desire as his lips brushed each nipple, tonguing them and leaving them with the erotic coolness of saliva on each one.

Her head arched back in ecstacy now, hardly realising that he had dropped to his knees until she felt those fingers move downwards and part her denuded crotch. And then she knew exactly why that had been done. However embarrassing it had been at the time, it afforded him easy access to her inner sweetness.

Abbie ached for the dream to continue and not to end in frustration like so many other dreams. She was surely on the edge of fulfillment when some disturbance in the courtyard below woke her abruptly and brought her back to reality. She wanted to weep. Now she would never know how the act of seduction would have ended, and her own fingers did nothing to satisfy her.

* * *

Throughout the past days, in another part of the lonely and secluded house known as Villiers Manor, its owner had learned with satisfaction of the female ministrations to his new prize. He conversed with the old woman in her native tongue, and she reported faithfully that the girl was a virgin and more than ready to be broken. Maya had been too long in Villiers's service to be reticent about his needs and desires.

'Good,' Villiers said with a smile. 'Some English blood appeals to me, Maya, and I have been too long without.'

She nodded without speaking, and if she thought his words were a slight insult to the nubile Indian girls in his seraglio who so readily did everything he asked of them, she knew better than to say so. A Master with a healthy sexual appetite made his own rules, and those who served him loyally and without question were well treated.

'I will decide when to send for her, Maya. I want her physically recovered after the fall, but meanwhile see that she continues to be given sufficient sedatives to keep her relaxed and apparently dreaming.'

'It will be attended to, Master,' the woman murmured.

She left him in his chamber and gave orders that the jug of specially-prepared cordial was to be kept ready at the young lady's bedside for whenever she needed to drink. It was harmless enough, even if it produced a mild hallucinatory state. In Abbie's case, Villiers also considered it a necessary medication while she recovered from the trauma of the head injury she had sustained in her fall.

After the old woman had brought him her nightly reports as to the young lady's progress, Leon Villiers leaned back in his throne-like chair, well pleased with the turn of events that had come his way so effortlessly. He had never gone out of his way to procure an English girl, choosing discretion over the many delights he might have found there.

Besides, he had girls in plenty. They had accompanied him from India, some as gifts or handmaidens, and some as specially chosen concubines for his bed.

From the moment Leon Villiers returned to England after some years as a successful merchant in India, he had been determined to surround himself with the kind of harmony and beauty he had found there. In the southerly area where he had traded, the Mutiny hadn't touched the lives of the Indian princes with whom he had formed such good connections.

Any distant dispute with the British, however fiercely fought in the north, was also tempered in Leon's case by the fact that he had been instrumental in saving a young prince from a stampeding rogue elephant, managing to snatch him back from the brink of certain death.

From then on, the grateful prince was ready to give Leon anything his heart desired, and that included the sultry, beautiful young Indian women who were more than eager to surrender themselves to the handsome Englishman and pass on the ways of eastern seduction in which they excelled. He could own a fabulous collection of jewels, money, polo ponies, his own astrologer, peacocks and elephants if he so wished.

'Your Highness,' he had told Prince Khali regretfully, 'I am afraid there will be little call for elephants in deepest Sussex, where I intend to buy a secluded estate through a land agent in order to continue something of your own lifestyle.'

'But you do not entirely throw my generosity back in my face, friend Villiers?' the prince had said lightly, and Leon knew he must tread very carefully.

'I do not, Your Highness! And I will most humbly and gratefully accept the polo ponies and the rest of your gifts, including my choice of the concubines for my seraglio. But I would prefer to decline the astrologer and the elephants.'

He waited anxiously for the response, for it would be

a serious breach of etiquette to his wealthy host if he refused his gifts. But the prince laughed, slapping him on the back and calling him a jolly good fellow.

'Then we will choose our women together, and I trust you will not be returning to that cold little island for a good many years yet.'

And to their mutual indulgence Leon had spent the remainder of his years in India living a life of opulence and luxury in the prince's palace, beloved by all as an honorary brother, enjoying the riches, the orgies with the skilled concubines, the bountiful pleasures that were all his for the taking.

But even though the delights of the eastern women were like ambrosia to a young and virile man, it was almost inevitable that in time the searingly hot, dry days and even hotter nights began to pall despite all their pleasures. He began to long for England, and when the news came that his father had died it gave Leon the perfect excuse to break the silken chains of India and return home.

But he never returned to the ancestral home in the north of the country that had been in his family for generations. It was sold, and this present house, known now as Villiers Manor, had been purchased discreetly and privately on his behalf with the fortune he had been left.

Leon Villiers did not come home alone, nor without the wildly bohemian and unconventional ideas that would have had his father turning in his grave had he known how the isolated Villiers Manor, hidden within its vast, wooded environs, was to be used for unadulterated pleasure.

Chapter Four

*A*bbie was well aware that the sweet cordial was like
nothing she had ever tasted before. She had
deduced from all that the old woman told her that she
had been badly concussed when she had been thrown
from her mare, and that the potion had done much to
aid her recovery.

But although the cordial had the effect of making her
feel pleasurably drowsy, at the same time it seemed to
expand the capabilities of her mind. All her senses
seemed to be heightened, and coupled with the aromatic
scent of the perfumed candles she felt as though she
was capable of seeing beyond the rainbow into a magical
world of colour and light. With the feeling came a
sensation of eroticism such as Abbie had never known
before.

She lay on her bed, totally relaxed in this house of
strangers, and felt as if she had been here always. It was
the most unreal feeling she had ever known, but she
was totally unable, or unwilling, to question it. Something stronger than herself was telling her that this was
her destiny, and that she should let herself be drawn
into its caressing currents as if she drifted in a warm

blue ocean wherever it led her. It wasn't Abigail Richmond's style, but she no longer knew exactly who Abigail Richmond was.

When her door opened, she turned her head slowly, as if by now each movement was a great and deliberate effort. Her hair was spread out on her pillow in a shimmering sheet of silver, and somehow she sensed that someone had attended to it while she was half-sleeping. The vague sensation of soothing hands brushing out the silky strands, and of delicate fingertips massaging her scalp, had been as potent as an aphrodisiac.

She saw the older woman approaching her bed. Behind her came several of the young girls she had seen before, with their beautiful, expressionless faces.

'It is time for you to be bathed, lady,' the old woman said. 'The Master commands you to his presence in three hours, and there are many preparations to be made.'

Abbie became fractionally more alert at her words.

'What preparations?' she asked. If she was to be sacrificed to this so-called Master, then surely they had already done all they had to do.

She remembered the flashing blade of the knife as it had begun its work between her open legs, and she gave a small shiver of apprehension as another thought struck her. Whatever the Master intended doing with her, she supposed she should thank God that these women hadn't resented her, for they could certainly have mutilated her beyond measure at that time.

Her hands moved involuntarily as if to shield that part of herself, and the old woman gave a slight smile.

'The Master desires purity above all things, lady, in mind and body, and you will come now to the bathing chamber. There is no need for you to question.'

Abbie rose numbly from the bed, knowing she had no choice, and that even if she did question, she would receive no satisfactory answer. By now she knew better than to disobey. Each time her bedroom door had been opened, she had already glimpsed outside the huge, dark-skinned guard dressed in eastern garb, and she hadn't missed seeing the curved, evil-looking sword at his side.

Her legs felt unsteady, and she suspected that was also because of the cordial she had been taking. Feeling more sensible now, she guessed that assuredly it would have contained powders to keep her relaxed, and probably some medication to help heal her bruised body from her fall. Whatever the potion was, it had certainly done that, she mused.

She had drunk deeply and frequently, day and night, for the room was so hot with its overpowering scents. But although her muddled head no longer hurt, it felt full of wool.

The old woman took her arm, and spoke a mite more kindly as she was led towards a door leading off the bedroom.

'Do not be afraid, lady. As long as you do exactly as you are bidden, you will find that the Master is generous to his chosen ones.'

The implication of being this unknown man's love-slave was not lost on Abbie, and she felt a spurt of anger.

'And what if I refuse to do as I am bidden?' she said.

Behind her she heard the young girls gasp. Whether or not they understood her words, she knew they guessed by her voice and her attitude that she was not as subservient as themselves. But she had already begun to wonder if one or two of them understood far more than they allowed her to believe.

'You will obey, lady,' the old woman said, in a silky, menacing voice. 'If you do not, you will regret. And your recent concussion will not be considered an excuse for disobedience.'

She didn't elaborate further, but the unfinished sentence

chilled Abbie as much as if she had made a definite threat of pain or death. There was something about this woman and her apparently fawning obedience to do the Master's wishes, even to procuring young English girls for his pleasure, that she found totally repellant. But she realised she was right in one thing. She had been concussed, and that was partly why she felt so disorientated. It was a slight relief to know it. There was always something sinister in feeling light-headed for an unknown reason. But she also knew that a blow to the head could account for much strangeness.

She was gently pushed through the door of the bathing chamber, and then she was the one gasping at the opulence of it all. She could not recall having been brought here before, though she realised it must have been these girls attending to her ever since her arrival here, however long ago that might be. They knew her intimately in every sense of the word. She had been massaged and pampered in her bed with oils and sweet preparations, and if she had been brought to this bathing chamber before, it had been erased from her memory.

Time had no meaning for her any more, she realised with a sudden stab of alarm, and she seemed to exist in a suspended state from which there was no immediate release. Perhaps she had truly been too frail to be moved after her arrival, but despite her lethargy, she now felt less frail in body than in spirit.

She breathed in the steam that arose invitingly from the waiting bath of seductively scented water, and the temptation to step into its caressing heat was almost impossible to resist. She made no demur as the girls removed the light garment she had been wearing.

Nor did it occur to her to wonder at how readily she seemed to have lost all modesty. No one had ever seen her naked before, and in her uncle's household it had been strictly understood that she bathed alone. The housekeeper had once told her that Brindley Richmond considered the sight of another's naked body to be encouraging the devil's works.

Abbie frowned, knowing she should remember something very important about her uncle, but these flashes of memory only came to her now and then as if to tantalise her, and were as quickly forgotten.

She glanced at the girls helping her into the scented water. She had deduced by now that they were all of Indian descent. What she saw in their eyes was open envy of her untried young body, so alabaster-white in contrast with their own honeyed skin. Her full breasts were firm and rosy-tipped, the thighs rounded and womanly, and the crotch pouted enticingly without its silky triangle of hair.

Abbie felt a sudden dart of excitement run through her as she lay back in the bathtub, coupled with a sense of mischief at seeing the reaction of these nubile girls. The old woman had left them for the moment, and the girls were obviously to be the only ones attending her.

'You like?' she said, in what she hoped they wouldn't think ridiculous pidgin English. But from the slightest smiles by way of response, it was obvious to Abbie that they did indeed understand what she said perfectly well.

One of the girls picked up the wash-cloth, and spoke softly for the first time as she trickled the aromatic water over Abbie's breasts.

'Lady is most beautiful,' the girl said in the awkward manner of one who had acquired a second language with some difficulty. 'She will please the Master greatly.'

'And have you pleased him?' Abbie said swiftly, unwilling to admit how much she was enjoying the sensual effect of the hands moving over her body now.

Another girl raised Abbie's feet and legs out of the water in turn, and gently soaped them with her palms, while yet another massaged her back, running her fingers down the length of her skin in feathering movements. A fourth girl stood waiting, and Abbie had no idea what her particular function was to be as yet.

She hardly cared. She was too busy concentrating on what was happening to her, and trying to stop her eyes from dilating with pure pleasure. Her nipples had peaked now, and she could do nothing to stop them betraying her feelings.

'We all please the Master when we are called, lady,' the first girl said in her slow, sing-song voice. But just for a moment Abbie thought she detected a rare flash of expression in the girl's black doe eyes – something that might have been jealousy or searing resentment, when seconds before it had been merely envy.

'Why won't you call me Abigail? It's my name, and you might tell me yours,' she said, in an attempt to show a spirit of friendship, but the girl shook her head at once.

'It is not permitted. Also, our names are chosen by the Master, and he alone can say what we are to be called.'

'He's not God, is he?' Abbie said, suddenly irked by all this servitude to a man she hadn't even seen yet, but who was apparently to have such influence on her life. They all seemed to be obsessed with pleasing him, as if everything in this place revolved around him and his needs and desires.

The girl didn't answer, and Abbie realised that the fourth girl was moving forward now. Before she knew what was happening, the others held her arms and drew her to her feet, and the one she silently referred to as number four was gently and deliberately parting her legs and applying a wash-cloth to her most intimate parts.

Abbie closed her eyes, never having experienced such a thing in her life before. She was uncertain whether or not she should protest or complain, or scream, or shout, or merely to stand and submit.

After a few moments, number four knelt on the floor,

discarding the wash-cloth in favour of her own slender fingers, inspecting her closely as she worked, as if to ensure that every particle of her most private area was as spotless and virginal as that of a new-born babe. She was still held captive in the other attendants' surprisingly strong arms, and she knew she should be outraged – but it was all far too erotically shocking for her to utter a single sound.

She was also aware of an almost irresistible temptation to thrust herself forward into the girl's face to offer an even closer inspection, and the thought that she might do so was suddenly alarming and shameful, so she purposefully kept her eyes fixed on a point on the wall and tried to make her mind a total blank. At last she felt her legs being released from their bondage, and both the bathing and the inspection were over.

'Lady will please step out now,' the first girl instructed, and when she did so, Abbie was immediately enveloped in warm towels and escorted back to her bedroom to be laid on the bed where the girls carefully dried every part of her.

Then came the same anointing with aromatic oils that she remembered from before. Many hands massaged her now, and as the oils penetrated her softened skin, they transformed her body from its natural translucent hue to a pale glowing amber. Her eyes closed as the ministrations went on.

'Not too much. You know the instructions.'

Somewhere from the depths of her delirious pleasure at the proceedings, Abbie heard the voice of the old woman. She hadn't even been aware of her entering the room, but she heard her speak sharply to the girls now.

'The Master wishes her to remain white-skinned. If you anoint her too deeply, you risk a lashing.'

She spoke to them in English, and Abbie wondered just how often in her first days here they had spoken in their own tongue simply to keep her from guessing where she could possibly be. She still had no idea whether or not she had been taken on board some ship to a secret eastern destination, as she half-suspected. But the combination of the mild hallucinatory state induced by the sweet-tasting drink and the perfumed candles, the sensual handlings in the bathing chamber, and now this, meant that she no longer cared.

She looked slowly down at her own body. It was no longer marble white, but a softer, more delicate hue. But at the old woman's words the girls were quickly taking off the intensity of the oils now, and leaving her soft and pale and fragrant.

'You will be dressed now, and await further instructions,' the old woman said. 'On no account must you attempt to leave your bedchamber until you are sent for.'

Abbie felt a growing, intense dislike of the woman. The girls themselves seemed like mere puppets, obeying her will or that of the Master himself. But Abbie was sure this one had an evil streak in her.

But she made no argument as the girls dressed her in diaphanous white garments similar to those they themselves wore. Her face was meticulously made up, with subtle colour being applied to her cheeks, and a vibrant blue on her eyelids. Her eyes were then heavily kohl-rimmed, amd her mouth was painted crimson. Many rings adorned her fingers and toes, and before they had finished with her there were jewels around her neck and arms and on her forehead. A glittering ruby was placed in her navel. She had no idea how it was attached, nor whether or not the gems were real or paste.

Her long hair was left free and loose, and when she was shown her reflection in a mirror, she gasped at the voluptuous woman she had become. Her blue eyes and silvery hair were a stunning contrast to the eastern artefacts. Finally, a veil was positioned over the lower part of her face held in place by a silken cord, and the

60

transformation was complete. She was someone she no longer recognised, and she was Abigail Richmond no longer.

'What am I supposed to do now?' she asked huskily, when she could think of nothing else to say, and assuming there was no response expected to her changed appearance.

'You wait,' the old woman said again. 'And when someone comes for the one who is to be called White Dove, you will go where you are taken.'

Abbie started violently, her mouth drying with shock. White Dove – it was the same name the man in her dream had given her. But had it been a dream after all, or had it been real? She trembled at the knowledge of a coincidence that could surely not be a coincidence, but something far more sinister. Had it all actually happened?

She desperately wanted to ask more, if she could only have stammered out the words through her dry lips. But before she could gather her wits, the old woman had clapped her hands imperiously. She and the attendants left the room instantly, and Abbie was alone.

But White Dove – she couldn't get the name or the shock of hearing it out of her mind now. How had the Master come to call her by that name? And how could she possibly have known of it? The only logical explanation was that the cordial she had been taking so regularly, since it certainly eased the ache in her head, had produced such a hypnotic effect that she had actually gone through all the actions in the dream and never realised it was actually happening.

And if that were so – Abbie felt a wanton thrill run through her veins. A well brought-up young lady should never admit to having such feelings or such dreams. But if it had all been real – She fought to remember the sensations and images she had experienced. Seeing a man's body for the first time in her life, touching and being touched, kissing and being kissed, in intimate places where she had never been touched or kissed before –

As if she was only just emerging from the dream, Abbie slowly sat up on the bed where she had been laid so attentively. No – almost reverently, she amended, as if she were to be some sacrifice to a superior being.

Rushing into her head now came snippets of the lascivious tales that Sophie the kitchen-maid had told her. She had completely forgotten Sophie until this minute. It was as though memories of everything that happened before she came here had been erased from her mind, and were only gradually returning in these annoyingly tiny flashes of remembering, just as the haunting, elusive memories of a dream returned.

But suddenly she remembered clearly Sophie's tales of this screwing that was such a forbidden word for the respectable Miss Abigail Richmond to use, but which seemed to be such a mutually enjoyable experience between the kitchen-maid and her lusty Tom.

And in the telling, Abbie recalled that there had never been a hint of one of them being superior over the other. They took mutual pleasure in their love-making, and Abbie was very sure that Sophie had never considered herself a sacrifice. Nor would she ever have submitted to such a thing!

In that respect it was the kitchen-maid who was far superior to herself, since Abbie was quite convinced now that subjugation was to be her destiny. As the thought entered her mind, her spirit instantly revolted. She totally rejected the idea of being any man's love-slave, no matter how seductive and charismatic the lover. And as yet she still didn't know for certain if the man in her dream was the Master, or a figment of her imagination – or even if it had all been a dream after all. It frustrated her beyond measure.

'But I can find out,' she said defiantly. 'I don't have to be treated like a puppet, for those women to do with me what they will. I need to know what's in store for me, and to find out exactly where I am.'

Just saying the words aloud made her feel more like her old self, and her thoughts were clearer than before. She slid off the bed and walked silently across the room on her bare feet. Evidently, shoes were not considered necessary for the introduction into eastern life. She opened the door cautiously, and at once her way was barred by the huge guard, and she saw the gleam of the heavy curved sword at his side.

'I've been summoned to the Master's chamber,' she said quaveringly. 'Please be good enough to show me the way.'

She held her breath, wondering at once if she was being naively foolish, for he must know that no one had sent for her, and the sword in his hand looked all too menacingly sharp. He didn't answer. He merely stared at her with his blank, dark eyes, then stood aside, and pointed towards a long, dimly-lit corridor.

'Thank you sir,' Abbie stammered, hardly knowing how to address him, but certainly not wishing to offend him.

She sped away down the corridor as fast as she could. The guard terrified her, and she had no idea what race or nationality he was, but his very size, and even more so his silence, was totally unnerving.

She moved farther down the corridor he had indicated, and the flickering candles in their wall-sconces seemed to grow dimmer as she tried to stay calm and to walk more slowly. She glanced back once, but by now her guard had seemingly vanished, and she was entirely alone. It had all happened so smoothly that she couldn't quite rid herself of the brief suspicion that he had been alerted to let her leave her room if she wished to do so, but she dismissed it from her mind.

She hesitated now, as the corridor divided two ways, unsure which direction to take. One side was better lit than the other and looked the more inviting, and as she crept along it she passed many rooms with closed doors. Each room had a latticework grille in the door, which was presumably for ventilation, although the entire house was almost stiflingly perfumed and the scent became heavier the farther she wandered into the maze of corridors.

Through the grilles, she could glimpse the costly silk furnishings of bedchambers and other rooms. The whole place seemed to shriek of some Indian temple of pleasure, and although Abbie tried not to let herself think of it, from such places there was surely no escape. At the far end of the corridor it was somewhat brighter, and as she moved nearer she could see light spilling out through the grille in one particular door.

With her heart pounding now, Abbie pressed her face near to the grille to see inside the room. As she did so she felt a wild stab of alarm, for the room was the same as the bedchamber in her dream. There were the mirrored walls and ceiling, the enormous bed with its black satin sheets.

Even while she was digesting this information, her startled eyes took in the fact that there were three people on the bed, and she recognised one of them instantly. It was the handsome man in her dream, wearing the white robes she remembered. Two young girls were attending him, offering him grapes and wine. The mirrors magnified the number of people there, and if she had had any experience of a Roman orgy, Abbie thought this must surely resemble it.

She felt numb with shock, not only that she was now being an unwilling voyeur, but also with the knowledge that this bedchamber was exactly as she remembered. She was positive now that it had been no dream. Somehow she had been brought here, and undergone the ritual dancing and preliminary initiation into whatever the Master required of her, even without being fully sensible. That anyone could have such control over another person's mind and body was barbaric.

As she made to back away from the scene inside the bedchamber, she saw and heard the Master clap his hands and without a word being spoken between them, the girls began to disrobe him, although they remained fully dressed in their own flimsy garments. Abbie paused in her first instinct to take flight.

Despite the memories of her so-called dream, she was now seeing a naked man in the flesh for what she considered to be the first time. And what flesh! She was mesmerised by the firm rigidity of his body, from the muscled torso down over the flat belly to the half-erect phallus below. It was just as she remembered, but it was so much more real now.

She caught her breath, realising that as the Master lay half-prone on the bed the girls were starting to massage his body with oils in a similar fashion to the way Abbie's body had been anointed. The erotic aromatic scents permeated the bedchamber, teasing her nostrils as she pressed even nearer to the grille, and she found it impossible to look away as the female fingers moved delicately around the intimate parts of the Master's body. As the ministrations continued he became fully erect, and Abbie felt her mouth go dry.

Suddenly, she heard him give a groan, and then he spoke.

'Enough. You know what I require of you.'

The fact that he spoke first in their own language to them, and then in English, should have surprised her, but she was too sexually aroused by the sight of all that was going on to really notice it. He pulled one of the girls down over him, and gestured for the other to come nearer.

Abbie saw the first girl take his erect phallus into her mouth now, while the second one straddled his face.

An instant memory of Sophie's hoarsely excited words shot into Abbie's mind.

'Then we do the sixty-nine, which means I lie head to feet over him, takin' his cock in me mouth and givin' it a good old suck, and I'm over his face, so he can tongue me at the same time. I tell you, Miss Abbie, until you've played the game of sixty-nine, you ain't lived.'

Abbie knew that what she was witnessing now wasn't exactly the same, but maybe it would be beneath the Master's dignity to contort himself into a different angle to pleasure these girls. It seemed that what was required of them was simply to be there to pleasure him. Though she could hardly imagine how either of the girls could be unaffected by what they were doing, or having done to them.

Without warning, she felt the wetness in her crotch, and she was throbbing so fast she drew in her breath sharply with the pulsations that accompanied it. What had Sophie so eloquently called it? As wet as washday – that was it, and Abbie knew now exactly what she meant.

Her eyes were closed tight with the sheer ecstasy of it, and then she had the uncanny feeling that she was the one being watched. Her eyes flew open. The girls had stopped their activities now, and stood on either side of the bed, while the Master gazed directly towards the grille, just as if he knew she was there. And from the lack of surprise or anger on his face, her heart leapt as she wondered if he had known it all along. As if this was the reason he had spoken to the girls in English, as if allowing her to be the voyeur was all part of the libidinous games he played.

He clapped his hands once more, and the girls instantly covered him with a sheet and sped towards the grille, to slide it shut. Abbie was as stunned by the speed with which it had all happened as by the alacrity with which the girls obeyed his every command. It was terrifying to think that one man had such power over them. Terrifying, and excruciatingly exciting, because she was realising more and more that this was part of another world she hadn't even known existed. She had wanted adventure and escape from the dullness of her life, and she was getting it in full measure now.

She turned blindly, then gave a cry of terror as she found herself grasped by the guard who had stood outside her door. He had evidently followed her here. He would know what she had been doing, and somehow he would relay it all to the Master. And she was certain to be punished.

All her common sense and her genteel upbringing fell away from her in an instant, and she could only blubber out a plea for leniency to this tyrant who seemed to tower over her now.

'Please,' she gasped in terror. 'I meant no harm. I lost my way. I didn't mean to pry, and I didn't see anything –'

It unnerved her even more to register that he still never spoke a word, nor did his expression ever change. He just continued to stare down at her with those dark hooded eyes. From somewhere in her memory of school-room facts when learning about eastern ways and customs, she dragged out a snippet of information about eunuchs. Her tutor had quickly glossed over such unsuitable information in a young lady's education, but Abbie hadn't been able to help pitying those poor creatures who were emasculated by being castrated, and then had the further indignity and pain of having their tongues cut out as well, to ensure complete loyalty to their masters, and to prevent them betraying any secrets.

She swallowed hard, wondering if such a powerful-looking fellow as this could really have suffered the humiliation of being castrated – and for what reason.

'Can you speak?' she said hoarsely.

He shook his head unsmilingly, and she sensed that her surmising was true. It was nothing short of bestial, and if this Master was responsible for such an outrage, then not all the charismatic seduction in the world would enable her to warm to him.

The guard put his hand on her arm, pulling her away from the bedchamber grille, and she deduced from his motioning gesture that she was to be escorted back to her room.

She nodded meekly, thanking God that all the wanton feelings that had assaulted her body had quickly subsided, and she could at least walk back through the corridors with some semblance of dignity.

'Thank you,' she said to the guard, but he didn't even acknowledge that she had spoken. Once inside her room, she all but wilted with shock and reaction to all she had witnessed and learned.

She was certain now that she hadn't dreamed the experience of dancing in front of the Master. Nor had she dreamed up his warning words that he expected her to be a virgin, and that if she was not – Abbie shivered. But of course she was a virgin! It was what every gentleman expected of his bride – though she doubted that in the eyes of God what the Master did with his many women could be construed as anything more than an unholy travesty of wedlock!

Even as she sank down on her bed and thought of the words, she knew that not every young woman of her age was the same, or desired a respectable marriage – Sophie, for instance, who knew more about the ways of loving and men than Abbie had ever imagined. She desperately wished Sophie was here now, so that Abbie could tell her in a lofty, superior way that she knew all about screwing and the ways of pleasuring a man.

But she didn't, of course. Not yet. Not all of it. And

she hardly imagined that the Master would refer to joining with a woman as screwing or even fornicating. He was too educated, too grand, and too much a gentleman for coarse talk.

Abbie felt like childishly stamping her foot at the thought. It was so ironic to think of such a heathen as a gentleman. But even so, there was something about him that belied all the crassness of the acts he performed and expected others to perform for him. If it didn't seem so bizarre, there was something quintessentially English about him that not all the quasi-eastern trappings in the world could disguise. She couldn't place it yet, but she would discover it in time.

She turned restlessly on the bed, wondering how long it would be before she was sent for. No doubt it would be a while, and the three hours the old woman had mentioned were not yet up. She would try to sleep, and not to dream. She eyed the jug of cordial by her bed. Whatever was in it was anathema to her now, and, asserting her own strength of character, she knew she would take no more of it.

While her head had been woolly and concussed it may have done its work, but she no longer wanted to feel dependent on it. She needed to be in control of her own mind and thoughts. Impulsively, she rose from the bed and tipped the liquid into the little washbasin in her room, refilling the jug with plain water. Such a simple little act made her feel remarkably better, as if she was once again Miss Abigail Richmond of The Grange, defiant to the last over what was to become of her.

Chapter Five

*B*rindley Richmond cared little for his ward's female activities. Just as long as she appeared for her meals and otherwise kept out of his way, he was satisfied. He hadn't wanted her here, but a sense of duty and concern for what his betters might think of him had he not taken her in after her parents' deaths, had made them form an uneasy alliance.

So it was predictable to his cynical household staff that once Brindley found that his ward had flown the coop he would be more incensed than worried, because now there was far more at stake than his own reputation. The bride-price promised to him by his old friend Lord Eustace was slipping out of his grasp, and he knew that even if the chit was brought home again, there would be a great question mark over whether or not she would be acceptable to the old rogue.

A doctor's examination would determine if she had been tampered with, of course, but having to enlist someone's service for such a task was unsavoury, to say the least. Brindley veered away from the very idea of having to find some discreet practitioner to perform the task of seeing if the girl's maidenhead was still intact. It would be a further outrage to Eustace if such a thing were to be ordered, putting a definite doubt in his mind over both the girl's virginity and modesty and therefore her suitability to bear his child.

Twenty-four hours after Abbie's disappearance Brindley still hadn't informed his old friend, and had contented himself by merely making curt enquiries among the staff, which eventually exploded into his more usual volcanic wrath. The following morning he summoned all of them to the drawing room, where most of them stood shuffling their feet, clearly feeling like fish out of water in this environment.

'You all know why you're here,' Brindley thundered. 'My niece has gone missing, and somebody – probably one of you – must have some idea of where she's gone. You all know that her mare was found with a broken leg and had to be destroyed. And by God, if I find out that one of you has aided and abetted her, the same fate may well await you!'

'He's hardly goin' the right way about making anybody own up to helping her, is he?' Sophie said out of the corner of her mouth to Cook.

Brindley rounded on her at once, his eyes narrowing as he took in her bulging shape beneath the coarse cloth of her workdress. She was a slut of the first order, he thought with distaste. But she needed to be questioned, like all the rest.

'You there, girl. What do you know about it?'

'I don't know nothin',' Sophie said defiantly. 'I've passed the time of day with the young lady if I've seen her in the garden, and that's all. She was always far too fine to waste time talking with the likes of us.'

'And so say all of us,' the young gardener breathed darkly from further along the line of servants.

Brindley's eyes raked over the motley lot of them. He paid meagre wages and rarely came into contact with any of them, and he preferred to keep it that way. That he had to appeal to them at all in this respect was an affront to him, and the bold look in the kitchen-maid's hot eyes was the worst affront of all.

'Get out of here, all of you,' he finally snapped. 'But I'm putting you all on your honour that if you hear anything, or think of anything that might help, you're to come to me at once. Anything could have happened to Miss Abigail, and if she isn't returned by this second nightfall, I'll have no alternative but to alert the constables. If that happens, you'll all be questioned again, so think very carefully. If you've forgotten anything that could be of use in finding her, and bringing her home safely, you're to come to me at once.'

They all knew his words were both a warning and a threat. If any of them was found to have helped Abbie get away, they'd be for it. And being interrogated by the constables wasn't a prospect any of them relished. More than one of them had come under their rough scrutiny before now.

But he'd left it a bit late to start sounding concerned for Abbie's safety, Sophie commented indignantly to Cook, once they had all been dismissed. It had been no more than an afterthought, and showed how little he really cared for her. It was only for proprieties' sake that he was making such an almighty fuss, when everybody knew he couldn't wait to be rid of her when she turned eighteen. And to some dreary, ancient, dried-up husband too.

Cook continued thumping away at the pastry case for the evening's pigeon pie, eyeing Sophie thoughtfully.

'And I'm wondering just how much you really know about the little escapade, miss?'

Sophie put an innocent look on her face. 'No more than I said upstairs. I was as flummoxed as anybody when I heard she'd gone missin' –'

'But you weren't tellin' the whole truth just now, were

you, my girl? I've seen the two of you with your heads together in the shrubbery, more than once.'

'You wouldn't tell on me, would you, Cook?' Sophie said with a scowl. 'We were only talkin', and there's no harm in that. She don't get many other folk to talk to, poor dab.'

And such juicy talking it was too, she added silently.

'Well, you just get on with your work and stop dawdling, and I might just forget what I've seen,' Cook said tartly.

But it soon became the talk of The Grange, and if Brindley hoped that Abbie had merely wandered off and would soon come dutifully home, there was one person who was equally certain that she wouldn't. Sophie couldn't wait to speed across the fields after dark, eager to confide the whole story to Tom in the warm, musky atmosphere of their secluded hay loft.

By now they were cocooned in the warm bed of straw high above the stalls in the barn where the cows were bedded down for the night, and for once there was something on her mind other than Tom's searching fingers.

'Where do you think she can have got to?' she said excitedly. 'I wouldn't like to think she was hurt, but the stable-lads went out looking for her, and although they found the nag, there was no sign of Miss Abbie anywhere.'

She knew Tom was far more interested in undoing her bodice than hearing about the missing Abigail Richmond, but he was perceptive enough to see that his girl was really concerned about the disappearance of the young lady.

'What I think is that it's likely no harm's come to her if they haven't already found her dead or maimed,' he said lazily. 'You've probably been filling her head with such stuff lately, I daresay she went off to find some of her own,' he added with a lecherous laugh.

'Do you really think so?' Sophie said dubiously. She gave a nervous giggle at the thought. 'Gawd, if she practises some of what I've been preachin' to her –'

She giggled again, for what was the use of worrying about it when there was nothing in the world she could do about it? And meanwhile, there were far more interesting things to do right here and now.

'Just what have you been tellin' her, wench?' Tom said with mock aggression. 'I thought what we did was private.'

He had freed her accommodating breasts now, fondling them in his hands and feeling their ready response as they strained towards him. Sophie arched luxuriously, giving him more access, and urging him on silently.

'So it is, but the poor bitch knew nothin' and needed a bit o' teaching, see, and I decided I was expert enough to give her some.'

'Oh aye, I'll agree that you're an expert all right,' Tom said with a grin, his fingers starting to tantalise the tips of her nipples in soft, circular movements. 'So just what did you tell her?'

'Well, all sorts,' Sophie said, beginning to breathe more heavily as Tom's lips brushed her nipples and licked the area surrounding them. 'About this, for a start. The poor young dab had no idea what she was missin' until I told her.'

'And about this?'

She felt his hand suddenly clamp over her dress in the region of her crotch. The layers of workdress and petticoats were between them, but his farmworker's hands were large and rough, and he worked his fingers sensuously over the area while she squirmed with pleasure.

'About all of it,' Sophie said, seconds before his mouth

left her breasts and sought her lips, clamping over them in a tongue-thrusting kiss. At the same time his hand raked up her clothes and found the moist, willing flesh, opening her at once with his probing fingers.

'And how did my lady react to the thought of a man screwing her?' Tom spoke seductively against her lips.

'Oh, she liked the idea of it all right. She's more than ripe for lovin, Tom,' she said with a moaning gasp as the probing went deeper into her, releasing her juices so that they flowed and sucked all around that jabbing finger.

'I reckon that's where she's gone then, to find a man,' Tom said, with a leer.

'My Gawd, you don't really think so, do you? But that means I'm responsible for her disappearance!' At the frightening thought, she almost leapt away from all the delightful things her lover was doing to her now.

'No you ain't. And stop thinkin' about her, can't you? I don't aim to spend my evenin' worryin' about no missin' floosie. I'd rather concentrate on the one I've got.'

He was getting impatient now, and Sophie knew it was high time she stopped talking about Miss Abbie. And there was no point in thinking about what might have happened to her either. It was like bringing a third person into their love-making, and she had no truck with any of that.

Besides, she heard Tom's trouser fastenings ripping open, and gave up thinking about anything but what was happening here and now. There was nothing they could do about it, so what was the use of wasting this precious time together? There were far more important things to do.

Tom had already grabbed her hand and was pushing it inside his trousers, and Sophie grasped him tight, grazing her thumbnail down the hard shaft of his cock, knowing what he liked and hearing him grunt with satisfaction as she yanked it out into the air. Her eyes glittered with lust, her tongue sliding around her lips in anticipation of what was still to come. Sometimes it was good to strip off completely and take their time about things, and sometimes it was good to pretend they were about to be caught in the act and had to do everything rough and fast – and she knew from Tom's aggressive attitude that this was to be one of those times.

'Turn over,' Tom said harshly. 'On your knees, wench.'

She obeyed at once, elbows and forearms flat on the blanket-covered straw and thrusting her rump high in the air. She could feel the coolness of the air on her buttocks as Tom thrust her skirts upwards and fondled the rounded globes for a minute, the calloused roughness of his hands doing nothing to lessen the excitement surging through her. He positioned himself carefully before he penetrated her inner recesses, even though she knew how impatient he was for her now. But she gave a small squeal as he thrust slowly into her, for despite her wetness, the initial entrance to her core in this fashion always felt a little unnatural. But once he began to move she relaxed, knowing that this gentle introduction wouldn't last more than a few seconds, and nor was it necessary. It always fired Tom up to poke her this way, and almost immediately he was thrusting into her hard and viciously. And she was much too excited by his panting breath and the way his fingers were digging into her buttocks now to think of anything but the thrill of the game. If there was anything better, Sophie didn't know of it. And she was coming so fast –

'Tom,' she gasped out warningly, knowing all about the risks of making a baby. Even for a kitchen-maid, the disgrace would be hard to overcome, especially in a household as strict as The Grange, with a tyrant of an employer.

'I know,' he grunted, lingering just long enough for

her to finish, then pulling out of her to spill his seed on the straw, while she collapsed in a heap on the blanket.

Seconds later, he had turned her onto her back and was lying across her, but his trousers were safely buttoned up again now. That was the only thing about a quick screw, Sophie thought mournfully. Once he had come, that was the end of it. But not for her –

Her skirts were already rucked up to her waist, and she felt his tongue tease its way into her belly-button, circling the little knub of it as if he was already where she most wanted him to be. She pushed his head down, squirming as the little licks and nips trailed over her rounded belly and down to the fleshy, bushy mound below.

It was still engorged, still as wet as washday, she thought jubilantly, remembering how she had told Miss Abbie that that was how a woman needed to be for a man. Tom finger-poked her now. He was still rough, but it was how she liked him. Not for her the soft touch of an aristocrat, and despite herself, she found herself thinking fleetingly of Miss Abbie again, and praying that whatever she had found, it was something as good as this –

And then her eyes closed and her panting breath pounded as Tom's tongue continued what his fingers had begun, and the luscious love-spasms began all over again. And she couldn't think of anything else but him.

'I suppose I'd better be gettin' back,' Sophie said eventually with great reluctance, knowing she would far rather remain here all night in the sweet-smelling barn, locked in her lover's arms. But knowing too that Cook would be keeping a weather-eye out for her if she didn't get back to the servants' quarters before midnight.

'Just one last feel, then,' Tom muttered, as if he couldn't get enough of her. But she knew that one last feel could often start up something that lasted an hour, and she daren't risk it with all the fuss going on at The Grange. She clamped her hand fast over his as it reached for her crotch.

'You've had quite enough for one night, Tom Peach,' she said severely. 'Let me be now, or I might not turn up tomorrow night to pleasure you –'

She squealed again as he pushed her back on the ground, pinning her arms to the straw, his eyes hot and glittering.

'You'd better, wench,' he said arrogantly. 'You'll never find a better stud than me, so don't go thinking you will.'

'Don't I know it! And I didn't mean it, you dolt. I was just teasing –'

'That's all right then,' Tom said, his small burst of temper dissipating as fast as it came. He leant forward and kissed her mouth. 'Do you want me to walk part of the way back with you?' he said generously.

'What for? You've never wanted to before. Don't you think I'm capable of findin' me own way back?' She was perky now, thankful his good humour was restored.

Tom laughed. 'I think you're capable of anything, you lust-bin,' he said, pulling her to her feet before they descended the rickety ladder in the hay loft. Once they were at the farm gate where they would part company, he gave her a friendly whack across the backside, sent her on her way and went off whistling. It was the nearest Tom Peach ever came to saying he loved her.

'Cheeky bugger,' Sophie thought cheerfully as she trudged back across the fields. She didn't mind his lack of sweet talk. They both knew what they wanted and they got it from each other in full measure.

It was a good two miles between the farm where Tom worked and The Grange, but the fields were moonlit now, and sparkling with the night-time dew that heralded a fine warm day tomorrow. And in any case, Sophie knew the way as well as she knew the back of her hand. She quite liked to be alone after a lusty session with Tom. It gave her burning cheeks time to cool down, and her throbbing parts time to subside properly. And it gave her a bit of breathing-space before she had to meet the eyes of that old harridan, Cook.

She was humming a little tune when she suddenly sensed that she was no longer alone. It was no more than a feeling, but it was very real, and her heart began to pound sickly as she realised she was virtually in no-man's land, halfway between the outlying farms and the distant shadowy outline of The Grange's environs. She stood perfectly still. She strained her eyes to see if there was anyone lurking in the ditches, or behind one of the big oak trees along the hedgerows, and trying to detect the slightest sound of breathing. But all she could hear was her own, raggedy and hoarse. She summoned up all her resolve.

'Whoever you are, I've got no money, so you're wastin' your time stalkin' me,' she said as boldly as she could.

To her horror she heard a thick, guttural laugh from the direction of the shadowy oak tree nearby, and knew that someone had been following her all right.

'Well now, me beauty, that's a real invitin' word to be usin', so it is,' she heard him say.

'What word?' Sophie spluttered. All her bravado was gone in an instant, and she knew she would never outrun the man, whose powerful shape she could see perfectly well now as he stepped out from the shadows.

'It's quite a while since I've had the chance to be stalkin' a pretty maid such as yourself,' he said coarsely, and Sophie knew instantly what he meant by the word.

A dart of fear ran through her, but it was coupled with a wicked and unbidden thrill as the fellow came nearer, and she could see that he was roughly handsome – and a rogue of an Irish tinker if ever she saw and heard one, she thought.

'If you come near me, I'll scream,' she snapped.

'Will you now? And who's to hear you, I wonder?' he taunted. 'Not that stuff-bucket of a gent at the big house, to be sure, and nor would he care what happened to one of his minions. But if you're another sample of the goods the place has to offer –'

Sophie was nothing if not quick-witted, and she was alerted at once by the sly words.

'What goods? Have you seen Miss Abbie? Where did you see her? If you've harmed her –'

The words died away and she felt increasingly alarmed now as the fellow laughed again, his attention caught by her agitation.

'Sure and I've seen her,' he said carelessly. 'And had a quick sample of her tempting curves. But I'm thinking a servant-girl will be more appreciative of a lusty fellow than a rich man's sprog.'

Sophie stepped back as he approached her, but he was too quick for her. Before she could protest he had grabbed her in his arms and yanked her head back with one powerful hand, raking her mouth with his tongue, while his free hand reached for her breasts. She struggled to free herself, even while the thrill of this unexpected moonlight encounter was not lost on her. A roguish Irishman could be an exciting lover, and Tom would never know. Nor would it be the first time she had strayed, and she didn't doubt that he had done so too when the the opportunity arose. But there were more urgent things on her mind at this moment, and she wrenched herself out of the Irishman's embrace.

'Where did you see Miss Abbie?' she gasped. 'It's important that I know where and when.'

For the present, she wouldn't let herself imagine the worst. Nor that it had been this oaf who had done something ghastly to her mistress. For all that the girl was such a simpleton when it came to worldly matters, Sophie was fond of her, and wanted no harm to come to her. She was so dainty and so innocent of the ways of men, and she would have been frightened half to death if this one had tried anything on.

'Well now, before I tell you that, we'll have to consider what reward I'm to get for the information, won't we, sweet thing?' the man said lazily.

Sophie fumed. Men could be so stupid at times, and he must be wearing blinkers if he couldn't see that this was important to her. But the idea of herself getting some reward from Brindley Richmond if she went to him with positive information about Miss Abigail's whereabouts wasn't lost on her either. She stamped her foot on the damp grass, feeling the wetness seep through her thin shoes and stockings.

'We'll discuss that when you've told me what you know,' she snapped.

'We'll discuss it now,' he said, suddenly aggressive. 'Do you think I was born yesterday, me darlin'?'

'All right. You can have a kiss –'

He hooted with laughter now. 'A kiss? Is that right! It's worth more than one paltry kiss to tell you what I know about the pretty miss.'

'Well, you can state the terms, as long as it's within reason – and as long as the information's worth it,' Sophie added, knowing she was being reckless, but having gone too far to back out now. He'd never let her go without *some* kind of reward.

'I'll have a taste of you and a quick stalkin', and then I'll be on me way like I intended doin' a few days ago.'

She gasped, but she knew there was no help for it. If she didn't agree, he'd take her anyway. He was big and powerful, and he could easily overcome her struggles. And if he really *did* know where Miss Abbie was, it would be worth submitting, and a quick fumble beneath her petticoats wasn't going to set the world on fire.

'So where did you see her?' she demanded, but he was obviously intent on getting part of his reward first.

He propelled her back into the shadow of the oak tree until her back was pressed against it, and she stood impatiently with her legs parted while his hand roamed up her skirts and pressed against her protruding knub, rubbing it right and left in a rocking manner. Her pulses jolted into life at once. His fingers were blunt-ended, and they rubbed her with a different touch from Tom's. Different and exciting.

'That's me fine beauty,' he grunted, as her breathing became more laboured and heavy. 'All ripe and ready for the pluckin', aren't you? And 'tis a lovely bush you've got down there to guide a fellow inside –'

'You promised to tell me,' Sophie said faintly.

'All in good time. Don't tell me you ain't enjoyin' yourself. I can tell you ain't no shrinkin' violet, nor new to the game.'

She couldn't argue with that. The chance encounter had taken her by surprise, but she was already very aware of the bulge at his crotch, as stiff as a ramrod now, and exciting her more by the minute.

'I ain't lyin' down in the damp grass,' she said, trying to keep some control over her swimming senses as the wetness flooded through her again.

'There's no need. I'm quite partial to a stand-up fuck meself,' he said crudely, making her gasp. Even Tom never used such words, but somehow just hearing them made her throb with excitement and anticipation.

She realised he was pulling his knob out of his breeches now, and she could see it quivering in the light of the moon. It was huge and damp and bulbously purple at the tip. Her eyes gleamed at the sight of it, and without even thinking what she was doing, she grasped it, sucking in her breath at the very thought of it entering her.

She knew there would be no more finesse about him than there was with Tom. No pretence that this was anything more than a quick poke and then he would be on his way – but there was something he'd promised to tell her, and even though her senses were swimming with lust now, Sophie fought to remember what it was.

Miss Abbie. Dear God, she had to find out what he knew about Miss Abbie.

'That's it, girlie. Guide it into that luscious hole,' he said hoarsely, and then he was bending his knees to get better access and pushing his cock up into her without more ado. It was so rock-hard and swollen that for a moment it felt as if it was near to splitting her in two.

To stop herself from falling over she was forced to cling on to him as he pumped into her, and with a last semblance of sanity she gasped out that he musn't come in her. If she ever had to have a sprog, it should be Tom's, and not this oaf's.

'Don't fret, me darlin', I'll pull out in time,' he gasped. 'I've no wish for any little encumbrances.'

He suddenly did just as he said, withdrawing so fast that Sophie nearly fell over. She clamped her legs together tightly now, feeling more bruised than pleasured, and furious that she had let him touch her at all. But it had been for a reason, she reminded herself.

'So now tell me about Miss Abbie like you promised,' she snapped, once he had finished himself off and tidied himself.

'I seen her down at the stream,' he said. 'She's a fine piece of skirt for a toff, but not so willin' as yourself, of course,' he added, in what was supposed to be a compliment.

'But when?' Sophie almost yelled, thinking him stupid indeed if he couldn't tell her what she wanted to know. And then she felt more than a stab of fear at his mention of the stream. If he had done anything bad to her mistress – And if he had, then he could very well do something equally bad to *her*. The fact didn't escape Sophie, and she slid quickly away from him as if ready to take flight. She spoke more quickly.

'You know the constables are going to be searching for her soon, don't you? If you know anything, you'd better tell me now so I can forestall them if need be –'

She yelped as he strode forward and grasped her arm.

'What do you mean, slut?' he snarled. 'When I saw her she was well enough, so if she's gone missin' don't you go layin' no blame at my door for anything that's happened to her.'

'She's been missing since yesterday,' Sophie said through terrified lips. 'And you said you'd seen her –'

'So I did, and she was fine and well when I left her,' he snarled again. 'But if you go pointin' the finger at me, I'll be after tellin' the constables how you came and had a fine old time with me, and were after gettin' your revenge now I'm going away and won't take you with me.'

Sophie's eyes dilated. He was an Irish story-teller all right. And if such a tale ever reached Tom's ears, he'd finish with her like a shot, and she couldn't bear that.

'I'm not pointin' the finger at anybody. I'm just concerned about my young lady, that's all,' she said.

He laughed again, reverting to his roguish manner.

'Well, from what I saw of her, you needn't fret yourself too much over that one. If she's got away from that old stuff-bucket in the big house, then by now she'll be havin' a high old time of her own, you mark my words. Now, how about one more kiss before I go on me way?'

Sophie twisted away as his beefy arms reached out for her. She couldn't bear the sight or the smell of him one second longer, and her feet flew like the wind over the soft damp grass as she yelled back at him.

'You've had your fun, you bastard, and you'd best be on your way before I meet my friend,' she invented wildly.

For a minute she was afraid he was going to run after

her, but she only heard his coarse laugh following her, and the sound of his words ringing in her ears.

'He's welcome to my pickin's, darlin'. But you can tell him I approve of his choice.'

She ran on, half-sobbing now. She'd learned virtually nothing, except that the Irishman had seen Miss Abbie, but she was pretty sure now that it had nothing to do with her disappearance. Such louts were always boasting of their conquests, and he'd not have been able to resist telling some of it to Sophie. And she had had to put up with his pawing and poking for nothing.

Even as the thought slid into her mind, Sophie began to slow down. The outline of the estate with the big house in the background were coming into view now, and she couldn't deny that the encounter hadn't been entirely unpalatable.

In fact, it didn't harm anybody to have a change now and then, as long as Tom didn't know, and she certainly wasn't going to tell him. Besides, she thought, almost crowing to herself, it wasn't every girl who had two lovers in one night, and such lusty lovers too.

Tom was the best, of course, she thought hastily, but she soon found it easy to forget the indignity of the other one's assault, and to preen herself for the fact that she might be no more than a plain-faced kitchen-maid, but when it came to loving, she had all and more of what was required to keep a man. She could even feel a mite sorry for Miss sweet-faced Abbie Richmond, knowing that she was by far the superior when it came to loving. And despite all her teachings she doubted that my lady would ever be able to forget her prissy upbringing enough to enjoy such earthy pleasures.

Chapter Six

*A*bbie recovered quickly from the erotic scenes she had witnessed and the fright of being discovered. She had been excited beyond measure, and now felt an increasing hunger to experience this unknown art of seduction for herself. In her innocence, she believed she was already as moist and ready for a man as she would ever be, and it wasn't in her nature to be patient. But even so, she knew better than to leave the bedchamber again. She dare not risk it for a second time.

If what she suspected was true – that the Master had known she was peeping through the lattice grille, and had fully intended her to witness his debauchery – then he would also expect her to be waiting for his command to go to him. Her nerves were alive with impatience and excitement. She felt more restless than she had ever been in her life, far too restless simply to lie on her bed and wait obediently.

She rose now, ripping aside the confining veil that was still fastened across her mouth and was suddenly stifling her, just as the whole atmosphere of the house did. She needed air, and she needed it now.

She sped across to the window and tried to wrench it

open, but it was stuck fast, and she could see nothing through it, she thought in surprise. Until this moment she had never realised that the glass was opaque, confining the person inside the room even more. She was truly in a beautiful, evil prison, she thought with renewed alarm. The knowledge made her feel even more claustrophobic, and she rattled the window fastening in frustration.

And then it gave way, opening outwards so fast that she almost fell out after it. But as it did so, the fragrant purity of apple-scented air assailed her nostrils, and she simply closed her eyes and breathed in deeply for ecstatic moments before she looked down.

Her heart jolted with shock as she did so, and the suspicion that she was indeed in some foreign place lodged even more firmly in her mind. The vast courtyard below was surrounded by tall trees that blocked any view beyond. It was comprised of little sections and arbours separated by white-painted arches. Each arbour was filled with trees and bushes. As well as the familiar apples that she recognised, most of the trees were loaded with exotic fruits of a kind Abbie had never seen before. An oval pond was edged with a tiled border of white and gold that glinted in the sunlight, and in its crystal blue water she could see darting gold and other brilliantly-hued fish. Several white peacocks paraded elegantly around the courtyard, and even as she watched, awe-struck at all this unexpected magnificence, she heard their raucous cries, and wondered fleetingly how something so beautiful could utter such jarring sounds.

This *had* to be some eastern place – yet another, more logical thought presented itself, for how could it be? She had surely not been away from The Grange long enough to travel distances over sea and land.

'The lady will come away from the window now,' she heard a voice say behind her. She whirled at once, to find the old woman standing perfectly still in the centre of her room. How she hated these silent entrances, Abbie raged, invading her privacy.

'Is it forbidden that I even breathe fresh air, then?' she said angrily. 'I cannot think that even the most tyrannical Master would deny me that!'

Maya gave a grimace of a smile. 'You need not fear such things. The Master is generous to his favoured ones.' She intoned the words Abbie had heard before as if it were a mantra.

Abbie scowled in a way that was disapproved of in a young lady's etiquette, but by now she no longer cared about such things.

'Has he sent you to fetch me, then? Am I to be his next sacrificial lamb?' she said, oozing sarcasm.

Maya looked at her silently, as if she did not know what to make of young English women who defied everything she had been indoctrinated to believe in. She walked stiffly towards the window and closed it firmly, and when she continued to say nothing, Abbie became more incensed.

'If you are to take me to the Master, how do you know I am quite well, and will not defile him by my uncleanliness?' she asked sarcastically.

She had never imagined saying such things to anyone, but such sensibilities seemed far out of place now, when this woman knew her body as intimately as she knew it herself.

'Your monthly functions took place almost as soon as you came here,' the old woman said. 'It has all been attended to, and the Master is well aware that the time is right for the joining. You would not be taken to him otherwise.'

Abbie gritted her teeth amid the fury and indignity of her words. No matter what she said, the old harridan seemed to be one step ahead of her. Even so, the thought slid into her mind that if there had been only one monthly function, her suspicion that she had not been taken to some foreign place must be correct, for such a sea voyage would have taken many weeks, if not months.

'I would like to know what has become of my own clothes,' she said imperiously now. 'It's unthinkable that I remain here in this place, garbed and painted like some concubine –'

Maya's eyes flashed, and Abbie could see that she had offended her, and that she regarded the words as an insult.

'You are mistaken, lady. You are not garbed as a concubine, nor are you housed in the *zenana*. You have already been given special treatment, and five pieces of the jewellery that adorn you are a bride's favours.'

Abbie's heart jumped uneasily again. 'You're not telling me this Master intends to marry me, are you? The last thing I expected of him was an honourable attachment! And what is this *zenana* of which you speak?'

'You would do well to be more humble, White Dove,' Maya said sharply. 'The *zenana* is the women's quarters. As for marriage – no, it is not to be one of your feudal English marriages. But the Master indulges himself in whatever fantasy appeals to him at the time, and more especially with a prize such as yourself. So he has commanded that you come to him suitably adorned.'

'I don't understand you' Abbie said, not liking the sound of this at all. Anyway, she certainly had no wish to marry a stranger – although, on reflection, there was no comparison between all she had seen of the Master so far and the aged Lord Eustace, whom her uncle had chosen for her. She shuddered at the memory of those ancient groping hands, and pushed down the frisson of excitement at the thought of the Master's young, virile body. She concentrated on what the old woman was telling her now.

'There are certain requirements for a bride to bring to her prince –'

'The Master is a *prince*?'

The old woman sighed. 'Only to those who serve him, lady. But here he is revered in the same way as a prince, and therefore we do him the honour of according him the same rituals that would apply to one of noble birth.'

'What rituals are these?'

Abbie sat down abruptly on the edge of her bed now. Clearly the time had still not come for her summons to the Master's chamber, even though the little ornate clock by her bed told her that three hours had long since passed. This delay in sending for her was probably quite deliberate, Abbie thought. She glared at the old woman, who gestured to her that she should look again in the mirror.

'You see the *tilaka*, lady,' the woman said, pointing to the mark on Abbie's forehead that had been made earlier with sandalwood paste. 'This announces that you walk on the straight path, signifying purity. The ear-rings are to remind you that a woman's ears are weak and should pay no heed to gossip. The necklace ensures that you keep your head bowed in humility. The bangles on your right arm tell your hand to go forward in charity, and the anklets tell you to put your right foot forward.'

Abbie stared at her in silence. It all sounded so servile, and wherever this Master came from, he was obviously used to treating women as chattels.

But she was annoyingly intrigued by the things she had been told, never thinking that the wearing of jewellery might have any particular significance in this way.

'Is that all?' she said at last, when the woman said no more. 'You mentioned five pieces of jewellery.'

'The Master thought it unsuitable for his English White Dove to wear the nose-ring –' At Abbie's gasp of outrage, she paused, then went on, '– and from your

90

face, I see that he was right. It is not an accepted custom for your countrywomen, I think.'

Nor was dressing her up in strange garments and jewels and transporting her to a different world, whether physically or mentally, Abbie thought keenly, but she let that pass.

'That is why the ruby is placed in your navel instead,' the woman continued. 'It symbolises blood.'

Abbie felt her stomach clench. She was still not convinced that everything here was simply a sexual pleasure-dome, or that something more sinister might not take place in these surroundings.

'You need not be afraid,' Maya went on. 'It is merely the symbol of the life-blood coursing through your veins. The Master is strongly opposed to necrophilia –'

'To what?'

'The lady clearly does not know the term,' Maya said in her smoothly sing-song, infuriating manner. 'It means that a person is attracted to the sexual pleasure of dead bodies. The Master considers such an act of defilement to be an abomination. And you need never fear for your life providing you are humble at all times.'

Abbie knew her eyes must have dilated in horror at hearing such a ghoulish tale. She licked her dry lips. The more she heard of this Master and his practices – even those that he didn't indulge in – the more she feared him. And this sycophantic old crone had far more command and understanding of the English language than she had believed at first.

'There is one more thing that White Dove should know,' Maya said now when Abbie continued to be silent.

'And what's that?' Abbie said sullenly, wondering just what else was to be required of her.

By now she freely admitted to herself that she had expected to be swiftly taken to the Master and to be swept along in an orgy of sexual gratification such as

91

she had already witnessed. The fact that he was apparently in no hurry to receive her after all, was just as swiftly turning her feelings to frustration and anger.

'The ruby placed in the centre of your body decrees that as your life was saved by the Master, it now belongs to him. You are as bound to him as if you were in chains, but providing you always behave with humility and respect for being so honoured, such a thing will not be necessary.'

The words outraged Abbie, intimating that she was to be just another love-slave, which was what she considered the Indian girls to be. Except that she had been given the bride-jewels – but even that made a mockery of all that was decent in English society. They were probably given to every new conquest the Master made, and she chose not to enquire further.

'What of this bangle?' she said instead, fingering the single heavy ivory circle on her upper left arm.

'This is a symbol of the Master's esteemed worth. It shows that he is brave enough to kill an elephant, as he has done many times. It is a matter for great pride to be given such a bangle to wear, and unless he agrees to it, it should not be removed except for sleeping and bathing.'

Abbie had heard enough. By now it all seemed like a lot of superstitious nonsense – or would have done had it not been said with such solemnity. Whether it was all part of some ancient pagan rites or just mumbo-jumbo, the fact that Maya related it all with such conviction was unnerving in itself. It was all beginning to undermine her fragile self-confidence. This Master, whoever he was, would seem to have total control over everything in his kingdom, and Abbie Richmond was his newest prize.

Before she could say anything more, her door was opened again, and two of the young serving-girls entered. Each of them stood with their hands held together, fingers pointing downwards. All their actions seemed those of servitude, and she was beginning to find it as tiresome as it was alarming. Even in her uncle's household she had never felt so much in the grip of something she couldn't control. But these girls seemed to have no wills of their own, and the worst part of it all was that they accepted it so readily.

However near or far from The Grange she had been taken, it was to be plunged into a different culture from the one she had always known, and she felt a sudden desperate longing for the healthy, blessedly normal English way of life she had always known. Even life at The Grange.

'It is time,' the old woman said, even as Abbie opened her mouth to demand to know exactly where she was.

Behind the two girls she could see the eunuch guard in the open doorway now, and assumed that he was not allowed right inside the bedchamber. Not that his presence could possibly affect a woman, she thought wildly, for what could he do with his castrated testicles and flaccid penis, and his tongue cut out? All the things she had witnessed, and the memory of the lusty things Sophie had told her about with such eager excitement, filled her with sudden pity for the man who was no longer a man. She felt obliged to avert her eyes quickly before he could see the knowledge of his plight reflected in them.

But evidently he was to be an additional escort as Abbie was taken to do the Master's bidding. She rose from the bed on unsteady legs, and allowed the girls to re-fasten the veil around the lower part of her face. They each took one of her hands and moved silently towards the door, with Maya preceding them in queenly fashion.

It was almost farcical, Abbie thought, with rising hysteria, as Maya led the way along the maze of corridors where she had gone before, with herself and the two serving-girls following, and the guard bringing up the rear. It was an almost regal procession – and ending with what? To share the Master's bed for an allotted time and be his plaything, attending to his every desire and obeying his every whim, and then being discarded until the next time. Or until the next woman was plucked from the *zenana* to pleasure him.

Abbie shivered suddenly. She was totally inexperienced, and she recalled how those other girls had known exactly what was required of them. Knowing her own inadequacy made her extremely nervous and agitated. She was sure she couldn't do any of those things to a man's satisfaction. She was such an *ingénue*, and he would be angry with her. And if that happened, she had no idea what punishments there might be in store.

But there was always the memory of the dream that wasn't a dream. In it she had been guided and instructed by the Master himself, and a primitive mating instinct had supplied her with the knowledge she needed. That and her own awakening sexuality that had done the rest.

The procession finally ended outside a door. Abbie couldn't be sure it was the one she had seen before. In the maze of twists and turns to reach here they all looked the same, all with their latticed peep-holes through which light spilled out into the dimly lit corridors.

'You will enter, lady, and stand inside the door with your head bowed. You will remain there and await the Master's instruction to go to him. On no account will you raise your eyes until you hear his voice.'

Abbie wanted to laugh out loud at such an absurdity. She had been taught to be ladylike in a gentleman's presence, but to be expected to obey such commands was almost ludicrous. But as she felt a small grip on her arm from the old woman's talon-like fingers, she decided that discretion was better than flaunting disobedience, at least until she knew what was in store for her.

And even then, how could she disobey, when she had no other choice?

Almost before she knew it, she was inside the room and the door had closed behind her. And suddenly too terrified to do anything else, she kept her eyes tightly closed and her head down. Unconsciously her hands assumed the same downward steepling position used by the Indian girls.

She despised herself for allowing such manipulation. But by now she was aware of an insidious, exotic enjoyment in playing the part of the concubine, and until that moment, she had not even realised that it could be so, or that, provided she could think of it all as merely playing a part, then she could be whoever she wanted to be and do whatever the Master wanted of her. Inside herself she would still be Miss Abigail Richmond, and no one could take away the fact of her own identity.

'Won't you look at me, Miss Richmond?' a voice invited.

Her eyes flew open in astonishment, as much from hearing her own name as the length of time it seemed she had been standing there. She had not dared to move a muscle, but now she blinked in the seductive lighting all around the room and the softly candlelit table in the centre of it.

Her mouth dropped open as she registered that this was not the bedchamber with the black satin sheets and mirrored walls. This was a dining-room, and the most splendid one she had ever seen, with its blue and gilt-painted ceiling adorned with cherubs and peacocks in a seemingly heavenly setting. The walls were hung with exotic carpets, while the floor was patterned in exquisite mosaics that echoed the colours and shapes of the ceiling.

But while she took in all this magnificence and the feast that was apparently awaiting her, her eyes were drawn to the Master himself, coming towards her now with his hands outstretched. He wore the white robes that sat on him so majestically, and at his throat was a huge ruby that matched the one in her navel. To Abbie, the matching seemed symbolic, and not knowing whether or not she was meant to address this magnificence, she stammered out the first thing that came into her head.

'I thank you for using my given name – Sir.'

He smiled, and she thought she had never seen such white teeth – or perhaps it was merely that they appeared so in contrast to the darkness of his skin. Yet, at closer quarters now, she was quite sure he was not Indian. It was rather the effect of living in hotter climes that had deepened his skin colour, she thought swiftly, remembering several male acquaintances of her uncle who had done the Grand Tour and had appeared in the same healthy condition.

'I thought it would put you at your ease for a moment,' he said, with what Abbie considered to be a vast understatement. 'But from now on, we will play the game of Master and conquest.'

So the brief moment of empathy she had imagined was not to continue.

'If we must,' she muttered, half-amazed at herself for even daring to say anything so feebly defiant, when she was quite sure none of the other women in the *zenana* would dare to do such a thing. Then, seeing a sudden surge of irritation in his eyes, she swiftly remembered that she had been given special treatment, and a luxurious bedroom of her own, and she was not being treated in quite the same way as them – yet.

'I'm sorry. You must forgive me. I am not used to this situation.'

To her astonishment she heard him laugh. He had

come closer to her now, and she noted the aromatic scents surrounding him. It was extremely pleasant to be near to a man who didn't smell of tobacco or horses, or even more unsavoury things. Daringly, she spoke to her captor again.

'Is it permitted to smile?'

He took her hand and raised it to his lips, and it was such an old-fashioned, gentlemanly gesture that it brought a glimmer of tears to Abbie's eyes. Seconds later he had gently removed the veil from her face, and with great tenderness he slowly ran his finger around her lips. Surely a man who could show such sensitivity could not be *all* bad.

'I hope that you will smile often, White Dove, for I have seldom seen such a tempting mouth as yours.'

Her smile became a little crooked then, not missing the innuendo in the words. She had hoped fervently that all this nonsense was over, and that he would continue acknowledging her English name and upbringing and acting with an English decorum. But clearly such hopes were not to be. He held out his hand, and without thinking, she put her own in his. His fingers curled around hers, caressing the soft skin between them.

'Come. We will eat first, and then we will have a different feast. And you will call me Master.'

His words instantly reinstated their different roles, thought Abbie. Just for a moment, in some peculiar way, she had managed to pretend they were equals, but this was obviously not to last either.

She walked with him to the damask-covered table, loaded with dishes of meats and vegetables on small raised stands that had enclosed candles burning beneath them to keep the dishes warm. She had been brought food at intervals ever since she arrived here, but she recalled that it had been bland, nourishing food, and she had sometimes longed for something tastier. Now she was almost dazed by the spicy aromas assaulting her nostrils, together with the delectable presentation of foods that she didn't instantly recognise, and her mouth watered in anticipation.

She was told to sit at one end of the table while the Master sat at the other. He clapped his hands, and instantly two large eunuchs seemed to appear from nowhere, silently serving the food to them and then quickly retiring from sight. Abbie hadn't been asked what she would like – but nor could they ask her, she remembered, and she was presumably expected to taste everything. As she stared down now at the several plates in front of her, the Master spoke again.

'I promise it will not poison you, White Dove. You will find that the food is of the highest quality, and the ingredients include some of the most effective love potions available. We may linger over it as long as you wish, since we have the rest of the night at our disposal.'

Abbie started at the words, her face flooding with colour. This was just the preliminary then, and he meant to seduce her by every means available, biding his time, since there was no escape for her. She was his prey, and when they had satisfied one hunger, the other feast to which he referred was to be herself.

'What exactly is this food?' she murmured with a quaver in her voice.

'Oysters and venison and honey, spiced with coriander and peppers,' he informed her. 'The chicken dish is cooked in lemons and wine to appease your English taste buds, should the other prove too hot for you. The vegetables you will find very palatable, and they are also steeped in wine and spices. After we have had our fill of these, we will share a dish of ripe grapes, bananas and passion fruit, mulled and spiced with ginger and honey to quicken and fire the blood.'

She had never heard a man speak with such authority on food, but this was evidently meant to be a meal with hidden properties to inflame the senses. And despite the enticing lusciousness of his descriptions, his last words served to dry her mouth again. But her initial suspicion of the food disappeared, even though she knew that this was seduction in the most primitive manner, and a world away from Cook's dreary concoctions at The Grange. It was also like nothing she had ever experienced before, and her resistance to all the new things that were happening was fast beginning to crumble.

Beside her plate a goblet of red wine had already been poured out, and there was a large carafe of it awaiting them. As the Master saw her eyeing it, he nodded.

'Drink freely, White Dove, but not so much that your senses are dulled. I would not wish you to be unreceptive to all the delights we have in store. And now we will eat.'

Abbie decided she needed to sip the wine before she could taste a morsel, and the deliciously fiery liquid coursed down her throat. But it hardly matched the hot fire of the food. It made her gasp at every swallow, but it was so meltingly succulent that she ate her fill, even if she was obliged to take frequent sips of wine to offset its potency.

Through the haze of candlelight in the centre of the table, she could see the Master's outline becoming rosier by the second. She was well aware that the effects of the food and wine were having a relaxing effect on her, but whatever aphrodisiacs were in the food were nothing compared with the sheer sexuality of the man himself.

When they were sated with the meats and spiced vegetables, the Master came to sit close beside her, and began to spoon-feed her with the rich confection of fruits and honey and wine. With his dark eyes burning into hers, Abbie thought weakly that short of being physically seduced, this was the most erotic thing that had ever happened to her. And she was quite sure that there was much, much more to come.

She felt a trickle of honey and fruit juice run around

the corners of her mouth, and before she knew what he was about, he had leaned forward and slowly and sensuously licked it off, tasting the curves of her lips with his tongue. Her mouth was slightly parted, and she felt the merest touch of his tongue enter it, teasing her inner flesh before it withdrew again to savour more of the sweet liquid that still clung to her velvety skin. It was as if to say that it was not yet time for the full exploration of the virginal Abbie Richmond – or White Dove, or whoever she was, she thought, her senses reeling in sweet delirium as her heartbeats quickened and her loins pulsated and throbbed.

She had never known the skilled art of seduction before, and this was certainly something that Sophie had never mentioned. But it had already begun to dawn on Abbie that there were very different ways of love-making, and that Sophie and Tom's lusty thrashings would be vastly different from that of a practised seducer like the Master.

But she no longer wanted to think of them, nor could she. Not now, when there were tantalising fingers touching her face and gently caressing the curves of her nose and cheeks and ears, as if he would know every inch of her by touch. Abbie closed her eyes once more, caught and held by the lovely sensations he was awakening in her. She was drowning in pleasure and she swayed towards him as she breathed in his body scent, and felt the strength in those marvellous hands – hands that could kill an elephant, she recalled, and just knowing of such a feat was enough of an aphrodisiac in itself. She gave a long, shuddering sigh, and at the sound the movements paused and stilled.

'I think my White Dove is more than ready for the next course on the menu,' she heard him say softly now.

He pulled her gently to her feet, and she was aware of the dampness between her thighs. It embarrassed her, knowing that he must soon be aware of it too, but since that was what he would desire in her, she tried not to let it concern her. Her legs felt weak as she walked slowly with his helping hand beneath her elbow towards a door at the side of the room, but it was due less to the wine and all the exotic foods that had so excited her taste buds, and more to the sensual power of the man himself.

As the filmy garments she wore moved in the slightest breeze, she felt as if she floated across the room. Then he opened the door and she gave a small gasp, not so much of surprise, for she had instinctively known what to expect, but knowing the time had now surely come for her to explore all those mysteries she had yearned to discover for herself.

'Are you afraid?' the Master asked, as her eyes took in the mirrored ceiling and walls, the black satin sheets on the huge bed, and the way the room was so subtly lit after the lighting in the dining-room. The half-hooded candles gave off a seductively rosy glow and warmed the bedchamber. Abbie shook her head dumbly, and he gave a small smile.

'And why should you be, when you have already seen this room and something of its occupants?'

She couldn't tell from his tone if he was mocking her or being censorious, and she stammered out a response.

'I didn't mean to pry – Master. I really didn't. But I was born curious – my parents always said as much – and I had never seen a man unclothed before –'

Her voice died away in horrified embarrassment, realising that she sounded like something out of the schoolroom now. But instead of becoming impatient, he was openly laughing at her. And she *had* seen him, she remembered, in the dream that wasn't a dream.

'It's no matter. I like what I have seen of you – and you, I think, like what you have seen of me?'

She blushed. 'Is it seemly for a young lady to say so?'

'It's desirable for her to think so,' he said dryly,

relieving her of the temptation to say she had found the sight of his taut male body so aggressively stimulating. She had hardly noticed that while they spoke he had been deftly stripping away the gossamer garments that the women had so carefully draped around her, until she finally stood, naked and trembling except for the jewellery. She lifted her arms slightly, spreading her hands and tentatively displaying her charms – ignoring the urge to clasp her hands modestly about her. She knew instinctively that he wanted to look, and she wanted him to look, and to be beautiful for him.

'You are the most ravishing creature it has ever been my pleasure to seduce,' he said. 'And, by God, I had almost forgotten how incredibly refreshing it would be to make love to an Englishwoman.'

Abbie's swooning senses were alerted at once.

'I am not the first then?' she said faintly, seeing that he was stripping off his own robes now, performing each action slowly, as if to allow her to savour every movement. She had felt a moment's raw jealousy at his words, just as if it mattered to her whether or not she was his first Englishwoman, when he had had so many women. But the moment passed, and her eyes feasted on the display before her.

He stood a few feet away from her. His body was so firm, so in contrast to a woman's softness. His muscled chest was broad, tapering down to a slim waist and flat belly, and below it Abbie saw that he was already fully aroused, the engorged bulbous tip quivering slightly in response to her quickening breath. The base of the stalk was crowned with a thick bush of dark hair that served to expose the sinewy evidence of his erection even more proudly.

Her innocent eyes were awed by the sheer size and proportions of it. The temptation to run her fingers around that smooth tip and caress it was sending shivers through every nerve-end now, and she could feel the pulses racing in her neck with anticipation of what was to come.

'I will possess you now, White Dove,' he said arrogantly, and Abbie knew he was impatient for the ultimate in pleasure.

The heat in her body was overwhelming, and there was no longer any thought of resistance. He held out his arms and she went into his hungry embrace, and the distance between them no longer existed.

Chapter Seven

*H*e scooped her up in his arms and carried her to the bed. His arms were taut, the veins and sinews standing out as proudly as she had glimpsed on that huge protuberance below. Abbie could feel it pressing against her body, and shivered with a wanton thrill at the power and strength of it. She quickly ignored the stab of anxiety at being able to accommodate such a magnificent love-tool, for at last she was to learn the mysteries of a man and a woman's loving that even the lowest serving-girls and the basest animals knew.

However, she preferred not to think of such connotations, for there was nothing like such bestiality here. She knew instinctively that the Master intended to initiate her more considerately into the rituals of loving.

Even so, she felt her lips tremble as he lay her down on the satin sheets and passed his hand in feather-light caresses over her velvety skin, first from throat to shoulders, then lingering over the curves of her breasts and just grazing the budding tips with his finger-nails until they rose obediently. His hands moved gently downwards over her belly, and she caught her breath as his knuckles gently kneaded and stroked the shaved entrance to her secret core.

Abbie still hated the enforced nudity of it, and longed for the natural downy covering of silky hair to return. But presumably this was intended to be less of an encumbrance to a man, at least a man of the Master's persuasion. And she had already noted that he was not shaved there. The thick, bushy black hair curling around the base of his penis gave it even more prominence and importance.

'You please me greatly, White Dove,' he murmured, and just for a breathless moment she thought he dropped his guard a little, and looked at her as a man would look at a woman he loved. But it could not be so, of course, and such a desirable and romantic state was all in her young girl's imagination. His only need of her was to gratify his lust, and love didn't enter into it.

She didn't know if any response to his words was needed, but in any case, she was too numb to reply. By now, his fingers were stroking between her thighs, sending the hot, tingling sensations rushing through her. Involuntarily, she opened wider, unconsciously arching her back so that her crotch was urging upward towards him, inviting him in. Her hands clenched, wanting to hold him, but not daring to do so.

She heard his indrawn breath, and then she felt the tip of his finger enter her. It remained quite still for a moment, and then began a slow, sensual circling on the outer labia of her vulva. At the same time she felt his thumb move to the little knub at the top of the lips – what had Sophie called it? She couldn't recall it, but she knew it was something ludicrously out of place in this temple of sensuality.

'Your delicious little pearl of desire is moist and ripe, White Dove,' the Master said. 'But I think a little more pleasuring would aid the deflowering.'

He leaned over her, sliding down on the satin sheets

and opening her wide with his fingers. She saw him run his tongue slowly around his lips, and the next moment it was seeking entrance to her vulva, and she felt the heat of his tongue alternately curling around the erect knub of what he so delightfully called her moist pearl of desire, and licking the slippery sides of her labia.

By now, Abbie was almost delirious with pleasure, her senses fully aroused to the sight and the scent and the feel of him. She ached to do something with her hands, to join in the mutual excitement and pleasure. Involuntarily, her fingers reached for the hair at the nape of his neck and entwined in it, caressing its softness. Her head moved from side to side in something approaching ecstacy. As she did so, her eyes took in the images on the mirrored ceiling above the bed. She knew then just why they had been installed in this room to add to the lascivious pleasure being enacted on the bed below. The reflected images were as abandoned as it was possible to be, she thought weakly; the powerfully-built man with his dark head burrowing between her open legs; and herself, with her shining silvery hair spread out around her, her face flushed with passion. Her oiled breasts were sheened like beautiful golden orbs, and her eyes glittered to rival the jewellery she wore.

Just when it seemed as if she could hardly bear the exquisite touch of the Master's tongue a second longer without squirming wildly, he removed himself and slid upwards to tease and caress her breasts. He took each nipple into his mouth in turn, tweaking and tugging, and sending little spasms of excitement coursing through her loins each time he did so.

By now she couldn't stand her own inactivity a moment longer, and without knowing if it was permitted to do such a thing without the Great One's permission, Abbie's hand reached downward and tentatively touched the stiff stalk of his manhood. At first she simply touched it, wondering at her own bravado. Then slowly she gripped it more tightly, easing her fingers around the shaft and caressing it firmly.

She heard his momentary indrawn breath, but he didn't stop what he was doing to her, and nor did he complain or instruct her. As her grasp on the stallion-head became stronger, she thought that perhaps this was a game she had to learn for herself. If so, it was a game of hedonistic pleasure that went far beyond the games of childhood.

Again, she felt her eyes being drawn to that mirrored ceiling, and then to all the images in the mirrors around the walls, and her throat clenched with a feeling of wanton lust. There were dozens of images of him suckling her breasts and of her hand caressing and stroking and rubbing, allowing her fingers to run over the swollen crest of his erection and feeling the tiny spurt of moisture there. She gave a sudden gasp as strong spasms of climax assaulted her in rippling, uncontrollable waves, and she felt the love juices trickling out of her.

'The time has come,' the Master said, his voice suddenly thick, and then his body was covering hers, and he was opening her with his fingers again before pushing the tip of his phallus inside her yielding softness.

She caught her breath, half-closing her eyes, but still watching him through her lashes. He paused just briefly.

'I promise you the discomfort will be of little duration, White Dove, for never was there a more willing pupil than yourself. A moment's pain, and then all the pleasure in the world will be yours.'

She hadn't even thought about pain, she thought faintly, but before her senses could consider what he had said, she felt him push more strongly, and she was so moist and ready that there was only the smallest feeling of tearing before he was surging inside her. But despite the way she now felt she knew him physically, she had never expected it to feel so large, or to fill and stretch her so much. The pain he mentioned was so slight as to be almost non-existent. Besides which she wanted this so much, she wanted *him*.

'Raise yourself up slightly to meet me,' he whispered against her cheek. She did as she was told, and after a few moments she found herself pushing with him, meeting every thrust with one of her own, so that they moved effortlessly together in the sweetest unison. He gripped her buttocks tightly, squeezing and fondling all the while, pulling her in to him even more, and her finger-nails dug gentle grooves in his powerfully muscled back.

'Look at the two of us,' she heard him command, and she realised his head had turned sideways now, to watch the thrusting movements in the mirrors. She saw how her own arms clung to him, and how her legs had somehow wrapped themselves around him, so that they were no longer two people, but one. Her breath caught at the erotic picture they presented. Then he was pressing his mouth to hers, forcing it open, and his tongue was foraging inside her in a savage replica of what his glorious shaft was doing to her. Abbie's own tongue slithered and interwove with his, increasing the joy she was feeling.

Briefly, she wished her experience had been greater, so that she could give him as much pleasure as he gave her, but instinctively she allowed her muscles to tighten around him and from his small groans she knew she had pleased him.

After an age of pleasure, when she thought she was surely drowning in her own juices, she heard his breath quicken, and he removed his mouth from hers to nuzzle his face in the nape of her neck. Abbie was fully aroused now, and her own passion was inflamed as the movements below became more frantic. She could no longer keep up with them, and nor could she even try.

Shock-waves of sensation were gripping her loins, her muscles pulsing and holding him so tightly now that she cried out with the sheer pleasure of him filling her. Then she felt him twist and strain against her, as if he would enter her very soul. Seconds later a hot gush of his life-fluid surged inside her, adding impetus to her own writhing sensations.

He sprawled across her, spent but still inside her, as if loath to move away. Abbie lay motionless as the soft tears trickled down her face. She dared not speak, sure that she shouldn't let him see how affected she was. It was not with distress or pain, but with the most sensational flood of emotion she had ever felt in her life. As yet she couldn't even begin to analyse what those feelings meant.

The Master slowly raised his head and looked down at her. She couldn't read his expression. Had she offended him by her weak woman's tears? Was he so angry that she would be due for punishment in some way? Was he disappointed in her, when he was used to so many expert hands touching and holding him and bringing him to the point of ecstacy?

'You will sleep now,' he said, his voice deeper than usual. 'The first time was necessarily quick, out of consideration for your virginal state. But now that you are broken, the next time we meet we will explore even more sensual pleasures, White Dove.'

She felt the touch of his fingers wipe away the silent tears, and she closed her eyes, fighting back the sudden craving to reach out and hold those fingers to her lips that had done such delightful things to her. She kept her eyes closed, pushing down an even more possessive desire to hold him fiercely to her once more, knowing it must surely be forbidden to be so familiar, and that it was highly unlikely that he would permit such intimacy.

She didn't hear him leave the bedchamber, yet she

had the feeling he stood watching her for some moments before he gently covered her with the satin sheet. She was so very tired now, never realising that her own emotions and the intense pleasure he had given her could produce such a sweet lethargy.

But she must have slept for a while, because the next thing she knew the old woman was gently shaking her arm, and she was accompanied by the two girls who had brought her here.

'You will be taken back to your chamber now to continue your night's rest, lady,' Maya said.

So it was still sometime in the night. Abbie had lost all sense of time, but as she sat up slowly, her senses dulled from sleep, a robe was placed around her and a silken cord tied at her waist. She tried to rouse herself from her stupor, wondering if she would ever resume sleep as the memory of all that had passed between herself and the Master came rushing back to her.

But once she had traversed the maze of corridors to her own room, she was told to wash herself with the sweet-smelling warm water in her wash-stand, and she was thankful that this time she was not to have other hands doing the task. The women waited with eyes averted now, and finally she was helped into a night-gown, and she slid between her own bedcovers.

'Will you please tell me where I am?' she asked huskily, for want of something to say, finding the mere attendance of the three women unbearable. They would all know what had occurred in the Master's bedchamber, in what should surely be a very private happening between two people. And she didn't expect an answer to her question, she thought wearily, save for an evasive one.

'You are in the home of Leon Villiers,' the old woman said, and at the smooth reply Abbie's mouth simply dropped open in shock. The thought swept into her mind that whoever this Villiers was, he was obviously as debauched as the Master to allow his home to be used for such libidinous purposes.

She wondered fearfully if Leon Villiers would be the next man to come for her, now that the Master had had his fill of her. Was there to be no end of them? The idea of being used as a plaything or a novelty by a group of men sickened her, but she smothered her terror and tried to stay rational.

'But where is this place? Have I been taken very far?' she asked thickly. The old crone had made no move to leave her immediately, although the girls had departed silently now.

'About as far it would take a horseman to accomplish in a comfortable afternoon's ride,' Maya said, looking at her steadily.

Abbie's eyes opened wide, and she sat up in bed, alert at once, her thoughts whirling.

'But that surely means I can be no farther than about ten or twelve miles from home,' she almost spluttered.

The woman remained enigmatic. 'You have been told all that you need to know, except that I would remind you that this is now your home, lady. You owe your life to the Master, and it belongs to him, as you do.'

She turned and left Abbie alone, closing the door firmly behind her, but not before Abbie had seen the guard positioning himself outside as usual. It was not so much a home as a prison, she thought bitterly. But her amazement at all the woman had told her had got the better of her, bypassing the immediate need for sleep.

If she was so near to The Grange – which she had naturally referred to as home – then she was still in the county of Sussex, and this temple of sin was no more the princely abode of an eastern potentate than the humblest of country farms. She lay down again, finding the whole idea of it bewildering. And presumably this

Leon Villiers must know what was happening here, and was a part of it.

It was also obvious to her now that Maya had been instructed to give her this information and no more. The Master had known she would be curious, and had allowed her this much, as if carelessly throwing her crumbs.

Suddenly furious at being such a pawn, and with the erotic excitement of the deflowering already fading, Abbie leapt out of bed and returned to her wash-stand. Without a second thought she picked up the wash-cloth and soap and scrubbed at all the powders and paints on her face, until it was as pale and innocent of colour as it had always been.

Quickly, she removed the bangles and anklets, the necklace and earrings, leaving only the ruby in her navel and the heavy ivory bangle on her upper left arm, hardly daring to remove these so-called symbols of belonging.

Only then did she feel really clean. And only then did she feel able to lie down on her bed again and fall into an exhausted sleep.

'You told her?' Leon Villiers asked the old *ayah* who had accompanied him from India. Maya inclined her head.

'As you instructed, Master, and no more.'

'And what was her reaction?'

Even as he said it, he thought impatiently that the reaction of the English girl shouldn't matter to him. But since she was the first to come into his possession and his bed in many a year, and since she was one of his own countrywomen, he felt an odd kind of responsibilty towards her. The very thought angered him, for in common with the prince who had taught him the art of seduction, he had learned to look upon women as mere playthings for a man's pleasure.

But he doubted that even Prince Khali had had such a

woman in his bed as Miss Abigail Richmond – and the fact that Leon recalled her name so readily instead of the more exotic one he had given her, was an added irritation in itself.

He could almost hear Prince Khali telling him sternly that there was no room for sentiment in the pursuit of physical pleasure. Until now he had agreed with him wholly. But now he was admitting that the prince was of a different culture and a different caste, while at heart Leon was still an Englishman with an Englishman's sensibilites.

'Her reaction, Master, was as expected,' Maya replied.

For once he was irritated with her as well. She was as loyal to him as an old servant could be, despite the fear and awe the women in the *zenana* felt towards her – and White Dove too, he suspected. Poor child – at times she seemed little more. Yet he wasn't a pervert, to ravish children. Perhaps it was simply her innocent, fragile beauty that disturbed him so.

'Please be more specific, Maya,' he snapped, knowing he was truly in danger of letting sentiment get the better of him, and reacting strongly against it. 'She did not weep or protest that she must leave here immediately?'

'She did none of those things.'

'And what has been found out about her? She gave her name in her delirium, but nothing more, and we deduce that she came from the gloomy old dwelling to the south. Has she relatives who will be searching for her?'

'Only an uncle who wishes to be rid of her in marriage. She attains her eighteen summers in less than one week's time, and she will no longer be his responsibility.'

'I see. You may go now. But see to it that the orders I have given are carried out.'

And if she thought it odd that he thought to reward a woman for favours given, when such a thing was unheard of in the *zenana*, Maya knew better than to say so, and nor would anyone defy his orders.

'One more thing. She will be removed to the west wing tonight, and I shall not require her again for three days.'

Why the devil he should even consider the girl's feelings he didn't choose to think. It was enough to let her believe he was allowing her to settle down before she came to him again. In the meantime, there were plenty of others to entertain him and to be entertained.

When Abbie awoke the following morning, she couldn't readily identify the strong perfume in her nostrils. She opened eyes that were still heavy with sleep, and as she did so, the sight of a huge white bird in her room made her give a little scream of fright.

She cowered beneath the sheets, then quickly realised that it was not a real bird, but fashioned in the shape of a dove with flowers of purest white, a white dove, like herself. She felt overwhelmed by the gesture, thinking, as before, that maybe the Master wasn't all bad after all.

She had certainly not had any such thoughts on the previous night. The memories surged into her mind again, and she pressed her hand lightly over her warm crotch, to the place where he had been, wishing she could experience it all over again to remind herself how spectacular the sensations had been.

But she was destined to do so, she reminded herself with a leap of excitement in her heart. And he had told her that the next time it would not be over so quickly. There might even be an entire night of exploration ahead of her – providing that the next time didn't involve the lecherous Leon Villiers, whose house was given over to such practices, she remembered.

She even felt able to forgive the Master now, for he had been the one to bring her such exquisite pleasure. And she dared to hope in her heart that perhaps the fact that he insisted that her life belonged to him might mean that she wouldn't be passed around to others in a game of pass the parcel. Abbie made herself believe it, and was content to rest with her dreams until someone appeared to tell her what to do.

It was Maya who came, as she had expected, but not with the words Abbie longed to hear, that she was to be summoned again to the Master's bedchamber that night.

'You are to be moved to different quarters, lady,' the woman said, and Abbie felt her spirits sink.

'Am I to be despatched so soon to the *zenana* then?' she asked bitterly, thinking how quickly he must have tired of his new sport.

'You will put on the robe you wore last night and follow me,' Maya said without further explanation.

'And may I take the white dove with me?' she said defiantly, thinking that at least in this house where she was directed like a chattel, she should have the floral tribute that clearly belonged to her alone.

'It will be brought to your new quarters,' she was told.

Impotent with rage at what she considered very much a lowering of status, Abbie obeyed with her lips clamped and her hands shaking. She had no wish to eat and sleep in a cat-house with those painted women who never spoke to her or cared for her and probably actively hated her, she thought in a fright. They might even do her some harm.

When she was ready, she stalked out of the room ahead of Maya with as much dignity as she could muster, and the guard stood back to let them pass. As before, she had no idea where she was going, and the corridors were just as long and winding, but as she walked she knew they seemed different. There was more light, and less of the cloying perfume that was as sickly as it was titillating to the senses.

Finally, the old woman stopped outside a door and

opened it, and then stood back for Abbie to go inside. As she did so, she gasped, for gone were the salacious trappings of the love-chamber. There were no mirrored walls or ceiling, and no black satin sheets on a vast bed that was obviously intended for one purpose. And certainly no hint of a kind of women's dormitory.

This was an English bedroom, with English furnishings and fittings, and a serviceable if richly patterned carpet on the floor. There was a white quilted counterpane on the four-poster bed, and the window was uncluttered by outer shutters or opaque glass. Through it Abbie could see green lawns stretching away into the distance, and a forest of trees beyond. The morning was as misty as an early summer morning in the Sussex countryside could be, and she felt her spirits soar at the pastoral scene.

She turned quickly to question Maya further, but even as she did so, the door was closing again and she was alone. But she no longer cared. It was blissful to be in something approaching her own environment again, after however long it was that she had been incarcerated here. And having expected to be taken to the women's *zenana*, she was humbly grateful.

Not that it was in her nature to be humble for very long, and for the first time in what seemed like weeks she began to feel something of her old zest returning. There were no barriers to the windows either, and she threw them open with a feeling of delight, as the scent of English roses drifted up from where they were entwined around the arches in the arbours below.

Next she turned to the closets in the room, and found to her surprise that there were racks of gowns in sensual silks and satins and in every hue; chemises and matching silk stockings. But before she became too carried away with euphoria, Abbie discovered other garments. There were lacy petticoats in scarlet and virginal white, and wasp-waisted black satin corsets with scarlet laces of a type she had certainly never seen before, nor ever envisaged wearing. She fingered the garments gingerly, unable to imagine herself wearing them.

But just as quickly came the thought that these were the clothes of a strumpet or a high-class prostitute. So if they had all been put here at her disposal, and in this very different part of the house, she was presumably expected to act in a very different role from that of the seraglio women — and with a different partner, or partners.

Her heart began to beat painfully fast, and the brief sense of complacency at her good fortune in being moved to these quarters quickly faded. She waited with trepidation for someone to send for her.

There was no sign of the Master during the next three days, by which time Abbie was almost distraught. Half the time she felt close to weeping with frustration and self-pity for her plight, and alternately she raged against this tyrant of a man who could seduce her so thoroughly and then leave her wanting.

She had quickly learned that once the flood-gates of passion had been opened wide, there was no turning back from them. She was hungry for more, and trying to find some release from tension in touching and stroking herself afforded little pleasure, for there was still a lingering soreness from the first invasion of her body by a man.

Maya was her only visitor now. She was brought food and drinks at intervals, and there was an adjoining bathroom for her personal needs, though it was nothing like as elaborate as the one she had used previously. She was also invited to try on any of the garments she found pleasing.

All of this alerted her suspicions that she was indeed to be used for someone's pleasure when the time came.

117

She resisted the temptation to try on any of the clothes for at least twenty-four hours.

But because she was a woman, and a very feminine one at that, the temptation finally overcame any scruples. Just fingering the silks and satin gowns and the delicate lacy undergarments sent waves of pleasure through her, especially imagining the reaction of a man who saw a woman wearing such things that would have been utterly taboo at The Grange.

But by now Abbie knew she had long since left behind the essence of the young girl who had fled her uncle's tyranny in such a fright. He would have a blue fit to think of her posturing about like a whore, she thought — and that alone put a sudden rebellious sparkle in her eyes.

There was a long mirror in one wall. On each side there were various portraits, which were presumably intended to break up the starkness of the mirror and form a kind of montage. Abbie didn't altogether care for the way the eyes in the portraits seemed to follow her around the room, but she decided to ignore it and concentrate on amusing herself for an hour or so with trying on the various garments.

Once she began, she couldn't stop. Her own modest cotton chemise and petticoats, fine fabric though they were, were as coarse as sacking compared with the luxurious feel of the others. It was hard to decide which she liked best, and she remembered how she had dolled herself up the night Lord Eustace came to inspect her, and then scrubbed away every vestige of powder and paint.

She wasn't tempted to do the same now, but there was hardly any need. Her cheeks were suffused with heat, and her flushed cheeks and mouth echoed the scarlet of the gown in which she twirled now. She lifted a dainty stockinged foot, loving the silky sheen of it, and laughed with sheer enjoyment. She raised the skirt higher, revealing the matching red satin garter at her thigh before the lacy stocking-top met her skin.

If this was how it felt to be a trollop, Abbie thought wildly, then it was a remarkably good feeling – though she resisted imagining all the other things a trollop had to do in her chosen career. Pleasing different men every day of her life, and lifting her skirts for a quick fumble in return for a few pennies – but then Abbie reasoned that no street doxy would be dressed as finely as this!

These clothes were for a far better class moll. She laughed out loud at the devilment the words evoked inside her, throwing back her head and pouting prettily at her reflection in the mirror. With her new-found knowledge of the ways of men, she felt suddenly reckless, and whirled around the room in a crazy dance.

By the third day of boredom in her new room she was constantly dressing up and posturing in front of the mirror, and had favoured a delicious sapphire blue gown that enhanced the colour of her eyes. After the usual preening at herself in the mirror, she flopped down on her bed, laughing at her reflection. She was so hot that her skirts were rucked up around her knees in a froth of blue silk and white lace petticoats. Seeing how abandoned she looked in the mirror now, the laughter changed to a secret smile as her hand went downwards to rub gently the part of her the Master had entered so satisfyingly.

And where was he now, when she had believed he would come for her to continue his teaching and seduction! She sat up quickly, thinking petulantly that she must have been a disappointment to him after all, and that he was taking his pleasure with the nubile girls who knew how to entice him far more than she did.

Her heart suddenly skipped a beat, for surely, *surely* the eyes in one of the portraits around the mirror had moved. It happened in less than a moment and then the eyes looked as flat and painted as before. But unless the sunlight from the window had been playing tricks on her, then she was perfectly sure that someone had been watching her all this time.

She had stripped off everything to slide into the tight-waisted corsets and felt a searing excitement at seeing how the little pouting mound between her legs had been shown to such advantage. She had twisted this way and that, so that the creamy swell of her buttocks had been offered towards the mirror, wiggling them enticingly.

She had lovingly cupped her breasts, finding a carnal delight in seeing how their fullness was accentuated by the upward thrust of the boned satin. She had donned the stockings lovingly, relishing the sensation of silk against her skin, and let her fingers brush her inner thighs with more than a frisson of excitement as she did so.

While she was still stunned by the force of her own sensuality, she fought to gather her wits as her door opened. Her face burned with rage and embarrassment, and she threw her hands to her face, hiding her eyes as if to ward off the presence of this unwanted visitor. She tried frantically to remember just how she had been indulging her senses for this past hour – and these past three days.

She felt utterly humiliated now, to think that someone might have been *watching* her all that time.

'Why do you stop, Miss Richmond? I've seldom taken such pleasure in watching a lady cavort in her bedroom without taking part in it myself.'

She should have known, Abbie thought, for of course, it had to be him. It could be no one else. Her hands slowly dropped away from her burning face, and then she gaped.

It was the Master, as she had expected, but it was the Master as she had never seen him before. Gone were the eastern trappings, the princely robes and flamboyant jewellery. In their place was a gentleman of quality, elegantly attired in tight-fitting trousers and well cut jacket. The neckcloth at his throat was fastened with one large pearl pin, and apart from a ring on his finger that sported a large diamond, it was his only concession to jewellery.

Abbie's mouth dried as her eyes took in this so-fashionable gentleman, and immediately her own flushed face and sensuously bright gown made her feel overdressed.

'What do you have in mind for me now, sir?' she said with rising hysteria. 'Are we to play a different game?'

He laughed, coming towards her with deliberate slowness, so that she felt obliged to back away from him. But there was nowhere to go until she felt the edge of the bed behind her.

'I had the distinct impression that you approved of my games, Miss Richmond,' he said.

He was no longer calling her White Dove, but using her own name, Abbie realised. But such a formality seemed no more than a mockery, for she was still a prisoner here – a prisoner in chains, no matter how silken and alluring.

He looked so much the English gentleman now that she could hardly believe the scenes she had witnessed between him and his concubines, nor that she had allowed herself to be so thoroughly and delectably seduced. She knew now that she was not in some foreign place, but right here in her home county. And that all of it was no more than a splendidly orchestrated charade.

Whatever he wanted of her, she had no choice but to obey, and she could do nothing to stop it. But there was one thing she had to know.

'Who *are* you?' she whispered.

Chapter Eight

*H*e reached her side and held her tightly, while she stood as if mesmerised. She could feel his hands sliding over the sapphire silk gown as he gently moved them down her spine and caressed her buttocks.

'Don't you know? I thought you were a woman of intelligence as well as beauty,' he said mockingly.

'How can I know! You bring me here and tell me I owe my life to you, and then you appear in different guises, and expect me to be clairvoyant enough to understand exactly what's going on here. Well, I don't!'

As her voice rose, her eyes flashed as blue as her gown, and she heard him draw in his breath. If she had angered him now, she no longer cared. It seemed that she was no more than a plaything to him, and her feelings didn't count.

'I hadn't expected you to be quite such a little fire-brand,' he said, more mildly now. 'But it pleases me not to have you so servile, and to see that you have all the makings of the coquette.'

For the moment she ignored the implications of his remark. 'So it was you watching me,' she said instead, although she had instinctively known it all along.

Who else would be allowed to inspect his private property in such a voyeuristic fashion? Unless that was part of his sport too, to allow his gentlemen friends to watch her dressing and undressing. The thought of being such a peepshow for their entertainment made her freeze with rage.

'Does it offend you to know how exciting I considered your performance to be?' he said now.

'It was not intended as a performance,' Abbie snapped, less afraid to speak her mind to him in this garb than when he dressed and acted the role of the potentate.

'Oh, but it was, my dear,' he said in a silkier tone. 'It was a delight to watch.'

Abbie shivered as he bent his head, just allowing his lips to touch hers. No matter what he said, or how he dressed, she couldn't deny the rampant sexuality of the man. But for the moment she refused to rise to the bait.

'You still haven't answered my question. Who are you?'

She breathed the words against his skin. It wasn't smooth like a woman's skin, she thought. It was excitingly male, not coarse, but with just enough roughness to ignite the senses. She pushed aside the thought and stared up at him unblinkingly.

'Haven't you guessed?' he countered.

Abbie fought to move away from him then, but he was too strong for her, and he held her captive in a more rigid embrace.

'How can I guess?' she stormed. 'I have no idea where I am, apart from the old woman's garbled words that I'm not so far from home – but I'm not sure I can believe anything she says! And the only other name that's been mentioned is someone called Leon Villiers who sounds like a Frenchman –'

She stopped as he laughed.

'I admit the name has a French ring to it, and my

123

paternal grandfather did come from that Godforsaken country, but I assure you I am as English as your sweet self, Miss Abigail Richmond.'

'*You* are Leon Villiers?' she echoed stupidly.

'The same,' he said gravely. 'And now that we have been formally introduced, I have no intention of wasting this lovely afternoon in idle chit-chat when I am intent on bedding you.'

Abbie gasped. In a moment, it seemed to her, he had changed with chameleon-like speed to the typical English rake, and she had seen all too many of them eyeing her lasciviously at her uncle's house. Then she had been under Brindley Richmond's protection, and for all his intention to see her married off and be rid of her, he would not have entertained any lewd happenings under his roof.

But here she was helpless to stop it. Whatever Leon Villiers wanted – either as himself or in the guise of the Master – he would have.

'Then if that's what you have in mind, I have no way of preventing it,' she said stiffly.

His eyes narrowed. He had been staring thoughtfully at Abbie for so long that she began to feel decidedly uncomfortable. And she couldn't deny that her own words – practically inviting him to take her here and now, as he assuredly intended doing – had sent the now-familiar surge of sexual excitement coursing through her. But this prevarication was making her nervous, and when she was nervous she spoke more quickly and more boldly than usual.

'Well, sir?' she snapped.

To her surprise he laughed again, throwing back his head and slapping his thigh with one hand, while still retaining hold of her with the other.

'By God, Abigail Richmond, but you do me a power of good,' he drawled. 'I'd almost forgotten how refreshing it could be to have a verbal thrust and parry with an Englishwoman.'

Abbie looked at him suspiciously. If this was a compliment, it wasn't the kind she expected from him. It was almost tantamount to saying that he liked her – and the only time she thought those sentiments applied to women were when he had them in his bed, and under his control. But from what she had seen, liking – or loving – didn't really come into it then, as long as his sexual appetite was satisfied.

'You look doubting,' he said now. 'Do you think me incapable of conducting a proper conversation with a woman?'

'In my experience, sir, conversation is the last thing on your mind where women are concerned.'

She said the words before she could stop herself, and then stopped abruptly, for surely none of the golden-skinned girls from the *zenana* would dare to speak to him like this!

In answer, he pulled her into his arms again. The sapphire gown she wore had the smallest of puffed sleeves, and her slender arms were bare, save for the ivory bangle she had been afraid to remove. Leon ran his fingers down the length of her arms with the lightest of caresses, and when his finger-tips met hers he lifted her hands and brushed them with his lips.

'That's certainly the case where you're concerned, my sweet,' he said. 'But we will delay our more delightful pursuits for a short while. I suggest you throw a light shawl around your shoulders, for there's a cooling breeze outside.'

Abbie's eyes shone at the unexpected words, forgetting everything else. 'I'm actually going outside?'

She knew she sounded like a child being given a treat, but it would be such a welcome novelty to be out in the fresh air after so many days of hibernation in this cloying atmosphere that she simply couldn't help her reaction.

125

'I have something to show you,' Leon said, 'and it's rather too large to bring inside the house.'

It would be some other prized possession, she presumed half-scornfully, intended to show her just how fabulously wealthy and powerful a man he was. But she did as she was told, draping a light gossamer shawl about her shoulders and followed him obediently, out of the lovely bedroom and traversing more corridors and stairs. And all the while Abbie thought that this house must be not only a veritable fortress, but one of palace proportions.

She had no idea how far they had gone, or in which direction, but she forgot all other concerns when at last Leon opened a door, and they stepped out into the sunlight. She gulped in the fragrantly scented air like someone long starved of oxygen.

'Has it all been so terrible for you, Abigail?' he said, watching her face.

Abbie blushed, fighting down the urge to tell him that she had found everything she had been searching for here, and discovering the art of love had been more spectacular and sensual than she had ever dreamed it would be. Sophie didn't know the half of it. And even though Abbie knew how disastrous it would be to allow herself the normal feelings of a woman for a man, she couldn't deny that she was more than half in love with him already.

Or maybe a woman always felt that way about the man who seduced her with such consummate skill and finesse, she thought, aware of her own inexperience in such matters.

'Since you don't answer, I must assume that it has been,' Leon said abruptly.

'If you mean, has it been terrible to waken from a state of unconsciousness to find myself apparently in some eastern place, and having unspeakable things done to me by strange women, then yes! It has been terrible,' she said heatedly to cover her embarrassment at the direction her thoughts had been leading her.

'And the rest?' he said softly.

She blushed again. 'I hardly think that's a suitable question to ask a lady!'

'Then your heightened colour gives me sufficient answer enough for now. Do you like what you see, Abigail?'

For once, it wasn't a blatantly sexual question, but that of a man displaying his achievements to his lady – if that wasn't an all too fanciful interpretation.

She looked around her at the beautifully kept lawns and flower beds. This was a totally different garden to the one she had seen from her bedchamber overlooking the Indian-style pagodas and arches. This was an English garden, though there was no more sign of anyone tending it than there had been in the other part.

'It's beautiful,' she said, thinking that at least she could answer this honestly.

'And so are you.'

Before she could think how to respond to this, he had offered her his arm. He was such an enigma, Abbie thought. One side of him was the arrogant, flamboyant Master – and this more gentle, yet no less charismatic side was the perfect English gentleman. When he changed from arrogant to gentle, it tugged at her very heart-strings. She walked beside him in silence now, accepting the arm he offered, and feeling her own hand tucked firmly in the crook of his.

But she also suspected that this very softness could be like the calm before the storm, and her nerves were stretched taut as they walked in apparent harmony together.

'Where are you taking me?' she muttered, when they had seemed to be walking a long way without a sign of anyone.

He gave a slight smile. 'Don't tell me you think I'm about to abduct you?'

'Why should I not, since you've already done it once!'

'You're quite wrong. I did not abduct you. If I hadn't found you dazed and weeping, and brought you here, you might well have fallen foul of ruffians long before this. Or suffered an even worse fate.'

After all the humiliations she had suffered at the hands of his servant women, to say nothing of being subjected to his own sexual fantasies, she couldn't believe this arrogance. She quickly revised her feelings about him. Master or gentleman, the arrogant streak was all too evident. It was quite obvious to her that Leon Villiers thought he owned the world and everything in it.

She wouldn't give him the satisfaction of answering his comments. Instead, she tossed back her long fair hair over her shoulders where it curled in soft silvery strands in the sunlight. Leon noted the gesture and gave a half-smile.

'My lady has a fine way of showing her temper without words,' he commented. 'And that glorious hair of yours is tempting enough to wind itself around any man's heart.'

'It will soon be put up, and then it won't tempt anyone,' Abbie snapped.

'Ah yes. The eighteenth birthday approaches, and the child will be a woman. But there will be other times when all its glory will be revealed to me.'

She didn't doubt what he meant, but she was more struck by something else that he said.

'How did you know about my eighteenth birthday?'

'I know many things about you, Abigail. When you came here you were dazed enough to say far more than you intended, and Maya's skilful questioning provided the rest.'

She looked at him with active dislike. These people

were despicable, and she wanted nothing more to do with them. She made to pull her hand away from his arm, but he held her fast.

'There's nowhere for you to go, my sweet one, so why do you try?' he said smoothly. 'Do you not think we make a very handsome couple strolling in the sunlight?'

They probably did, he in his elegant gentleman's attire, and she in her sapphire blue silk gown. They looked the epitome of the wealthy English couple, gloriously happy in each other's company, and without a care in the world. Abbie wilted slightly against him, wishing for one wild unimaginable second that it could all be true – and knowing miserably that it could never be so, not while Leon Villiers was intent on transforming himself into the rampant Master of his seraglio.

'Where are you taking me now, since I obviously have no choice but to do whatever you want?' she asked sullenly.

'To see your birthday gift,' he said calmly.

She stopped walking so suddenly that he was obliged to stop beside her. Before she could say a word he had gathered her in his arms and held her fast, pressing his mouth on to hers and running his fingers down her spine once more in the way that made her shiver with an erotic pleasure. When his lips were a breath away from hers, he whispered against them.

'If you persist in looking up at me with those huge, beautiful eyes, and that luscious parted mouth, you must expect to be kissed, if not ravished, at every available opportunity, Abigail.'

The words sent a rushing heat through her limbs, making her weak, making her tremble, so that she felt powerless to move away from him. And she felt the evidence of his rising passion against her, through the tight-fitting pants he wore. Leon felt it too, and without warning he thrust her hand downwards, to where she could feel the bulge all too well. She made to snatch her hand away but he put his own over hers, and massaged it gently so that she had no choice but to rub the tightly stretched pants at his groin.

'Why do you pull away? Does it not please you?' he said softly. 'And before your words deny it, let me tell you that your eyes are telling me something very different.'

Abbie fought to gain control of herself, even while the pressure of his hand over hers and the throbbing bulge beneath them both was drying her throat.

'Then if my eyes give me away, it would be useless to deny it,' she croaked. 'But it would hardly seem the time and place, sir!' But even as she spoke the thought of it happening in the open air in the warmth of the sun and the refreshing summer breeze was enough to stimulate all her senses.

'You think not? No one would dare to disturb us if I decided to ravish you here and now. But it can wait a little longer – just so long as you know what payment I will expect in return for my birthday gift.'

Abbie was outraged at the suggestion that she had to repay him for a gift. But she was young enough and curious enough to wonder about a gift from this man, and canny enough too, to know what his 'payment' would be.

They had walked a considerable distance from the house now, and when she glanced back she saw how enormous it actually was. It was built in a huge curving pile of stone, with a rotunda in the centre, and two great wings arching out at either side. No wonder she had been bemused by all the passages and corridors.

She wondered briefly which part of the house contained the *zenana* and the exotic bedchambers, and which were the conventional rooms of an English country gentleman. And she felt a sense of awe at realising just how well he had managed to create this environment for his own indulgences.

There was a long low building ahead of them, and from the whiff of straw and horse dung being carried on the air, Abbie knew they were nearing the stables. It must be her mare! she thought. They had restored her beloved animal to health, and her gift was to be allowed to ride her – under strict supervision, of course.

'Has that quick little brain of yours guessed yet?' Leon asked her.

'Perhaps,' she said. 'But I prefer to wait and see.'

As he laughed, she couldn't help thinking how very different he was when he wasn't playing the part of the Master. Different, but just as exciting. Or maybe that was simply because she was an Englishwoman, and all her instincts told her that this was how love between a man and a woman should be, wanting to be close to each other to the exclusion of everyone else; true to each other, with no sexual orgies to tempt the body and the senses. But even as she thought it, she dismissed the idea, for there was no love on his part, only the desire to have one more possession under his roof and in his bed.

He opened the stable door and stood back for her to go inside. The smells were familiar ones to Abbie. They were not sensuous and cloying like the scented bed-chambers of the seraglio, but just as evocative in a different and earthier way. They tingled in her nostrils and made her suddenly long for a normal, ordered life – with the right person to share it, of course.

'I don't see –' she began, when there was no sign of her mare, or any other animal, for that matter.

The loft above was full of sweet-scented straw, and she immediately thought of Sophie and her Tom, and the lurid tales she had been told of their coupling at his farm. She could hardly imagine that this had all been a ploy on Leon Villiers's part, bringing her here to indulge in a lustier form of love-making, for he had no need of such ploys. He could take her any time he wanted, and anywhere.

131

He walked ahead of her to the last stall in the stables, reaching for some sugar from a bag hung on the wall. Abbie followed slowly, her hand held by his, as he called softly.

As she watched, a sleek, pure white filly craned her neck forward out of the stall, whinnying softly before receiving the sugar from his hand. It was the most beautiful animal Abbie had ever seen. She drew in her breath at the affection that obviously existed between the man and the horse.

From long ago, and out of the past, she recalled her father telling her that any man who had a real rapport with an animal had at least some good in his soul. She stood dumbly, seeing the filly nuzzling against Leon's hand, and felt an absurd jealousy at witnessing such a freely given affection.

And somehow Abbie's mind was filled with the way those marvellous hands with their sensitive, questing fingers had touched her and opened her. She knew she must be mad to be thinking that way at such a moment, and seriously wondered if the man was bewitching her. After a moment, he turned and beckoned to her.

'Won't you come and say hello to your birthday gift?'

Her heart leapt, and then began to beat so fast she thought she might faint.

'You don't mean it!' she said huskily.

'When you've known me a little longer, my dear, you'll know that I never say anything I don't mean.'

She almost flew forward, just managing not to scream with excitement and frighten the filly. But it couldn't be true that he was giving this magnificent young animal to her! No one gave such a valuable gift to a stranger!

'But I can't believe it,' she said in bewilderment, reaching forward to stroke the filly's silky nose, and finding an instant response in her. 'Why would you do such a thing? You don't need to give me anything.'

Her face was hot with excitement, and she felt the

colour deepening, since he must know what she meant. He simply took what he wanted.

'I do it because it pleases me, and because an eighteenth birthday should be marked in some way. I am not all heathen, Abigail.'

She shook her head slightly, still puzzled. She accepted some more sugar from Leon's hand and offered it to the animal, establishing an instant friendship between them as the filly slavered gently over Abbie's fingers, breathing in her scent and acknowledging her.

'Am I allowed to ride her?' she asked.

'I think that goes without saying,' he said dryly. 'But not yet. Seeing the way she licks your fingers is stirring my blood. Later we'll ride around the estate together. But first, you will thank me properly.'

'Your reward,' she murmured, not finding such a thought quite so unpalatable now that she had seen her gift, and even more aware of a rising passion in herself at his words.

'Exactly.'

She assumed that they would go back to the house, and she patted the filly's head reluctantly.

'I'll see you again soon, my beauty,' she whispered, leaning her head against hers.

'You needn't worry. We'll not go far,' Leon said.

He had taken a riding crop from the wall, and she felt a brief moment of fear. But before she could guess his intention, he had motioned her to climb the ladder to the loft above the stalls. She did so tremblingly, lifting her skirts above her knees to climb the steep steps of the ladder. Just what devilment he had in mind now, she didn't dare to think.

Sophie had never mentioned anything like this. But Sophie's sexual education was far behind Abbie's own now, she thought. Nor could that simple soul ever imagine the debauchery that went on in the Master's bedchamber with the black satin sheets and the mirrors, and the women attending and pampering him.

Abbie shuddered, wondering if she too was going to be embroiled in such troilism, and hating the very idea of it.

'What are you going to do with me now?' she whispered when they had reached the loft.

'It's playtime, my sweet. I will be the stable-lad, and you will be the haughty lady of the house. You've succumbed to my luring you here, unable to resist a bit of rough horseplay with the handsome lad you've teased unmercifully. But once I have you beneath me, you remember your place, reach for the crop and whip me for my insolence.'

Abbie gasped, hardly able to believe her ears.

'You want me to *whip* you?'

In answer, he suddenly pushed her down in the mound of hay. As he tore off his jacket and shirt, heedless of the fine materials, his voice changed to a more guttural tone.

'I've waited for you for a long time, my fine lady, and you've teased me with those fine eyes and those luscious, inviting tits for long enough. I'll have you now if it's the last thing I do, and if you have me drawn and quartered tomorrow, it will have been worth it. You see what your taunting does to me?'

He grabbed her hand and thrust it on to his huge erection, and despite her shock at the speed of his change of mood, Abbie felt wildly exhilarated. Games like these were far removed from those of the schoolroom, and her eyes suddenly glittered. She was the lady, and he the earthy lad, lusting for her. She spoke imperiously.

'I'll have you whipped if you touch me, you scum,' she said, using an expression she had never used before. But she found it amazingly easy to enter into the spirit of the game, and she did so with rumbustious enjoyment.

He was ridding himself of the rest of his clothes now, and she felt the hot touch of his skin as his hands pushed the blue silk gown high above her waist. She still wore the silk stockings and the garter, and she felt him push her legs apart, before his fingers opened her wide.

'By God, but you've got a lovely little fanny there,' he gloated. 'And just ripe for the sucking.'

Abbie felt faint, for what he was doing to her now was dazing her mind. She felt his tongue roughly lick every inch of her satiny folds. He made a token stab at her love-bud, but it was obviously not his stable-lad's way to show any finesse towards his woman, and within seconds he was thrusting his tongue inside her, as if to lap at her very soul.

There was no preamble, no foreplay, and none of the skilful sensitivity of the Master, but it was infinitely exciting, taking her to climax so fast that she gasped with the sheer, spectacular lewdness of it.

She heard herself moan, and she was aware that she had thrown her arms wantonly above her head in the sweet-smelling hay. Leon removed his mouth from her throbbing core, and pressed himself heavily against her, so that she could feel his erection quivering against her moistness.

'Now then, my lady,' he said, in that strangely gut-tural voice that had all the earthiness of the serf, 'don't bother to scream, because no one will hear you, and it's useless to think of resisting.'

She suspected he said it to remind her of the game they were playing. And she entered into it willingly.

'I'll have you flogged to within an inch of your life for this, you bastard,' she grated.

'And who will take notice of a such a prick-tease as yourself?' he said, forging into her with a speed that made her gasp with shock. He filled and stretched her, moving roughly into her with long thrusting strokes. But because she had already come, she was just able to resist her intense feelings of pleasure at his roughness and to remember the game they played.

'You forget yourself, you bastard!' she snapped again. 'And I think the flogging should begin here and now.'

She had also managed to resist running her hands over his lovely body, and finding the little responsive male nipples. Instead she scrabbled for the crop he had left conveniently beside her, gulping for the merest second as she wondered if she dared do as he asked. But it was all part of the game to thrash him, and temporarily to hold the power of this strange relationship in her hands.

All the same, before she began, she sensuously ran her hands over his bare buttocks as they heaved over her. His beautiful, strong, bare buttocks – then, without another thought she brought the crop down against them, and heard him wince as she struck him. But although it was part of the game, she couldn't do it hard enough to wound, only to sting.

'You stuck-up bitch,' he growled. 'You'll pay for that.'

Without warning, he pulled out of her and sat on her chest so heavily that she could hardly breathe. The throbbing, gleaming head of his rock-hard phallus was right beneath her face now, and she could smell her own musky scent on him.

'Suck it, bitch,' he snarled.

'I certainly will not!' she snapped, still acting the lady, even while she felt a sharp thrill at the thought of it.

But her words were stifled as he pushed his shaft into her mouth and she felt its lovely hot smoothness against her tongue and her teeth. She circled it lovingly, and then gave it a little bite, remembering that she was supposedly forced into this against her will, when in reality she was guiltily glorying in the fantasy of it all.

'You cock-sucking whore!' Leon howled, and she

couldn't tell whether or not this reaction was from the pain of her biting, or a continuing part of the game. In any case, she was too far involved in the game now to pause. And once more the lady, she couldn't let it go on without whipping him for his insolence and degrading her like this.

She tried to bring the crop down against his buttocks again, but his position was such that it was a feeble strike, and hit the lower part of his back instead.

He reached back and grabbed the crop from her hand, throwing it out of her reach.

'Enough!' he said. 'Now, I'll have one more ride just so you don't forget what a real horny man feels like, before you return to your prissy house-guests. And when you're putting your food in your mouth, just remember what else has been there, wench.'

His weight was suddenly removed from her chest, and Abbie felt able to breathe properly once more. As he slid downwards over her again, she felt his swollen shaft opening and penetrating her, and she simply relaxed, forgetting the game and giving herself up to pleasure.

His hands were seeking her breasts now, pulling them out of their silky encasements as he buried his head between them. She felt his tongue sliding over her nipples, pulling them to peaking perfection with his teeth, and the ecstasy it evoked was almost too much – too much –

'Leon,' she gasped, using his name for the first time, and not realising that she did so. 'I can't pretend any longer. I can't hold back –'

She was moving rhythmically with him now, lifting her buttocks from the hay and clenching his own with fingers that raked his skin. It must be reddened and tender from the beating, but if it hurt him he never said as much, and her own sensations were so much more exquisite. By now they must surely be soaring in a sensual ride to heaven, Abbie thought wildly. And if there was anything better, she had yet to experience it.

'You'll have it all if I'm not careful, my lady,' she heard him say, and she knew he was still in the throes of the game after all. He pulled out of her quickly, and she felt the hot gush of wetness on her stomach as he spilled his seed.

She lay very still as he rolled to her side, panting, and she felt the strangest sense of loss at that moment. She had wanted all of him, and he had taken it away from her. And all that was left of his life-force was a sticky mass of fluid on her bare skin.

A silent tear trickled down her cheek, and she was held in such a mixture of emotions that she couldn't think properly. Leon saw the tear and wiped it away without a word, and the gesture was so sweetly gentle after the roughness of the past half-hour that she could have burst into noisy tears. And perhaps the lady of the house would do exactly that after being seduced by the brawny stable-lad.

But she could no longer think of him that way, and she struggled to cover herself. Before she could do so, Leon had taken a handful of hay and wiped away the evidence of his lust. He bent and kissed the satiny skin with infinite gentleness, and it was a gesture full of caring.

She felt a grudging admiration for the talents of such a man, who could change from being the all-powerful Master with his Indian Mogul tastes to the English gentleman to the lusty stable-lad. She closed her eyes, knowing that she felt a wild and guilty excitement in everything he did.

But for all that she knew his body as well as she knew her own now, she knew she had still not experienced the love of the English gentleman, and she doubted that she ever would. She should never forget that she was merely his plaything, his partner in his games of fantasy.

And when he tired of using her, there were plenty of others he could turn to for his sexual amusement. It would be fatal for Abigail Richmond to forget it and to begin weaving romantic dreams about him.

'It's time to go,' he said quietly, and she realised that while she had lain here with her eyes tightly closed, he had dressed himself again and had gently pulled the silk gown down over her.

Her eyes flickered open now, and she thought he looked down at her with an almost tender expression in his eyes. But it was quickly gone, and she sensed that there was little room for real sentiment in a man whose sole indulgence was in giving and receiving orgasmic pleasures.

She rose obediently, swaying a little and obliged to lean against him for fear of falling. She felt dizzy with all that had happened, and he held her tightly for a moment. It was a sweet moment that could have meant so much, given different circumstances, she thought wanly.

'What now?' she said huskily.

'Now we go back to the house and don our riding clothes, and in a little while you will try out your birthday gift.'

It astonished her to think that she had almost forgotten the reason for being in the stables at all. But he had that effect on her. When she was with him she could forget everything but being with him, being whatever he wanted of her; and doing whatever he dictated.

It was a frightening thought to be so enthralled by a man. It was the way she had always imagined in her girlish dreams that she would feel for the man she would marry. And it was surely disastrous to have any such thoughts about the well travelled and hedonistic Leon Villiers.

Chapter Nine

While Leon and Abbie had been indulging in their new-found sport, the bundle of rags in a far corner of one of the disused stalls had moved imperceptibly. The ruffian bedding down inside it was at first annoyed at being disturbed out of his drunken stupor. The voices hadn't roused him, but his fuddled senses had become increasingly alert as he heard the whack of the riding crop on bare flesh and realised just what was happening directly above him.

He should have been gone from this area long ago, but the long, hot summer was seduction itself. Beside which, the remoteness of this mansion he'd stumbled across, with its apparent lack of staff, had afforded him welcome shelter for a while longer. Then to be an unwitting eavesdropper on such an afternoon of stolen pleasure was enough to whet the appetite of the least lecherous man – and the Irishman had never fitted into that category.

He had almost choked at the realisation that whoever the lady of the house was, she was sporting with her well-hung stable-lad – and O'Reilly had been unable to resist giving himself a helping hand in that libidinous direction as well, reaching inside his breeches for his burning weapon and pumping in unison before disgorging his load over the straw in the disused stall.

It was only later, when the two love-birds had gone and he'd tidied himself, helping himself to some of the white filly's sugar for sustenance, that his befuddled brain began to clear a little and a sudden thought struck him.

There had been something about the woman's voice that stirred his memory, but the last time he'd heard it, he'd swear that it had been young and scared. He still couldn't rightly get his thoughts together on the voice, but it certainly wasn't the bold young servant-girl he'd encountered across the meadow late at night a while back. But just as quickly as he remembered that grand little piece and her willingness to oblige, he remembered how the girl had been asking him if he'd seen her missing mistress.

'Sweet Mother of God!' O'Reilly blasphemed out loud. 'It was the young wench stripping off at the stream!'

But she'd changed out of all recognition. He'd have sworn on a dozen Bibles, had he been so inclined, that the girl had been a frightened virgin when he'd chanced upon her. He instantly recalled those startlingly blue eyes and that look of fear in them when she'd stumbled and fallen against him, so soft and clinging, and the way her honeypots had popped out of her bodice. The very thought of her started the stirrings in his loins again, especially after hearing the way she'd carried on with the stable-lad.

O'Reilly frowned. If the girl and the woman were one and the same, then something had certainly happened to change her. And the bloke hadn't been one of the usual puny young lads who worked for a pittance in these surroundings, but a far lustier one than most, if all he'd heard was anything to go by.

It needed thinking about. There'd surely be a reward

out for anybody reporting the girl's whereabouts, but his own dealings with the constables made him revolt against running straight to them with information. There wasn't enough money in the world to tempt him into getting caught in that trap, and the guardian might be a much better bet. Except that a body such as himself turning up anywhere was always viewed with suspicion and turned away before he could utter a civil word. Either that or he'd be instantly accused of doing some mischief to the girl himself.

And there was something else nagging away at his gut. If the wench hadn't been as innocent as she'd pretended at the stream, then he'd been bloody well cheated. She'd been fair game after all, and he'd let her go because of those big, frightened eyes and that fragile, innocent appearance. Padraig O'Reilly was madder than a wild pig at the thought that he'd been taken in, and even more so at the thought that he might be getting soft.

'Hey, what are you doin' here?'

The young voice startled him, and he jumped back in the lee of the stables. The love-birds had gone out of sight by now, and he glowered at the lad who seemed to have appeared from nowhere, some riding gear over his arm and heading into the stables. O'Reilly leapt at him, catching him around the throat and giving his neckcloth a twist before he could cry out for help.

'Now then, me fine laddo, never you mind about me. You just tell me about the man and woman from the big house, and no harm will come to you.'

The boy's eyes bulged and his face whitened with fright.

'I don't know nothin'. Me and the others just get the orders from the old woman and look after the horses.'

O'Reilly's eyes narrowed. It wasn't the kind of answer he'd expected, and his instincts told him there was definitely something strange about this place, so isolated and seemingly deserted. It had suited his purposes, but now he felt decidedly uneasy.

'What old woman? I've only seen the one in the blue dress, you little scumbag. Do you know that one's name?'

The boy shook his head, his voice babbling with fright as O'Reilly shook him. 'Honest, mister, if I knew, I'd tell you. We just do as we're told and we get looked after. And right now I'm to saddle up the filly for the lady.'

The boy gulped, obviously thinking he'd already said too much. 'Please, mister, get away from here. If he thought I'd told you anything he'd thrash me, even though I ain't got nothing to tell!'

O'Reilly let him go, and the boy rubbed at his tender throat. There was more here than just a simple lovers' meeting, the Irishman thought, but he sensed that this one really didn't know anything. If he did, seeing how the snivelling wretch cowered, he'd have told him by now.

'Well, you just forget you've seen me, or I'll be back, and you'll be sorry your mother ever gave birth to you. Understand?'

The boy nodded, and O'Reilly gathered up his rags and lurched out of the stables into the sunlight again, blinking like an owl. He had to do something with what little information he had, if only to get some satisfaction over the way the bitch had fooled him with her innocent looks and was now seemingly so well set-up here. But as yet he wasn't at all sure what to do with his new-found knowledge.

Abbie walked steadily away from the stables, hardly knowing how to speak to Leon any more. He was three people, or he could have been a dozen, and she felt that she didn't know any of them. She burned with embarrassment at the way she had behaved in the hay loft, and knew that for all Sophie had told her, she was not made the same way as the kitchen-maid.

It had been an exhilarating and intense sexual experience, but there was guilt mixed with her pleasure at doing so readily all that Leon had asked of her. It surely wasn't natural for a man to want a woman to beat him – and would the time come when he would want to do the same to her, she thought in a fright? Even the dominating pleasures of the Master's bedchamber were more desirable than this.

'Why do you not speak to me?' Leon said, as they walked back towards the elegant mansion.

'I was taught to speak when I was spoken to, and I certainly thought that applied here,' she retorted, her sudden attack of nerves making her bold rather than reticent.

'Not to you, Abigail.'

She looked up at him then, this man who had turned her life upside down, who was so skilled in the art of love-making, and yet seemingly had no understanding at all of what went on in a young girl's head or heart. And since he wanted her to speak, she dared to ask what she most wanted to know.

'Very well, then. How did you come to be so expert in the ways of the seraglio, if it's not impertinent of me to ask?'

All the same, she felt her face scorch as the words tumbled out, for never in her wildest imagination had she ever thought she would be asking such a thing. But since her life was filled with new and undiscovered sensations and experiences now – and all of them due to him – it no longer seemed so outrageous to want to know. And she had been born curious.

After a moment's deliberation, when she thought she had definitely gone too far and would be punished for her insolence, Leon told her briefly about Prince Khali and the life he had led in India; and about the many costly gifts that had been poured on him after saving the young prince's life – and those that he had tactfully refused.

Abbie's mouth fell open at hearing such revelations. But it accounted for so much. It explained the deep tan to his skin that had to be due to spending many years in foreign climes. And if, as a young man eager for new experiences, he had been so well indoctrinated in the imperious ways of an Indian prince, it explained why he expected everyone to be so subserviant to him, including White Dove – but not, it seemed, Abigail Richmond.

'Prince Khali looked on me as a brother,' Leon went on, almost to himself, 'and I doubt that there's a young man alive who wouldn't have had his head turned by such lavish attention to everything he needed.'

'And he gave you the means for all this?' Abbie said, spreading her hands expansively, and wondering at once if she had gone too far in asking for such personal information. But he shook his head.

'Not all of it. My father was a wealthy man, and left me very well provided for. What I brought from India were the human gifts, the jewellery and artefacts, and a promise to Prince Khali that I should never forget the pleasures I learned from his teaching.'

Abbie noted the insidious way his manner had changed as he spoke of the prince who had obviously been just as dear to him as a brother. But the mention of human gifts was enough to turn her stomach. No man had the right to consider other people his possessions. It degraded them – and it degraded her to remember that he obviously thought of herself in the same way, after saving her life and bringing her here. She was no more than his property, his plaything, a new and varied amusement, and she was only one of many.

'And now I think you have heard enough,' he went on, his tone more forceful, just as if he was reading her

145

mind. 'If it were not for the way you please me, and the novelty of discussions with an Englishwoman, you would not have been told this much.'

They were hardly discussions, Abbie thought dryly. But he had quickly reverted to being the arrogant landowner again, and was clearly done with the conversation. But she couldn't leave it there.

'And do none of the other women have any idea of your true identity?'

'Only Maya,' he said, his voice clipped.

'But do they never wish to leave the house?'

He stopped walking, turning to face her with a heavy sigh. By now they had strolled through a wooded copse in the vast estate that discreetly hid the stables from the mansion itself. She saw now that they had walked in a circle, but she welcomed the breath of air, and the chance to get her breath back after the episode in the stables.

'I swear I never met such an inquisitive woman,' Leon said irritably. 'But since you ask, no, they do not wish to leave the house. They are unused to our inclement weather, and even the warmest summer days leave them shivering. They are content with the life they lead, and the ambience is as near as possible to the one they left.'

Abbie suspected that part of their shivering was due to the flimsy clothes they wore, but she declined to say as much. They walked on in silence, each with their own thoughts, and neither of them had noticed the hidden watcher creeping out of the stables, trying vainly to see the recent occupants, and to wonder if the woman could possibly be the one he suspected.

They entered the mansion by a door at one side, and Abbie guessed at once that this was the formal wing, while the other – but by now, she daren't ask any more questions.

Besides, as long as her door wasn't locked there was

nothing to prevent her from creeping out of her room and finding her way through the mansion again to observe what went on. She felt a quiver of excitement at the thought. And at least she was no longer being guarded by the eunuch. It was almost as if Leon Villiers no longer expected her to try to get away – and until that moment it hadn't occurred to her that she had not really thought of such a thing.

'You will find a riding habit laid out ready for you in your room, and I will join you again in fifteen minutes. Then you may give the white filly her head, and see how well you suit one another.'

'You're letting me ride off alone?' she asked. 'Aren't you afraid I'll simply escape?'

He leaned towards her and kissed her, running his tongue slowly around her lips for a moment before releasing her.

'You will not be alone. I shall ride with you. But as for escaping – you are not a prisoner here, Abigail.'

As he opened a door for her to go inside, she saw they had reached her comfortable bedroom again. And while this may not be his idea of captivity, it was certainly hers, Abbie thought indignantly. And there was nothing to stop her digging her heels into the filly and outriding him. But even as she thought it, she guessed she would never be able to do it, and a little later she knew why.

Hearing the clatter of hooves in the small courtyard beyond her window, she looked down, and saw a lad holding the reins of two animals. One was the white filly that was her birthday gift, and the other was a sleek, powerful Arab horse that was obviously Leon's.

She turned instead to the riding habit laid out on her bed to his instructions. It was made from a soft brown fabric and not the heavy velvet her uncle had ordered for her that was far too stuffy in hot weather. She quickly slid out of the blue gown, knowing she would always remember it with a special feeling after today.

Slowly she passed her hands lightly over her body, remembering how and where Leon had touched her and held her, and remembering the pounding of their two hearts and the rhythm of their love-making. And for an exquisite few moments the tremors of love surged through her again.

She turned away from the mirror where she had been gazing unseeingly, knowing too late how deeply she was falling in love with him and that it could only be a futile love on her part. Quickly she donned the habit, and was ready when he came for her, immaculate in riding breeches and jacket.

He gave a crooked smile. 'How demure you look, my dear Miss Richmond,' he said. 'And how rampantly and deliciously you belie that innocence.'

'Please don't tease me,' she said in a low voice, still caught up in the fantasy of loving him. 'You can do whatever you want with me, but please allow me a little dignity.'

Though there had been precious little of that in her involvement with him, she thought. He had shamed her and humiliated her and embarrassed her. And he had also taught her how to please a man and brought her to ecstasy.

'I'm sorry if it seems that way,' Leon said, and she felt somewhat surprised and found herself wondering how rare an occasion it was for him to apologise to a woman. 'Tonight you will have all the dignity you require.'

Abbie looked at him suspiciously. By now she felt she knew the kind of man he was, and she didn't expect him to indulge her, unless it was for his own reasons. Although, even as she thought it, she reminded herself that she didn't really know him at all, at least, not the real man beneath all the various façades.

He laughed at her expression as they proceeded through the house and into the fresh air again where the two animals stood tethered and waiting. There was no sign of any grooms.

'I see that you doubt me, Abigail,' he said lightly.

'Is it permitted to do so?' she couldn't help saying.

'If you must, but it will make little difference to the outcome of things,' he said, making her grit her teeth with rage at his arrogance.

Then she felt his hand caress her buttocks. She thought fleetingly that it seemed as if he couldn't keep his hands off her for more than a few moments, and that if this was his way of allowing her dignity, it was hardly that of a gentleman for his respected lady.

But of course, she was hardly that! And anyway, she thought, still with that hideous middle-class guilt that wouldn't quite leave her, she was beginning to realise that she didn't object to the touch of his hands anywhere on her.

In fact, far from objecting, she yearned for it every hour of the day. It was alarming to know how readily she was coming to depend on him, and how much she resented all those days and nights when he was away from her. As well as wanting him for herself, she was well aware of the jealousy in her soul, knowing he would be with those golden-skinned women and torturing herself as to what he was doing with them, instead of her. If she didn't *know*, and hadn't already experienced it for herself, maybe it wouldn't torture her so.

Leon helped her on to the filly from the mounting-block, although she would far rather have dispensed with the side-saddle altogether, as she'd done on the day she left The Grange. It seemed like a hundred years ago now, as if she had been asleep for all those years, and this was the only reality she had ever wanted. It was as if she had never been fully alive before. She waited while he mounted easily, looking as if he was a part of the horse, two magnificent animals.

'Have you thought of a name for the filly?' he asked,

as they cantered away from the house, heading through the copse and past the stables and towards the sprawling parkland beyond.

'Doesn't she have a name already?'

'Not until you give her one. She's your gift, Abigail, for you to name as you wish.'

Abbie stroked the silky white mane, finding a sensuous pleasure in the feel of the animal beneath her. She gave a secret, mischievous smile.

'She's so pure and clean. I think I'd like to call her White Dove,' she said innocently, and then she clapped her hands to her mouth in mock dismay. 'Oh, I wasn't thinking, and of course I can't call her that.'

'You can call her whatever you like,' Leon said with a dry smile. 'And I admire your choice. Whenever you ride her and speak to her, it will remind you of other times.'

She couldn't anger him, Abbie thought. He was always one step ahead of her, twisting her feeble attempt to annoy him into a suggestive comment of his own. But she was stuck with the name now. The filly was to be White Dove – and just as he said, whenever she used the name, she would remember.

'Let's give her her head,' Leon said, once they were in an open stretch of country. 'Show me what you can do.'

She thought he already knew that, but she resisted giving him back a barbed comment and dug her heels gently into White Dove's flanks and urged her on. The filly responded at once, and as Leon easily kept up with her on his more powerful horse, she felt an exhilaration comparable to almost anything she had ever known. Almost.

'That was wonderful and exciting,' she gasped, when at last they slowed down and the animals were panting as much as their riders. Her hair streamed out in the summer breeze now. Her eyes were glowing, her cheeks were crimson, and her mobile mouth was parted with unbridled joy.

'So are you, my dear Miss Richmond,' Leon said. 'And I don't believe you have any idea just how much allure you have in that delectable body of yours.'

Her heart began to pound as he slid down from his horse and came slowly towards her to lift her down. She was held close to him, and his hands moved downwards over her arms, his thumb softly pausing in the small crease inside her elbows, before he bent to kiss each one. It was sweetly erotic and sent her pulses racing as she saw the growing and demanding passion in his eyes.

She felt an irresistible urge to run her hands through his ruffled dark hair. Without any invitation, she found her fingers reaching upwards to caress his nape in gentle massaging movements where the hair curled into his neck, and she heard his indrawn breath as she arched towards him.

'My lady is something of a witch, I think,' he said softly, and she wondered for a moment if they were to enact the lady and the stable-boy again. But his voice was different now. It was gentle, coaxing, persuasive, and more like that of a tender lover for his sweetheart – at least, in her limited knowledge, Abbie believed it to be so.

'Am I?' she said huskily.

'Don't you know it?' he said, running his finger around the curve of her cheek and on to her lips, where she instantly captured it between her teeth, giving it a little nip. At his slight smile, Abbie knew he was thinking of the action in a different connotation.

'You fluster me,' she murmured, when he withdrew his finger and stroked the slender column of her neck. 'I never know how to take you –'

'Oh, my lovely girl, I think you know very well,' he said with heavy innuendo.

'Are you flirting with me?' she asked, finding the

whole idea charming, and so very different from the intense seduction of all the previous occasions they had been together.

'I thought you were flirting with *me*,' Leon said, 'and I didn't find the idea at all displeasing.'

Abbie would dearly have liked to ask him at that moment if his *zenana* women never flirted with him, but she already knew the answer to that. There was only one reason for their presence, and it wasn't for conversation.

She wondered suddenly if that was something he sorely missed, for he was obviously an educated man, and if, perhaps, he was only just realising it. The thought was at once heady and exciting, knowing that for all their sensuous accomplishments, Abigail Richmond could provide something the concubines could not.

'Then if I'm flirting with you, I insist that you call me Abbie,' she said, wondering at her own daring in insisting anything with him.

'Abbie,' he repeated with a small nod of his head. 'It suits you well, having a vaguely virginal sound.'

She blushed, for he of all people knew that a virginal state no longer applied to her. He had taken that from her, and she had given it so willingly.

'And I'm impatient to sample your charms,' he went on, 'and loath to waste this lovely afternoon in idle chit-chat. So what would my virginal, flirtatious Abbie care to do now?'

'That sounds very much like a hint at seduction, sir,' she said primly, since this seemed to be the direction the conversation was leading. A frisson of excitement held her now, as he caught at the reins of the two animals and tied them to a tree.

Then he turned and held out his hands to her. Abbie put her own in his, and felt his fingers curl around hers. Those marvellous, seeking fingers, she thought, that could weave such magic in their caresses.

'I want to lie on the grass with you,' he said quietly. 'I want to feel my youth returning.'

She felt her throat constrict at the simply said words. For a brief moment he seemed almost vulnerable, and lonely, as if he had been away too long in his fantasy world and was only starting to realise that even the best of fantasies eventually faded.

But she dismissed the idea from her mind, for Leon Villiers would know exactly what he was doing. This appeal to her for empathy, and the artlessness with which he spoke, was just part of the repertoire of amusements with which he filled his life. Nevertheless, she found herself warming to him as he drew her down on the sweet grass beside him.

He let his fingers run through the long, silvery strands of her hair, and then gently begin to massage the nape of her neck in the same way she had massaged his earlier. A sharp thrill ran through her and she gave a soft sigh, closing her eyes at the pleasurable feelings.

'Do you like that, my sweet Abbie?' she heard him whisper in her ear.

'Oh yes,' she breathed.

'And this?'

She was aware that one hand had left her nape, and was gently covering her breast in a feather-light caress. Although she had no experience of such an occurrence, Abbie knew instinctively that this was how the tentative touch of first love must be between a young boy and his sweetheart. If this was the new game they were to play, it was almost unbearably sweet, and she responded to it at once.

'Yes,' she whispered, doing nothing to stop him.

Somehow she was lying on her back, and he was leaning over her, a look of almost longing in his eyes, in just the way she imagined a young boy would look. At her mute acceptance of him his hands became bolder, feeling the contours of her breasts as if for the first breathless contact of a callow youth, palming them, cupping them, and gently squeezing her nipples until they sprang into obedient life.

'Abbie, will you let me – ?' he left the question unfinished, and before she could answer, his hand had strayed to her skirt, and was pushing gently upwards, moving ever so slowly over the silk-clad leg to her stocking-top, and into the warmth of her thigh. She heard him give a small sigh, as any young man would do in feeling the soft, moist folds and crevices for the very first time.

The whole experience was suddenly charged with emotion for Abbie, and she felt an almost unbearable excitement in this expression of adoration from a man, for she could think of it as nothing less. Even if this was no more than a sport to Leon, then in her soul she thanked him for it.

In leading her so gently into what she could only describe as the first discovery of sexual feeling between young lovers, he had somehow managed to wipe out all the degradation she had felt at other times. It probably wasn't intentional on his part, but it had had that effect on her.

'You're so beautiful,' she heard him whisper huskily now, as he leaned more heavily over her, and she couldn't miss the fact that he was fully aroused now. She had to force herself to clench her hands at her sides, because the temptation to once again rub her fingers over the straining fabric at his crotch was almost too much – but she was playing a part too, and she was the so-innocent virgin.

'Would you let me take a peek?' he begged her next. 'Please, Abbie, or I swear I'll die with longing for you.'

She couldn't speak, almost bursting with desire for him to do whatever he wanted with her. She gave a nod, and felt him lift her skirts higher, until she felt the cool air on her flesh. The sensation was as erotic as she had imagined it would be. Then his palm brushed the soft downy hair that was reappearing on her nudity, his fingers stroking either side of her pouting lips at first, teasing and tantalising.

Then he leaned down, parting her, and gazing into her, as if for the very first time.

'It's like a beautiful flower unfolding,' his young boy's persona said wonderingly, and he tentatively placed the tip of one finger in the moist opening. He watched her face then, as if to judge her reaction to his slightest movement.

But he must surely know how she was feeling by this time, Abbie thought wildly. How she longed for him to take her right now, and to have done with this youthful seduction, and to have him thrust into her like the man she knew him to be. Besides which, she could resist no longer, and without any warning her hand reached down for his swollen shaft. She squeezed tentatively at first, and then with increasing confidence and enjoyment; sliding her fingers down the erection and entangling them in the bushy hair that crowned its base, until they caressed the plum-like balls while the back of her hand gently kneaded the bulge beneath them.

'If you continue to do that, you know where it will lead, don't you, Abbie?' she heard him say, still playing his game.

'I know,' she said, hardly able to contain the ache in her crotch now, and hardly able to speak.

'There's just one more thing to do so that I won't hurt you,' he said, and then his tongue had replaced the tip of his finger, and he was licking her in long sensual strokes, just as if he had never done such a thing before, and then pushing inwards and upwards, revelling in the little murmurs of pleasure escaping from her throat.

'Now you're ready, my angel,' he said. 'And so am I. Hold still, now, and I promise I'll be quick, for I can't hold back much longer.'

She could hardly go on pretending that this was the first time when he was suddenly deep inside her, hot and thrusting. She clung to his back, moving rapturously with him, and soaring with him to a quick, tumultuous climax, as the hot gush of his life-fluid filled her.

He drew away from her almost at once, pulling her dress down over her with the clumsy embarrassment of a boy, and quickly fastening his breeches. And despite that sudden withdrawal, or maybe because of it, she sensed that the game wasn't yet over. He nuzzled his mouth into her neck.

'It'll be all right, Abbie. Nothing can happen the first time, so there's no need for you to fret, my sweet girl.'

For a second she couldn't think what he meant, and then Sophie's words came flooding back to her.

'– it's how you make babies, see?'

But this wasn't the first time, though she had become wise enough by now to know that her monthly timings had been calculated by that old witch Maya, and that there were certain times when it was unlikely for a woman to conceive a child.

Just as quickly, Abbie knew how fiercely she wanted exactly that. To have Leon's child, and to be the pivotal part of a loving, normal family unit was suddenly the most spectacular thing on her horizon.

It had once seemed like a distant, girlish dream to marry a man she loved, and to bear his child. But now there was only one man who could fulfil all her dreams – and she knew just as certainly that he would never be reckless enough to let it happen, and she might just as well ask for the moon.

Chapter Ten

The Irishman knew that some things couldn't be rushed. Being crafty was something that was inborn in him, and he contented himself in waiting and watching. He'd watched how the constables were half-heartedly combing the area, without the faintest notion that their prey was so near at hand. And for the next couple of afternoons, well hidden in the bushes, Padraig O'Reilly watched the delectable Miss Abigail Richmond going in and out of the west wing of the sprawling mansion.

He watched with lustful eyes as she swung with agility into the saddle of the white filly tethered for her near the mounting-block. His nether regions strained with even more lustful urges as he watched her straight back, her curvaceous shape and heaving breasts, and the way her cheeks were flushed with pleasure as her silver hair streamed out in the breeze as she cantered around the estate.

But O'Reilly was also nothing if not thorough. He had made his plan, and fornicating with this luscious piece was no longer on his agenda. It was the other wench, the lust-bucket from The Grange, who was going to see him right. Between them they would get some kind of reward for information out of the old fool there, if it was the last thing he did.

O'Reilly leered into the foliage of the bushes. No doubt the old boy would be glad to have his property back, no matter how damaged she was in the process. And the slut who was going to help him would do his bidding, or else, he thought, his hands clenching and his mood changing to one of menace.

Anyway, hadn't he already put the fear of God into her by threatening to tell the world the fiction that she'd wanted to go away with him? And that would finish her chances with her country yokel for good and all.

Late on the second afternoon of observation, O'Reilly finally slunk away from Villiers Manor, well pleased with the plan he was about to put into operation.

Alone in her room once more, after the daily ride by herself that Leon was permitting her now, Abbie felt oddly disorientated as she threw herself on her bed to relax. It was always this way, and by now she knew the reason for it. Tomorrow was her birthday, and in these last weeks, she had become more sexually fufilled than she had ever known she could be, but there was still something vital missing. It was love, she thought. Lust alone wasn't enough, when she yearned for so much more.

After that wild coupling in the stable, Leon had promised her dignity, she thought bitterly, but what dignity was there in being no more than a slave to a man's lust, however skilfully and inventively performed?

Not that she had seen hide nor hair of him since that day at the stables. And that in itself was an added frustration. All she'd had was a message that she was to be allowed to ride White Dove each afternoon. She knew at once that it was meant to test her, to see if she would flee, but the thought of it never entered her mind.

She lay staring unseeingly at the ceiling in her room, wondering where he was right now. What he was doing, and who he was with – and resenting the fact that he had such a hold over her, whether she liked it or not.

And dear God, but she *did* like it! Despite everything, she knew she wanted nothing more than to spend the rest of her days and nights with Leon Villiers, or the Master, or however he cared to style himself. If this was infatuation, it was on a grand scale. But she knew it was more than that on her part. She was totally in love with him, and willing to do his bidding, no matter what.

She turned her head, biting her lips, and wondering just what devilment was in her make-up for her to feel so besotted. But she knew it was all due to the undiscovered part of her that he had awoken so beautifully. She closed her eyes and tried to recapture the essence of him, hearing his voice in her head, breathing his breath in her mind, touching his body with her thoughts – and it was so very easy to do, when it was what she wanted so much.

A while later, a small tap on her door roused her from the drowsiness of her dreaming. She hadn't actually slept. Instead, she had just let the images of herself and Leon fill her mind the way he filled her body and soul. She turned her head at the intrusion, and gasped in shock.

'Tonight you will dine with Mr Villiers in the blue dining-room, and he requests that you play the piano-forte for him in the drawing-room afterwards, miss,' Maya said formally.

But this was a transformed Maya. Gone were the Indian garments that had made her look so sinister in Abbie's eyes, and instead she was garbed in the neat dark clothes of a European housekeeper in a gentleman's house.

'I don't understand –' Abbie stammered.

'It's very simple,' Maya said, as if Abbie herself were the one who was simple-minded. 'Mr Villiers wishes his guest to be with him, and begs that you will be ready at seven-thirty precisely. I suggest a demure gown for the occasion. Perhaps the claret with the cream fichu insert at the neck would be suitable.'

Abbie gulped before speaking. The old harridan was giving her firm instructions, no less, but she had to admit that in the formal housekeeper's dress, Maya looked far less formidable now than when she was weaving the sharp-bladed knife towards Abbie's crotch. She quickly averted her thoughts from the memory.

'Very well,' she said, more meekly than the spirited Abigail Richmond normally spoke.

'Someone will come to help you bathe if you require, and then help you to dress –'

'None of that will be necessary, thank you,' Abbie said quickly, wanting no sensuous hands on her body except those of Leon Villiers. But she pushed away the thought of him doing the tasks in the bathing chamber that the seraglio girls had done, knowing that such a thing would be far below a gentleman's dignity. All the same, just for a moment she couldn't resist letting her imagination soar, knowing how magical it would be to have his hands soaping her willing flesh, seeking out her curves and crevices, kissing her intimately in that heady, sensually perfumed atmosphere –

She swallowed hard as Maya stood waiting for her apparent dismissal from my lady's bedroom, and Abbie knew instantly that this was to be the new game. Tonight they were to be so very proper, the way a young lady and gentleman should behave. It gave her a frisson of excitement to imagine playing such a game, knowing how rampantly lustful Leon could be. And herself too,

Abbie admitted, knowing only too well now her own newly awakened drives and desires.

'Mr Villiers will present himself at your door at seven-thirty precisely,' Maya went on, still in the formal manner.

'Please tell him I'll be ready,' Abbie said unnecessarily, and the woman nodded and left her.

Abbie was galvanised into action now, all the lethargy leaving her. After the strenuous afternoon ride on her lovely filly, she longed to soak in a bath and make herself beautiful for him. And the sooner the time passed the better, for she ached to be with him again.

She had been delighted to discover that this fortress of a house had been filled with the very latest of luxury devices. The bathroom adjoining her room had a deep, ornate tub patterned with blush-red roses, and with gilt taps that produced instant hot and cold water without the need for heavy pails of water that strained the backs of many a young maid at establishments such as The Grange.

Thoughts of them reminded her momentarily of Sophie – not that a kitchen-maid ever had access to the more intimate quarters of a lady's boudoir. For a brief moment, Abbie wished Sophie could see her now, and that she could tell her everything that had happened to her since leaving The Grange. It wasn't only Sophie who had tales to tell – and none so wondrous and varied as Miss Abigail Richmond could relate!

But even as she thought it, she knew she could never tell Sophie everything. Nor anyone else. This house held secrets far too private and too incredible for anyone else's ears. But it would be good to tell the superior Sophie airily that Abbie too had a lover – and what a lover!

She laughed softly to herself as she stripped off the riding dress and undergarments and slid her arms into a silky robe before entering her bathroom. Its decor of soft blues and greens couldn't be more different from the white and gold chamber in which she had first found herself, with its strongly perfumed candles that dulled the senses. This was a lady's bathroom.

Abbie turned on the taps and tipped a handful of bath crystals into the water until it foamed and tingled her nose invitingly. She slipped out of the robe and stepped into the caressingly hot water with a sigh of pleasure.

As she soaped herself, she half-expected the door to open and for Leon to step inside. In fact, she knew how much she would have welcomed it to happen, but it didn't. She wondered if there were eyes watching her, and if the mirrored wall was a two-way affair enabling an observer to see through from the other side and watch her every movement. She had heard of such things, and if the observer had been Leon she would no longer have felt outraged. Nor was she shocked at her own feelings, realising how far she had come mentally, as well as physically, since knowing him.

And if there *were* such an observer – with a secret thrill she entered into her own game of pretence now, preening herself as the soap bubbles ran over her rounded curves, and sensuously and slowly squeezing her own breasts. She lightly palmed the rosy nipples until they stood proud, and felt her tongue run around her lips as if in anticipation of caresses from other hands and other lips. Then her hands moved slowly down over her softly rounded belly to the source of her pleasure, stroking lightly and fingering the opening just enough to feel her eyes dilating.

But even as her inner muscles began to pulse she knew she didn't want to feel the sweet thrill of climax again. Not like this. Not alone. Glorious though it was, by now she was discovering that the game held only half its seductive power when it was played alone. Abbie closed her thighs tightly together, willing the pulsations to subside before they took a real hold on her, and continuing more purposefully with her ablutions.

Unknown to Abbie, Leon Villiers' bedroom in the west wing of Villiers Manor was across the passageway from hers. He had watched with powerful binoculars as she took her afternoon rides, and his reward had been to see her return. There had been no attempt to escape.

By the second day of observation on the eve of Abbie's eighteenth birthday, he was attired in the conventional clothes of a wealthy gentleman, and he stared out of his window thoughtfully now, contemplating his vast estate and ruminating on just what he intended doing with the delicious Abigail Richmond.

In the wake of Prince Khali's doctrines and example, it had been his policy never to let a woman get close to him. But he freely admitted that during those licentious years of tutelage, even while he revelled in the art of seduction, he had been vulnerable and openly receptive to all the new experiences that came his way so effortlessly. That he was attractive to women he never questioned. That he was sexually insatiable had never been a problem, since there were always women in the seraglio ready to please and to perform whatever he required of them.

But now there was Abigail Richmond, the first Englishwoman he had bedded since his youth, and the only woman to get beneath his skin in a way he had never anticipated. He had told himself it was no more than a humane act to bring her here when he had found her so dazed and injured, but that impulsive gesture had quickly evolved into something else as he had toyed with the novelty of turning her into one of his devoted seraglio women, the one silvery-haired woman among the dark, honey-skinned others, the haughty Englishwoman tamed – and that in itself was a game, to see if it could be done.

Leon frowned, his finely-shaped brows drawn together as he thought of all the humiliations he had put her through. It was exactly the way Prince Khali had informed him a woman should be tamed, and that once she had been subjugated to all that a man demanded of her, she was his to do with as he would for the rest of her life. The young and impressionable Leon, blessed with a highly-sexed nature, had been thrown into a life of pleasure such as he had never known before, and it had seemed as if he had truly found a heaven on earth.

Later, when he finally yearned for England and home, he found it easy to reason that one of the prince's astrologers would have decreed that fate had led him here to find this isolated property. With all the wealth his father had left him, and the lavish gifts the prince had insisted on giving him, the means to perpetuate the indulgent life he could no longer do without had also seemed heaven-sent.

But now there was Abigail Richmond, he thought again. And he preferred not to consider too deeply just why he was finding it increasingly difficult, after all, to accept her into his harem. Nor why he allowed her liberties he would never allow the women who never left the *zenana*, nor showed any inclination to do so. In that, at least, he was confident.

But he never showered them with gifts, either, certainly not a valuable eighteenth birthday gift such as the pure-bred white filly. And then there was this piquant evening he had arranged for tonight – insisting that Maya wore the dress of an English housekeeper, and that the servants in the dining-room did the same. He wondered if he was going slightly mad to indulge Abbie's need for dignity.

With a semblance of the cruel disregard for women's feelings he knew Prince Khali possessed, he wondered if it wouldn't be far better to be rid of the girl for good, and send her off as a reciprocal gift to his old friend.

Leon turned away from the window, knowing that nothing on earth would possess him to do such a thing. She belonged to him. It was written in the stars that a life saved by another owed that life to the saviour in perpetuity. Prince Khali would recognise that, for it was he who had taught Leon as much. Except that in his case it was not so, for no one of royal blood could be tied in such a bond to a commoner.

Leon had been astute enough to see how easy it had been for the prince to get out of such a commitment, but it had also relieved his own mind not to have such a responsibility. Yet it had taken only a few seconds of gazing at the prone and dazed Abbie Richmond for him to exercise that right.

Angry with his own turbulent thoughts, he strode across his deep-carpeted room and wrenched open the door, quickly crossing the passage to Abbie's room and knocking peremptorily on the door before striding inside.

She turned with a gasp from the dressing-table mirror, where she was brushing her hair into cascading silken waves around her slender shoulders. Contrasted so vividly against the claret-coloured gown she now wore, it shone like silver. On her arm she still wore the ivory bangle that was the symbol of belonging to him.

'I'm sorry if I'm keeping you waiting,' she stammered. 'I didn't realise how the time had flown.'

He moved towards her as she made to rise, and eased the gilt-edged brush from her hand. For a moment it seemed as if she was afraid that he would strike her with it, and then as she felt the touch of his hand on her crown, and the long, sensuous strokes of the brush as he continued what she had begun, she half-closed her eyes in ecstasy at his touch.

'You have the most beautiful hair in the world,' he

told her. 'It will be a crime to hide it from public view when you reach eighteen tomorrow.'

'It seems to me that there are very few people who will see it, whether or not it's up or down,' Abbie said huskily, adding unexpectedly, 'unless you plan to release me after my birthday?'

'Is that what you want?' he countered.

'How can I even think it?' she replied. 'I'm ruined, and no other man will want me. My uncle would disown me for certain —'

'Then you had better stay where you're wanted,' Leon said, far more calmly than he felt at the sudden burst of bitterness in her voice. As he met those lovely, luminous blue eyes in her mirror, he suddenly felt like a monster, and it wasn't a feeling that sat easily on him.

Damn her, he thought irritably. He had been so beautifully set-up here, and she had been no more than one more bit of bed-sport — yet somehow she had wormed her way into the conscience he thought he had abandoned long ago.

'It's time for dinner,' he said abruptly. 'And afterwards, you will play for me.'

'I know. I've already had my orders,' she said.

For a moment their glances met and clashed, and Leon clenched his hands at his sides. Damn her again, he thought, for daring to try to get the better of him. Prince Khali would never have allowed a woman to speak to him so, and she would have been thrashed for her insolence.

Even as he thought it, he knew he wouldn't have wanted to see her beaten. All the same, there were pleasures she hadn't yet been initiated into, and it might be amusing to see just how she reacted to the flail and the blindfold. But that was for later. For now, he would show her the epitome of good taste, and she would be lulled into a feeling of *bonhomie* as they played the part of host and guest.

For just one moment more, his eyes lingered on the shimmering waves of her hair as it lay over her shoulders. Then, as if totally unable to resist it, he gathered it up in his hands in a twist and kissed the exposed nape of her neck.

His eyes met hers in the mirror, and with her hair no longer cascading downwards, the slender column of her neck and throat was more evident. Leon felt the wildest urge to slide his hands forwards, down over that creamy throat to the glorious mounds of her breasts, aching to feel her naked flesh. He restrained himself with an effort, angry for feeling momentarily as gauche as a young boy with his first girl.

But they had already played that game, he reminded himself. Tonight was intended for a different game. The moment passed, and he let her hair resume its flowing length and held out his arm to her.

'Your dinner awaits you, ma'am,' he said.

Abbie rose from her seat, her legs shaking as always when she was near him. She wondered what kind of dinner this was to be, and if it was to be a replica of that other time, when he had come to sit beside her, feeding her fruit and wine, and licking the honey from her lips. The sweet remembered imagery of it sent shivers of erotic pleasure down her spine.

He led her through the now-familiar corridors of the west wing, and down the curving staircase to a dining room. While she had been left to her own devices, Abbie had already discovered these lavishly furnished rooms. And she had no doubt that he was fully aware of her explorations, since there seemed to be little that she could hide from him.

He opened the door to the dining room, prepared as formally as any room Abbie had ever seen, from the gleaming damask tablecloth, to the sparkling cutlery and wine glasses. But she was more startled at seeing the attendants waiting to serve them.

Maya stood in watchful attendance, and several of the young seraglio women were dressed as demurely as the old woman, in the traditional black dresses and white caps and aprons of English maids. With their dark hair scraped back and swept up beneath the caps, and the exotic make-up removed, they would have passed for servants anywhere.

Abbie walked numbly to the chair that Maya indicated. Was there no end to this man's surprises? He was at once a flamboyant Indian prince, an English gentleman, a tentative young boy, a skilled lover, a rampant stable-lad, she thought, with a shudder of memory. He was a chameleon of a man, and the similarity between the word and his own name didn't escape her.

'Why do you smile?' Leon asked, as he seated himself at the far end of the table.

She looked at him through the haze of candlelight. There were people all around them moving swiftly and silently, like attendant bees to their queen, ready to serve them with soup and wine and the very English dish of succulent roast beef, the aroma of which was teasing her nostrils now. And because she was used to living in a gentleman's house where the presence of servants could be disregarded, she spoke freely.

'I was wondering just who you really are.'

He laughed. 'I'm whoever you want me to be, my dear.'

She shook her head faintly, knowing it wasn't true. He was whoever *he* wanted to be, and it would always be so. No woman would ever possess him the way he chose to possess them.

'Do you doubt me?' he asked pleasantly, but with the slightest edge to his voice. The girl ladling soup into Abbie's plate caught her glance for the merest moment, and she sensed at once that the girl was wondering if she would really dare to challenge his words.

And that in itself was a challenge to the rebellious Abigail Richmond, who had planned to flee from her uncle's tyranny and find lodgings with some kind, respectable family. Instead of that she was here, with a man she adored, who saw her as nothing more than another possession. Her chin lifted defiantly.

'I most certainly do! I think you dictate the terms in everything you do, and you expect everyone else to fall in with your needs.'

'Indeed? And may I ask what gives you the right to question anything I do?'

Abbie knew she was on dangerous ground. The serving-girls said nothing, but the atmosphere emanating from them was almost palpable. They would never dare to question the Master in this way. They were born to be servile – or servility had been indoctrinated in them for so long that they knew no other way to live – while she was different.

But he was not the Master tonight. He was Leon Villiers, her English host. She answered quickly.

'Only the right that as your guest I assume the respect any gentleman would accord a lady,' she said coolly. 'And that a lady and gentleman meeting at dinner on equal terms surely have the right to sharing intelligent conversation without either of them feeling unduly slighted.'

She spoke more boldly than she felt, for he could so easily turn against her and declare this pleasant *tête-à-tête* at an end – if *tête-à-tête* it could be called with so many secretly curious eyes watching them.

But he laughed again, and it seemed as if the whole room relaxed. 'By God, my dear Miss Richmond, but you do me a power of good. I'd forgotten the cut and thrust of real conversation with a woman, and every now and then you remind me most delightfully.'

Abbie wasn't sure how insulting the others in the room might find this, but probably not at all, she thought, briefly saddened for them. But since they were presumably so content with their comfortable lot, the brief sadness quickly passed.

'Then I'm glad I please you, sir,' she said demurely, her tongue in her cheek. 'So what shall we discuss now? The weather, perhaps? Or the state of the nation?'

She paused, for talking about the weather was banal, and she had no idea of the state of the nation, such was her ignorance of matters outside The Grange and the schoolroom lessons that usually avoided such things. It was an appalling admission, and one she had never even considered before.

Leon, with his widely travelled experience, was so much more worldly than she would ever be, and in other matters besides those of the bedroom.

'I'm sorry,' she added more humbly, and he raised a quizzical eyebrow. 'That was rather flippant of me.'

'I like you being flippant,' he said, astonishing her. 'In fact, I like you any way you choose to be, Miss Richmond.'

She saw him raise his glass to her through the flickering haze, and her cheeks became heated at once. As if she was reading his mind now, she knew what he was really saying.

'I like you soft and moist and pliant beneath me; or writhing in ecstasy; I like the touch of your skin, and the taste of your mouth, and all the other delectable places that give me entrance. I like my new plaything very much.'

Abbie kept her eyes lowered as the soup dishes were cleared away and the thick slices of beef were heaped on to her plate with the buttered carrots and tiny peas, and smothered in onion-spiced gravy.

She must be going mad to think Leon was thinking any such thing. Not that she doubted his liking for her. The proof of that was always evident. The real madness would be to think there was anything special in his liking for her. To let herself dream that this lovely evening, so genteel and civilised, could mean anything other than one more of his fantasy games. He was playing with her, as he had been doing since the moment he found her.

'I wonder just what's going on in that fertile little brain of yours now?' she heard him say.

'What goes on in a lady's head is not always for a gentleman to know,' she said, swiftly and coquettishly, and thankful that he didn't seem to be reading her mind right now.

'It's no matter. If it's of any importance I've no doubt you'll be unable to resist telling me. Frivolous young females can never keep secrets.'

At that, Abbie felt her face flame even more. 'I think you forget, Mr Villiers, that in a few hours from now I will no longer be classed as a frivolous young female.'

'Nor you will,' Leon said, so coolly that Abbie suspected he had been merely drawing her on to say exactly that. To remind her that he knew very well that tomorrow she would be classed as a woman, and beyond the clutches of her uncle. And to what end? To be forever in the clutches of a man intent on taking his pleasures from as many women as he could? The prospect was a dismal one for one reason only. Abbie was not born into a culture that condoned such behaviour.

But neither was he. That was the worst enigma of all. He was as English as herself, and all this – this play-acting – seemed suddenly so facile, so much the fantasy world of a man still searching for himself. And even as she thought it, Abbie despised herself for her stupidity, for if ever there was a man who knew exactly what he wanted, it was Leon Villiers, Master of all he surveyed.

'Is everything you see to your liking?' Leon enquired, and Abbie realised she had been staring at him for the past few minutes, while all the crazy notions ran through her head.

'Thank you, yes,' she said, deliberately misunderstanding and excruciatingly polite. 'The food is excellent, and the wine most palatable.'

He snapped his fingers at once, and the plates were removed, to be replaced by a huge platter placed reverently in the centre of the table, containing a concoction of crystallised fruits and sweetmeats in the shape of doves.

'Oh, how perfectly lovely,' Abbie breathed, and her eyes shone with pleasure, despite her efforts to behave in as adult a way as possible.

'But none of it can compare with your own loveliness, my sweet,' Leon said softly.

At least, she thought it was what he said, but his words were muted, and the serving-girls were gliding around the table and offering her a dish of the succulent fruits. And although she knew there would be no special seductive attention to her lips on this occasion, Abbie wondered if Leon was remembering that other time too.

She desperately wanted him to remember. She wanted to fill his mind and soul, the way he filled hers. She wanted him with a passion so strong that she ached and hungered with it. She would do anything he asked, and be whatever he wished, just as long as she could have him close to her. And despite all the fruits and the wine, her mouth went dry at recognising the depths of her own depravity. But depravity wasn't the right word for it, she thought swiftly. The word was love.

'If you've quite finished, we'll retire to the drawing-room, and you'll play for me,' he said, breaking into her dreaming.

Abbie started, having forgotten how this evening was to end. Or would it be only the beginning? She had no way of knowing what he might have in store for her, and she rose from her chair with her heart beating wildly as he came around the table and offered her his arm again.

Without another glance at the servants waiting to deal with the depleted table, they left the dining room and walked the few steps into the beautiful drawing room with its deep blue velvet couches and thick Persian carpet, the vases from the Orient, and the elegant grand piano standing in one corner of the room.

As she stood indecisively for a moment, Leon sat down in an armchair where he had a perfect view of the pianist's fingers on the keys.

'Will you please play for me, Abbie?' he said again. 'I'm intrigued to know what other accomplishments you have – in addition to riding.'

The words were bland enough, but the meaning in them was clear. But if she were the only one of his women who could play, then she might well be called upon more often than those others, at least when he felt the need for less exotic pleasures. She had her uses, Abbie thought wryly.

She sat at the pianoforte and let her fingers ripple over the ivory keys for a moment before embarking on a melody. She had always felt a special pleasure at the responsive touch of the piano keys, and this instrument in particular was especially fine, filling the room with pure, resonant notes.

Without warning, she knew exactly why she had always felt so attracted to this pastime. Touching and pressing the keys with a light or deepening pressure and feeling their instant response, was akin to feeling the delicate touch of a lover's fingers. She stroked the keys as if she stroked Leon's body, and her quickening breath as she reached the crescendo of the piece she played was almost climactic. Almost –

'You play very well,' he said softly.

Until that moment, she had been so mesmerised with

the music and her own turbulet emotions that she hadn't realised that he had risen and was standing right behind her now. She felt his hands on her shoulders, and his thumbs caressed the nape of her neck beneath her hair. Shudders ran through her body at his touch, and she had a violent urge to lean back against him, to beg him to tease her no longer, but to love her, as he surely intended this evening to end.

'This is your last official evening as a child, Abbie, although you and I both know that childhood is far behind you now. But on such an important evening it's an unwritten rule that you must be in bed before midnight,' he said.

'Is it?' she said faintly, because it was becoming all too clear to her now that he didn't intend coming with her. The disappointment was so intense that she could have screamed with the pain of it, assuming that he would finish off the evening with one of his other women instead of her.

He drew her to her feet and kissed her chastely on her forehead.

'I'll escort you to your room,' he went on, as if he had no understanding of the turmoil storming inside her. She *hated* him, she raged, for awakening all her dormant sexuality, and then casting her aside in this way. But short of begging him, which her pride prevented her from doing now, she had no choice but to let him escort her to her room and leave her there, to undress with savage haste into the white cambric nightgown laid out on the bed for her.

Once in her bed, she buried her face in the pillow and wept, hating herself as much as him, for letting herself be caught up in this nightmare. As she heard the chimes of midnight from a clock elsewhere in the house, she thought bitterly that this was her birthday, and never had she felt so alone and unwanted.

* * *

She was sure she hadn't slept – and yet perhaps she had, because the sound of her door being thrown open made her leap up and go rigid with fear. The night was still dark, and the moon was obscured by rain clouds now.

A figure stood in her doorway, dimly lit from behind by the candles in the corridor. Her heart seemed to be in her throat as it advanced slowly towards her. It was black from head to foot, and it didn't speak. She had no idea who or what it was, but she cowered back against her pillow, clutching the bedcovers to her chest.

'What demon are you?' she said hoarsely.

'No demon,' she heard Leon Villiers's commanding voice say. 'You will come with me now, woman.'

Before she could answer, he had hauled her out of the bed, tearing the nightgown so that it yawned open at the bodice, exposing her breasts. Her heart beat furiously, partly with fear and partly with exhilaration at whatever game he was playing now. Whatever it was, he was once more the Master, and she the love-slave, willing or not.

Chapter Eleven

*A*bbie felt herself being dragged along the dimly lit twisting corridors of the house. She put up no more than a token resistance, and that was only because she was sure it was what was required of her, but it did nothing to quench the wild and growing excitement in her veins.

Leon had let her think he was finished with her for the evening, when in reality he had planned all this, though whatever 'this' was, as yet she had no idea. But she realised that they eventually left the west wing, passed through the rotunda in the centre of the building, and were now moving into the scented corridors of his seraglio chambers.

But, her thoughts scattering wildly, she remembered that she hadn't been anointed or prepared. She hadn't been purified for the Master. That she could even think such pagan thoughts horrified her, yet just as quickly they became acceptable. She had become so acclimatised to all that he demanded of her that nothing seemed strange any more. If anything, it was the bland evening they had shared that had seemed all the stranger to her

176

senses now. She had been indoctrinated into his way of life so insidiously and sweetly –

They passed many doors in the corridors, but all were dark now, and she couldn't see the latticed grilles or anything beyond them. Finally he threw open a door and thrust her inside so that she almost stumbled and fell.

Abbie took in the scene quickly. It was the same seduction bedchamber that she had been in before, with the mirrored ceiling and walls. There were fewer candles lit, so that the room seemed more intimate. The candles were all pink-hued and seemingly scented with roses, adding to the sensual atmosphere, though she noted that much of the heady perfume was due to the actual carpet of rose petals strewn all about, and as they walked over them their scent permeated the heady sweetness of the room. The satin sheets on the bed were virginal white now, but delicately tinted with the rosy hue from the candles.

Abbie quickly took in the multitude of images of the room's two occupants. She saw herself, her hair wild and still tangled from sleep, her white cambric nightgown gaping open to reveal her breasts. If she hadn't looked so startled at all that was happening, it could easily have been the look of a wanton.

But as she looked at Leon, and saw the contrast between them, she knew instantly that her appearance was intended to be that of a captive. He was garbed totally in black, save for a jewelled sash at his waist. His luxuriant hair seemed even blacker than usual, his skin swarthier, and his eyes glittered with a piratical lust. To Abbie's eyes he was every inch the powerful, dominating Master.

'What are you going to do with me?' she whispered, her mouth so dry she could hardly speak. But it seemed that speech was not required of her. He pushed her towards the bed, his voice harsher than usual.

'Be silent, woman. You will speak when you are spoken to, and not before.'

Despite herself, Abbie couldn't resist letting a small smile creep around her mouth. So this was the new game, and one that was presumably intended as an introduction to her newly-aquired maturity. Another birthday gift, the like of which very few young women must receive.

Leon saw the smile and raised his hand as if to strike her. She cowered back at once, suddenly afraid, and unsure just how much play-acting this really was, or if he intended to ravish her more cruelly now. Was this, after all, a more sinister reason for the charade? Now that she was no longer a child, he'd be certain there was no court in the land who could condemn him for whatever he did to her.

She wished such a thing had never entered her head, for the last thing she would ever do would be to accuse him of rape or abduction. Not her lover, whom she adored with a passion –

'Lie on your back, woman,' he ordered, and she noted that she was no longer Abbie or Abigail or White Dove. She was nothing. But her innate curiosity got the better of her. If this was the game, then she must enter into it and do as she was told. And she sensed that she should not address him by name, either. He was her captor, and she was his slave.

And she had no doubt that the end of it would justify the beginning, for it would surely end in the sexual fulfillment she hungered for, and which only he could give to her.

Mutely now she did as she was told, quaking less with fear than with anticipation. But as she lay back on the cool satin sheet, Leon leaned over her and wrenched the remnants of her nightgown from her body, pulling it from under her and tossing it aside. She lay, naked and shivering, her hands pressed tightly to her crotch, as if to keep his lascivious eyes from seeing her most intimate places.

It was the way a frightened virgin would behave at being taken prisoner by an evil barbarian, she thought. And as he pulled her hands away from herself, she found herself wondering how such a heathen would react to the whiteness of her skin, and her still half-denuded parts, where the pale, downy hair was just beginning to re-emerge and curl softly over her pouting labia. Her mouth parted, and she ran the tip of her tongue around her lips, suddenly enjoying this game of captive and captor, and marvelling at this man's continuing inventiveness.

'You cannot hide yourself,' Leon said sardonically. 'And no one will hear you if you cry out. You cannot escape. But just to make sure –'

She had no idea what he intended to do until he swiftly reached forward to the bed-head that was adorned with white ribbons to complement the sheets. At least, Abbie had assumed that was their purpose. Now as Leon pulled one of her arms out straight, she realised she was going to be tied to the bed-posts. After her first frisson of shock she felt an unexpected and avaricious pleasure run through her, but in keeping with her role, she knew she should scream and struggle at this outrage. As she opened her mouth and wriggled to resist, he leaned over her heavily. The pressure of his jewelled sash dug into flesh, hurting her.

'Be still, and be quiet, or you will be gagged,' he ground out.

Abbie felt herself blanch at the thought of being gagged. She gave up resisting, fearful that he might really do such a thing. But perhaps it was no more than a threat, because if he did it, it would stifle every sound she made, including those of pleasure. And in her new-found experience of love-making, she had deduced that a man was further stimulated by hearing the gasps and cries and oral reactions from his woman, as well as the reactions from all the other regions of her body.

So she bit her trembling lips tightly together as if she was truly afraid, while her wrists were tied by these silken chains and then her ankles were similarly bound, so that she was spread-eagled on the bed. She saw how Leon stood back for a moment, watching her face, and she guessed that her pallor had vanished, and that she must be scarlet-cheeked with mingled embarassment and excitement.

As she expected, his intimate inspection didn't focus on her face for very long. Very slowly it went lower, lingering over her breasts and her softly rounded belly, from which the ruby had long been discarded, and down, down, down to the pleasure-zone between her thighs, where all the folds of her labia were opened to his gaze. Abbie felt a sudden spasm of pleasure inside her, and she tried desperately to resist, squeezing her inner muscles to stop the small gush of love-juice. But it was impossible, and he knew it and saw it.

'Not yet, woman. We have a long night ahead of us,' the barbarian said, as if mere words could dispel the tumultuous feelings inside her.

He slowly unfastened the jewelled sash and flung it to the floor, throwing off the black robes as carelessly. And Abbie drew in her breath at the sight of the man she had seen so many times before now, and would never tire of seeing. His body was firm and muscled, without an ounce of spare flesh. His powerful chest was broad and well shaped, and so smooth to the touch, as she now knew so well. His already erect phallus throbbed slightly as her gaze alighted on it, and the crown of dark hair around it was softly glistening like the rest of his body, as if anointed with what she guessed would have been sweet-scented oils.

Abbie's hands clenched within the confines of her bonds, until she could feel her own fingernails digging into her moist palms. Small beads of sweat dampened her forehead now, and she could feel the soft trickle of it in her armpits that she always kept scrupulously clean and sweetened with perfume.

Whatever he intended doing with her, she thought in crazy confusion, it was clearly going to involve some kind of sweet torture until he decided that enough was enough, and he forged into her. He held all the strings, and she was merely his love-puppet.

'You've seen enough to whet your appetite, woman. Just so long as you know that you have a stallion in store for you.'

As if she didn't already know that – but to her surprise he replaced his black robes once more, tying them more loosely with a plaited cord instead of the heavy jewelled sash. Presumably this was intended to establish even more indelibly just who was the master and who the slave, she thought faintly. As if there was any doubt.

He strode to a side table and opened a drawer, and when he turned around she saw that he had a blindfold in his hand. It was no ordinary piece of cloth, but an elaborate affair of the kind worn at masquerade balls, made out of white satin in the shape of a bird's wings, studded with tiny shimmering diamonds as decoration. Was this meant to be a token reminder of her role as White Dove? Abbie wondered.

'Have no fear. The underside of the mask is soft and will not hurt your eyes,' he said, in a rare moment of consideration. She guessed that this mood would soon pass, for such attention to her feelings would not be part of the game.

In any case, she had no say in the matter, and once he had fastened the mask firmly around her eyes, she was in complete darkness. For a moment, she panicked, her throat constricting with fear. But although she struggled wildly, the bonds at her wrists and ankles were tight, and every movement only served to tighten them more, so that she was forced to remain still, subject to his every whim.

She heard him rise from the bed and move away. Surely she was not to be left here like this – but she knew it couldn't be so. Leon was not a cruel man, whatever his taste in perversion, and he wouldn't leave her.

'Leon,' she croaked.

'Silence,' he commanded. 'And no names, woman.'

But his voice was nearer again, and she relaxed minutely, though all her nerve ends seemed to be stretched taut, wondering what was to happen, but knowing she had been right about the apparent anonymity of this seduction.

Seconds later she flinched involuntarily as she felt the slight sting of the flailing begin to assault her body. It could have been the lashing of thin leather thongs, or something completely undefinable. Whatever it was, it wasn't hurting her and he wasn't beating her, and she quickly realised that the soft, erotic thrashings simply rippled over every part of her body in a dozen moving fingers of sensation.

They began at her feet and ankles, and moved slowly upwards to her calves and knees, and then to her hips, and she felt her breath quicken in ever-excited anticipation, until finally the lashing trailed upwards along her inner thighs and reached the soft flesh of her labia.

She moaned aloud then, unable to stop the small gasps escaping her lips as the sensations captivated her in a way she had never experienced before. This was ecstasy on the grandest scale, she thought wildly, as the exquisite spasms of climax threatened to rush through her again. But just as she was on the brink, the erotic fingers of the flail left her moist, quivering core, and moved upwards to strike first her belly, and then her breasts.

Her nipples reacted at once. She felt them strain

upwards, and the darts of pleasure the flailing gave her speared through her to her groin and made her squirm as much as she could within the confines of her bonds.

But she could move her body if not her limbs, in fact it was impossible to remain still and her buttocks lifted from the bed and rocked from side to side in ecstasy as the flailing continued along the length of one arm before trailing beneath her chin and then teasing the other in similar fashion. She was drowning in pleasure, and her seeping love-juices must be perfectly obvious to him by now, Abbie thought wildly. But it was a thought that no longer gave her shame or embarassment, for it would be what he wanted to see.

When it dawned on her dazed senses that the lashing had stopped, she relaxed momentarily, though it was hard to do so when every part of her felt so tinglingly alive now, and she yearned to have him inside her, to finish what this sweet torture had begun.

'Please –' she gasped. 'How much longer must I be tied like this –?'

'Do you not enjoy it, woman?' his voice was still stern, and he was still the Master, the epitome of the Indian prince he so revered. And she knew that in their present roles, it would be the greatest insult – as well as a blatant lie on her part – to say otherwise.

'I can't deny it,' she said in a muffled voice.

He moved away from her, and she wondered if now at last he would untie her bonds and she would be able to do as she longed to do – wrap herself around him and hold him, and pull him into her, and love him, love him –

He had returned to the bed, and she felt it dip slightly as he leaned over her. Her breath came shallowly in her throat now, and then she felt the touch of something different on her skin. Something that was soft and light, feathery, seductively moving over her, stroking her, caressing her. She moaned and stretched upwards, her head wrenching from side to side in delirious ecstasy as the relentless teasing and tantalising continued – and as her head moved, so did the mask. It slid upwards just a fraction, but enough to afford her the merest glimpse of what was happening to her.

He was stroking her body now with a white peacock's feather, and the stroking and caressing and arousing that passed across her belly, teasing her breasts and her inner thighs, was made even more erotic now that she was aware of what was happening. But perhaps she was not meant to observe, merely to feel all the incredible tactile experiences he was bringing to her.

She closed her eyes as if obeying an unspoken command, knowing that this man, in whatever guise, had truly reached the soul of her, and that she would do his bidding, no matter what he asked.

The feathering seemed to continue for ever while she sensually writhed, her hands still clenching and unclenching, her toes curling, and she murmured indefinable little sounds in her throat. And then the feathering was replaced with a new and different sensation.

This time it was sensually cool, making her draw in her breath as it rippled across all the sensitive nerve-ends of her skin. Something was shiveringly cool against her breasts and her belly before it trailed down the long length of her legs. Again the urge to open her eyes was irresistible. She opened them very slightly to look beneath the mask until she could just glimpse what was happening.

A white silk scarf was being drawn slowly between her big toe and the next one now, and then it slid upwards over one leg until it reached her thighs, before being passed slowly down the other leg and through her toes once more. Almost at once, he passed the silk lightly across her breasts, back and forth, and the sensation of the cool sensual fabric against her skin was as erotically arousing as anything she had felt so far.

The gossamer-soft movements changed from slow to even slower, then to quick, then slowly again, moving from one sensitive part of her to another, so that she was never quite sure where one tingling sensation ended and the next began. And it only served to make her want to end the torment, until finally she could stand it no longer.

'Leon, for pity's sake –' she gasped.

Suddenly she felt his weight across her and his mouth ground against hers, opening it and thrusting his tongue inside it to forage inside her cheek and entwine with her own. She could feel his huge erection close to her belly, but not yet inside her, even though she strained to bring it to her, all modesty gone.

'Leon, please,' she begged, almost sobbing with frustration and longing now.

Without warning, he pulled the mask from her head, and she blinked, like a child coming out of the dark. But there were no child's feelings inside her, only those of a wanton, fully aroused woman, desperate for her man to love her.

'You belong to me, woman,' he said, still the Master, the barbarian, the captor. 'Say it.'

'Oh yes! I belong to you,' she moaned. 'I have always belonged to you. I always will.'

She closed her eyes again briefly, before he could see how deeply-felt were the words she spoke. She belonged to him, now and always. And it wasn't a cowering prisoner obeying her captor who said the words, but a warm and loving woman to her lover. That he didn't love her in the same way was a penance she would have to endure for the rest of her life – or as long as he wanted her.

He had thrown off the black robes now, and she could see that his glistening phallus was even more enlarged and eager. Almost delirious with her hunger for him, she realised he was untying her silk cords at last.

Her limbs felt unnatural and awkward after being held in bondage for so long. As if understanding, he massaged them gently with sweet-scented oils, his fingers continuing what the sexual artefacts had begun, but so very much more intimately.

His hands gradually moved up each leg from ankle to thigh, kissing the soft skin before every touch, and then she felt the oil being palmed into her flesh until at last he reached the centre where they met, and where she was so moistly ready for him.

The massage continued on either side of her nether lips, now so widely distended from their enforced parting, and he gently kneaded her pubic bone with the knuckles of one hand, while the other teased her opening. Finally, when she felt she could stand it no longer, his mouth sought the heat of her inner core, and she drew a great shuddering breath as desire swept through her as sharp as a flame.

Unable to prevent herself now, regardless of the role she was meant to play, she wrapped her legs tightly around him, so that she was the one holding him captive. Her hands raked through his hair, massaging his scalp and pressing him into her with her feet against his buttocks as his tongue flicked back and forth across her love-bud. Then she felt the full thrust of his tongue, surging in and out of her while she raised her hips with her hands to meet him.

'Leon, please don't make me wait any longer,' she gasped, her senses swimming with desire. 'Please love me now!'

And if she sounded the imperious one, the demanding one, she no longer cared. She wanted and needed him, and he had no right to continue this cruelty for one more moment – if cruelty such ecstasy could be called.

As if he fully recognised her aching need, he slowly moved up the length of her body until his softly oiled hands were circling her breasts, and then his mouth was seeking hers, his tongue erotically circling those other waiting, parted lips, and she tasted her own, musky love-juice on him.

'I hardly think either of us can wait a moment longer,' he said against her mouth, and his voice was oddly husky now. But almost before she could register the change in him, she felt the crest of his love-head enter her, and she gave a great sigh of exultation as the thick shaft of it followed, filling her. And then the sweet, familiar, rhythmic movements began, quickening spectacularly into burgeoning spasms of climax for them both.

Abbie had sensed that so much erotic titillation could not last for ever without their climax being reached too quickly, but she welcomed it, for to continue unabated would have been almost unbearable. As it was, she felt the flood of his heat inside her, and felt him twisting and straining to give her all that he possessed, and she heard him gasping with her as her own rippling sensations took her to the ultimate limits of pleasure.

Together. Complete. And the sweetest moment of all was that he gasped out her name as he reached his climax, although she suspected that he never even knew it.

'Abbie –'

They were both spent, both exhausted. Even Leon, her stallion, she thought wonderingly, as he made no move to leave the bedchamber. She knew by now that he never spent the entire night with any woman, but he made no move to leave her immediately, and although he briefly slept, she found it difficult to do so. She was still somewhere beyond the stars, still euphoric, and finding it hard to descend into a world of ordinary mortals once more.

But now she had the joy of cradling him in her arms while they were entwined together. His naked flesh was as close to hers as if they shared the same skin, and for these precious, vulnerable moments at least he was totally hers. He belonged to her, just as she had vowed she belonged to him. She could have no better birthday gift.

A small trace of tears touched her eyelashes, for how could she believe that any of her dreams would ever come true? This wonderful night had been just another game in his repertoire of amusements, and it would be madness to forget it. But he hadn't left her yet, and a thin dawn light was beginning to filter through the curtains at the window.

But even as she thought it, her heart sank as he stirred. She closed her eyes and pretended to be asleep, knowing it wouldn't humour him to have her watching him while he slept.

'You please me greatly, woman,' she heard him say softly. 'You will receive your reward when you awake.'

She felt him rise from the bed then, and wrap the covers more closely around her naked body. Her reward! As she heard him leave the bedchamber, the tears stung Abbie's eyes now, and she knew that her foolish dreams should have remained behind with her childhood. She was a woman now, and she had to accept that the man she wanted above all others, was a man of bizarre desires and practices. If she wanted to stay with him she must accept it all, even the seraglio and the women she must share him with. Distasteful though it was to her English sensibilities, it took less than the blinking of an eye to know that she would do so if she must.

She curled herself into a ball and finally slept from sheer exhaustion. When she awoke, it was to find something cold and hard around her throat. For a moment she panicked completely, wondering if she was in some kind of a vice and was to undergo a more evil torture for the Master's satisfaction. But when she looked above her to the mirrored ceiling, she saw that around her throat was the most exquisite pearl necklace.

She gasped, startled by the purity of such a costly gift, and finding her eyes stinging again with the unpredictability of the man. He had already given her the filly, White Dove, and this was surely not necessary. But before she could start to analyse his motives, the door of the bedchamber opened and the enigmatic Maya was there, holding out a robe, and waiting to accompany her back to her own room. And for the present, Abbie knew that the idyll was over.

Padraig O'Reilly had decided he had waited long enough. He was impatient to be off to new pastures, but his grasping nature wouldn't let him leave without first seeing what he could extort out of the old buffer at The Grange.

His information should bring in a few pieces of silver, little enough for his pains. Though since nobody else seemed to know of the young wench's whereabouts, he had the upper hand in it – providing they believed him, of course, and didn't welsh on any reward that was offered.

He scowled, knowing of old that few took any notice of a tinker's words, except to accuse him of the very crime he reported. Nor he realised had he heard any rumours of any reward being offered. Perhaps the guardian had really wanted to be rid of the wench. It would be bloody galling if it were so, after he'd hung about for so long, watching her movements when he should have been on his way long ago.

But he'd find out more about that from the kitchen slut. He knew just where to waylay her when she came tripping across the fields after dark, hot from her lover's arms and still reeking of sex. O'Reilly boasted to himself that he could take her any time he wanted. But any sexual interest he'd felt for her had waned, and his only hunger now was for whatever gain she could put his way.

He waited for her now, hidden from the moonlight that lit the fields and hedgerows that had long been his home. He knew she would come, fresh from her fornicating, and the minute her strutting walk reached him, he leapt out in front of her.

Sophie squealed in fright.

'What do you want of me? I've got no money, and nothing that would interest you –'

'I know all that, me darlin',' O'Reilly said lazily, and at the sound of his voice, Sophie gasped. She peered at him more closely and recognition dawned on her face.

'It's you, is it?' she spluttered, backing away. 'Well, you needn't think you can have your way with me any time you turn up –'

O'Reilly laughed, coarsely misconstruing her words.

'I ain't "turnin' up" for no second-hand goods, slut. Once was enough. But you an' me have got some business to discuss.'

'What business could I possibly have with the likes of you?' Sophie said scornfully.

O'Reilly spoke carelessly, making as if to move on as he threw the words back over his shoulder.

'Fair enough. If you're not interested in findin' your young lady no more –'

Sophie ran after him, clutching at his arm. 'Have you seen Miss Abbie? What do you know about her? If you've harmed her at all –'

He shook her off irritably. 'Sweet Jesus, I might have known that's how you'd react, the way they all do. I ain't never harmed her, not then, nor now, and if that's your attitude then I'll keep what I know to meself.'

'Please don't be offended,' Sophie said quickly.

'So what's it worth if I tell you where I seen her?'

'I've told you, I've got no money. The old skinflint only pays me a pittance –'

'But he'd pay to get his girl back, wouldn't he?' O'Reilly said slyly. 'And you and me could split the reward.'

He suddenly seized her arm, cruelly twisting the plump flesh and making her cry out.

'And don't try to do me out of my half, darlin', if you know what's good for you. If I don't get something for my pains, it'll be the worse for you – and for that horny young farmin' feller of yours.'

Sophie gasped, and spoke quickly. 'Where is she then?'

'There's a big house about twelve miles away, over the Downs, and well hidden in its own land behind a park and a forest of trees. She's well set up by the looks of her. I seen her riding a white horse and acting the lady – and havin' a fine old bit of dick-sport with her servants, if you get my meanin',' he added, sniggering with the memory of the woman whipping the man with the riding-crop.

'You can't be talking about Miss Abbie!' Sophie said at once, disbelievingly.

'No? Well, I ain't seen many other wenches with that long, silver-coloured hair and eyes as blue as the sky, and a shape to tempt any man to get her on her back –'

'All right!' Sophie snapped. 'So if you've seen her in this other place not too far from here,' she went on carefully, 'why haven't you told the police, if you're so concerned about her?

'Anyway,' she went on, 'I'm sorry to disappoint you, but there won't be any reward for informing old Richmond –'

She screeched out loud as the Irishman grabbed her again, shaking her until her teeth rattled.

'I warned you what would happen if you try to keep it all to yourself, slut –'

'It's not that, you bastard,' she yelled through her chattering teeth. 'It was her eighteenth birthday yester-

191

day, and her guardian's washed his hands of her now. He won't pay a penny to get her back, because she's no longer in his charge. She can go to the devil for all he cares.'

O'Reilly let her go so quickly that she fell to the ground. He towered over her, and she felt physically sick, all her bravado gone.

'Are you telling me the truth, bitch?' he snarled.

'I swear it,' she stuttered. 'The old fool made us all stand in line at the big house while he told us as much, just in case any of us had been keeping news of Miss Abbie from him. The constables won't give up looking for her though,' she added artfully. 'And you wouldn't want me to tell them who gave me the information, would you –?'

He yanked her to her feet, his rough, stinking hands around her throat. Sophie's eyes bulged, and she was so fearful for her life that her muscles slackened and she felt a gush of pee run down her legs.

'All right,' he snarled again. 'But from now on, you just forget you ever saw me. If not, it'll be the worse for you.'

'Yes, oh yes I will,' she blabbered.

He let her go then and blundered off into the night, cursing his luck.

Sophie staggered and wilted on the ground for a good five minutes before her natural pertness asserted itself. Then she scurried back to The Grange, buzzing inside with this unexpected news about Miss Abbie. She'd truly begun to wonder if the girl was dead.

And whether or not the old skinflint was going to throw her a few coppers for her information, she knew she'd have to tell him, and he'd be bound to tell the constables to follow up the information instead of letting them continue with their wild goose chases.

But that wasn't the only reason Sophie wanted to be

sure Abbie was safe and well. She was all agog to know if the story the ruffian told was true, if Miss once-so-innocent Abbie was really acting the lady in some fine gentleman's house, and making dick-sport with some of the servants, and just how much of Sophie's teachings she'd put into practice!

Her eyes glinted with lustful anticipation at the very thought of somehow renewing their garden talks, and she easily put any involvement with the Irishman behind her. All that Brindley Richmond need know was that a passing traveller, in conversation with the talkative kitchen-maid, had happened to mention seeing a pretty young woman fitting Miss Abbie's description, riding a white horse in a place not too many miles from here.

Chapter Twelve

Once Sophie got over the double shock of being confronted by the Irishman again and taking in all he had told her, she thought carefully. A kitchen-maid didn't go rushing to a stern employer with news from such an unlikely source. If she did, she was more likely to get her ears cuffed, she thought feelingly. Brindley Richmond was not known for his gentleness with servants, and Sophie didn't fancy a head-bashing on anybody's account, not even Miss Abbie's.

She let a couple more days go by before she decided exactly how she could deal with the information. If she'd been able to write, she'd have put an unsigned note for Abbie's uncle to find. But she couldn't write. Tom could manage his letters after a fashion, but she daren't confide in Tom, knowing he'd be instantly suspicious as to just how the Irishman had known where to find her.

But her eyes gleamed at the thought of what he'd told her about her young lady, and she was eager to know just what the pretty piece had been up to all this time. She couldn't even be sure that the Irish tinker had been telling the truth, or just blarneying away with the fairies.

Was Abbie really having a high old time and putting all Sophie's advice into practice, learning by experience, which was always the best way to learn.

'Now then, Miss Idleness, get that stupid look off your face, and see to that pan-scrubbing,' she heard Cook snap as she stood dreaming with a scrub-cloth in her reddened hands.

'I need to see Mr Richmond,' she snapped back before she could stop herself. 'I know something he'd want to hear –'

She yelped at once as Cook grabbed her by the ear, knowing she'd made a bad mistake. There could be only one thing old Richmond would want to hear – though Sophie doubted that he'd really want to hear it at all, now he'd virtually washed his hands of his charge. Still, he might pay something for the information – and Sophie had no intention of sharing it with anyone if he did.

But Cook was nothing if not sharp.

'Have you heard something about Miss Abbie, girl? If so, it's your duty to tell me –'

Oh yes? thought Sophie. And have the old fart go to Richmond herself and claim any miserable pittance he might throw her way?

'I ain't saying nothing except to him,' she yelled. 'It's none of your business what I know –'

Cook surveyed her disdainfully for a few moments then released her after a token slap on her backside.

'You'll have to go through the proper channels,' she said, as scratchy as a dog on heat. 'Miss Phipps will need to ask if the gentleman will see you for a few minutes. And if he will, you be sure to wipe your hands, and don't touch none of the furniture upstairs.'

As she turned back to her pie-making with a thump at the pastry, Sophie mimicked her waddling walk, scowling and primping, and making the other maids giggle at her daring. But her heart was pounding now, because she hated Brindley Richmond almost as much as Abbie did, and she wondered for the first time just what kind of disfavour she was doing the young lady by telling on her.

But she was cheered by the thought that at least he couldn't drag her back now her birthday had come and gone. In any case, it was too late to back out now, and later in the day, once Cook had set the necessary wheels in motion, Miss Phipps sent for her.

'You're to go to the study right away, and Mr Richmond will spare you three minutes,' the housekeeper said, clearly disapproving of such a liberty. 'You'll conduct yourself properly in word and manner, and then return to your duties immediately. Do you understand?'

Sophie resisted the urge to salute and said that she did. But the very stuffiness of the woman restored her courage. Brindley Richmond was only a man after all, and Tom had once told her that to lose her fears of any man, she only had to imagine him with no clothes on.

She hid a snigger, since she could have told Tom that it didn't always work! She certainly didn't want to think about Richmond in the altogether, and imagining how a brawny fellow like the Irishman looked when he was naked could put a girl into all kinds of trouble – She forced down the sudden throb of excitement at the memory, and vainly tried to make herself look as meek as possible as she followed the housekeeper to the study.

Naturally, she had never been to this inner sanctum before, and she gaped at the sensual smell of the soft leather chairs and the wood-panelled walls. The betters lived in another world from those who scrubbed and laboured for them, she thought indignantly, and instantly revised her ideas of asking for a piddling little reward.

'What is it you have to tell me?' Brindley Richmond said coldly. 'I've no use for time-wasters.'

But now that the moment was here, Sophie felt her legs go weak. This one could throw her out as easily as Cook threw out rancid meat for the birds to chew over.

'I've some news about Miss Abbie that might be worth a copper or two to you, sir –'

He leapt to his feet, his eyes blazing into her.

'What? What kind of insolence is this? I doubt that you've anything sensible to report, since the constables have searched the area thoroughly enough –'

'Somebody told me they'd seen her, sir, in a big estate some miles from here. She was seen out riding, and she seemed very friendly with the – the people there.'

She balked from saying any more. But she remembered how Cook had surmised that the constables had only been asked to search the ditches and hedgerows for Abbie. When no body had been found, they had informed Brindley Richmond that the girl had probably just run off, and he wouldn't have bothered instructing them to make enquiries at respectable properties.

'Who told you this cock-and-bull tale?' Richmond snapped.

'Just a – a passing traveller, sir,' Sophie babbled, seeing how his hands clenched together now. 'But I thought you'd want to know, and that it might be worth –'

'I don't pay for information from passing travellers or kitchen-maids, and nor do I believe a word of it.'

'Should I tell the constables myself then, sir, if you don't want to be bothered?' Sophie said innocently, with a burst of inspiration. 'It's my duty, I daresay – and maybe they'll reward me instead –'

She squealed as he came round to the front of the desk and grabbed her wrist in a vice-like hold. His face was very close to hers, and it was puce with rage.

'Don't you try to blackmail me, girl. I shall inform the constables myself, and if you're wrong, I'll have no hesitation in having you flogged for extortion. Do you understand me?'

Sophie nodded, her eyes wide with fright. She didn't understand the word, but she understood the threat in it. She escaped as quickly as possible, and raced back to the kitchen, realising she'd got nowhere, but simply glad to be away from the man – And having even more sympathy for Miss Abbie.

'Well?' Cook said, grabbing her. 'Now tell us what it was all about, Miss.'

There was no point in hiding it now, Sophie thought. She told the kitchen staff quickly, emphasising her idle chat with the fictitious passing traveller until she almost believed it herself. But it was done now. After her threat to tell the police herself, she knew Richmond would have to inform them, and they would have to check the information. And she prayed that if it all came out in the open – whatever it was – that Abbie wouldn't think too badly of her.

Abbie was experimenting with her hair. It was the accepted custom for a young lady of eighteen years to put up her hair, which announced to the world that she was now a woman and out of her frivolous years.

Not that there had been much frivolity during her adolescence, she reflected. It had been sombre and dull. The only highlights had taken place in recent months when she and Sophie had formed such an unlikely alliance.

She smiled at her image in her dressing-table mirror now, guiltily admiring her own swan-like neck that was revealed so elegantly by the lush silvery hair being piled on top of her head with combs and ribbons.

Such a small feeling of vanity couldn't compare with the guilt she knew she should feel at being such an eager listener to all the exciting things Sophie had told her about love and lust. But the emotion she felt most towards Sophie was gratitude, for preparing the way for her.

If she hadn't done so, Abbie knew she would never have entered into the fantasy world of Leon Villiers with such abandonment. Once the initial fright at what was happening to her was over, she had accepted everything he did, every word he spoke, every touch on her skin, and being with him was truly like being reborn, she thought euphemistically.

He had changed her life, and she never wanted this new life to end. Even as the words entered her mind, she wondered if she was tempting fate and sounding her own death knell, and she felt her shoulders wilt. Her arms fell to her sides as she gazed unseeingly into the mirror now.

For who knew how long this idyll could continue? How long was she going to be such a novelty to him? And how soon would he tire of her and return to his seraglio world of exotically painted women, so skilled in the art of pleasing a man?

He already gave her more leeway than she had ever expected, but she still didn't dare to hope that this meant she was anything special to him. She was allowed to explore the entire house whenever she wanted to do so now, and she knew that on the surface it was run like any wealthy gentleman's household.

There was a small army of servants who worked discreetly and silently, perhaps more than in most households. They were obviously totally loyal to Leon, which meant that he must treat them kindly and pay them very well, Abbie thought shrewdly. The only difference was that the majority of the servants were foreigners and she guessed they had accompanied him from India, but when they were garbed in their English attire their personas changed as easily as Leon's own.

He was a very remarkable man, as well as the most charismatic one Abbie had ever met or was likely to meet. She realised her heart was beating painfully fast at the thought, knowing she could never submit to another man's loving. He had spoiled her for that – if spoiling was the right word to use for the spectacular nights of seduction they shared.

And tonight, he had commanded her to be ready for him at seven o'clock for a very special evening. She smoothed down the cream satin gown that caressed her contours so lovingly, and fingered the exquisite pearl necklace around her neck. A gift from a lover was always special, and surely such a gift as this had to have been given in love, even if it was only love of a certain kind.

She turned away from the mirror, knowing that the hour had come and anticipating just what the game was to be this evening. As always her gown had been laid out for her, together with the stays and petticoats that befitted a lady, and one flamboyant garment that had shocked her when she had first seen it.

The drawers were not like anything she had seen before. They were made of the softest white silk, and they were adorned with red satin bows around the frilled and gathered legs. But what had startled her the most was that they were completely crotchless, like two separate garments merely joined at the waist. She had put them on, wearing only her stays, and gasped at her reflection in the long mirror as she stood with her legs slightly apart to see the effect. The pouting flesh at her groin peeped through the opening, and the glint of her downy, silvery hair caught the light from the candles.

Oh yes, Abbie breathed to herself. I can see just how these would appeal to a lover. She glanced at the portraits around her mirror, wondering if Leon was watching her right now. But the painted eyes never moved, and she felt a vague disappointment that he was not taking a voyeuristic enjoyment in her posturing.

And at the feeling, she knew how far she had come in his decadent world.

'Are you ready, miss?' she heard Maya's voice say as she still ruminated on the discovery of the garment she now wore beneath the very proper dinner gown.

She had grown used to the way the woman seemed to appear from nowhere at the appointed times, and smiled briefly.

'Quite ready. Will I do, do you think?'

She spoke artlessly, momentarily forgetting where she was and seeking approval for her new, mature appearance the way she would from any long-serving retainer. Maya looked taken aback for a moment and then nodded.

'The lady would please any gentleman,' she said.

'But him, Maya. Will I please him?'

She knew she shouldn't beg for approval like this, but who knew Leon better than this old woman? While not exactly a mother to him, she took on that protective role far more that anyone had ever done for Abbie, and for that reason alone she wanted her approval.

'You will please him, as always,' Maya said.

Whether it meant that Leon ever confided in her about his new possession, Abbie couldn't be sure, but she had to be satisfied with Maya's few enigmatic words as she waited to escort Abbie from her room.

She had fully expected to be taken downstairs to the blue dining-room again, since she was dressed so formally tonight, and there would be a sumptuous meal awaiting the two of them, perhaps to celebrate her birthday properly even though it had come and gone. Instead Maya merely walked across the passageway to an opposite room and tapped on the door before throwing it open and standing back for Abbie to go inside.

She saw that it was a bedroom, and she gasped in shock as Leon came forward to greet her, dressed as formally as herself. But if this was his own room, Abbie thought dazedly, then until that moment she had had no idea that he slept so near to her. She had only to walk a few yards and she could be in his arms, in his bed – or he could have done the same.

That he had never done so seemed suddenly like a great slap in the face. And she cursed the fact that while she had so curiously explored the rest of the house, she had lost interest in any of the doors on this floor of the west wing. In any case, she had found most of them locked and had assumed that they must be guest bed-rooms and therefore intended to be kept private.

Instead of which, except for however many times he had visited the east wing where his seraglio was housed, Leon had been no more than a few yards away from her every night while she slept.

Her startled eyes took in the rich decor of the room, the deep red wallcovering and carpet, and the matching bedcover. It was a hot, devil's colour, she thought faintly. And to add to the decadent appearance, the mirrored ceiling reflected all the garishness of the room. Against it, Abbie felt as if she stood out as pale as death in her cream gown. She immediately wished such a thing hadn't entered her mind, as the word 'sacrifice' filled her head.

'Are you surprised?' Leon said softly, as she stood rigidly without moving.

'Everything you do surprises me, but this is certainly different,' she replied carefully, trying not to reveal how unexpectedly emotional she felt.

What had she expected, for pity's sake? she asked herself. That he had been about to declare an undying love for her, and propose marriage? Such an eventuality seemed as remote and childishly fanciful as flying to the moon. She closed her eyes for a moment, trying to compose herself, and then felt Leon's fingers curl around hers.

'I assume you're hungry?' she heard him say.

As he led her to another part of the L-shaped room, she realised at once that it wasn't meant as a sexual *double entendre*. A small table was prepared for a meal for two, and a single servant waited to serve them. It was to be a very intimate *tête-à-tête*, Abbie realised with a dart of pleasure.

'I'm ravenous,' she murmured, and he could make of that whatever he wished. The small smile at the corners of his strong mouth told her he understood very well exactly what she meant. It had been two days, she fumed, two days since he'd presented her with the pearls and she had become a woman in the eyes of the world, and this was the first time she had seen him since then.

She felt a frisson of alarm at recognising her own frustration and annoyance, aware that she was starting to think like a wife. He still held her fingers, and now he raised them to his lips, and his eyes looked down into hers.

'Then we're both ravenous,' he said quietly. 'And we will eat our fill until our appetite is fully satisfied.'

And only a fool would have misunderstood the deeper meaning in his words, thought Abbie tremulously. The meal was to be no more than an *apéritif* before the main course. He held out a chair for her and she sank on to it, feeling as if her legs might not hold her up any longer. The servant swiftly served up the meal and discreetly left at Leon's command.

'I'm sure we can manage the rest for ourselves,' he commented to Abbie, and the meal progressed without incident, formally and discreetly. Finally he leant back in his chair, twirling his glass of red wine in his fingers.

'So tell me, Miss Richmond, how are you this evening?'

She sensed a faint mockery now, and she replied in kind.

'I'm well, thank you, sir –'

'And how do you sit?'

She stared at him, uncomprehending. And then she realised he must be referring to her lack of underdrawers, and she suppressed a wine-induced giggle.

'Very comfortably, if a trifle coolly,' she said in a stifled voice. But with a quite delicious sense of freedom in her nether regions all this while, she realised.

'But with sufficient heat to ensure a certain pleasure in wearing the garment, I trust,' he said, with no further attempt at archness.

'I find it remarkably pleasing,' she said, starting to breathe more heavily, her senses stirred by the strange formality between them when they spoke of such things. And Leon must be aware that she felt almost naked beneath the heavy petticoats and dinner gown, with just the gathered legs of the silk drawers confining her lower limbs.

'Then I should like to see my purchase, if you have quite finished your meal,' he said next.

'Would that be the garment, or the person wearing it?' she dared to ask without thinking.

Leon laughed. 'I had no need to buy you, sweetness. You pledged yourself to me of your own accord.'

At his urging, more like, Abbie thought, but what did it matter? Nothing mattered as long as she belonged to him, and he to her, if only for a little while.

He rose from the table and reached out to pull her to her feet. She put her hand in his, and he slowly stroked each finger in turn from base to tip. The simple caresses sent her pulses racing and her nerve ends tingling.

He led her directly to the bed. The last time, she remembered, she had been taken forcibly from her room and led to the Master's bedchamber in the east wing, to be bound and blindfolded, and to have all kinds of delicious things done to her. This was different. This was a more seductive kind of liaison – or so she believed.

'Show me,' Leon said.

Her mouth had gone momentarily dry, and she ran her tongue around it. As he saw the movement, he leant forward to capture her tongue between his lips, and tugged at it gently, sucking the sweetness from it. His mouth tasted as sweet as the wine, and the action sent an answering ripple of desire deep into her groin.

'It seems so immodest,' she murmured, not wanting to ruck up her skirts. 'You don't really expect me to –'

'I bring you a whore's drawers, so why do you not behave like a whore?' he said, suddenly ruthless.

Abbie gasped, her eyes stinging. But just as quickly, she blamed herself for not seeing it all before now. This was the game. This was presumably the way a gentleman behaved with a high-class prostitute rather than one of the lightskirts who apparently roamed the streets of every city and waterfront. This was the way it happened, being wined and dined, and then paying for the privilege.

'All right, sir, if you want to see the goods, you shall see them,' she said as airily as she could manage.

She quickly lay down on the scarlet bedcover, sliding out of her shoes and slowly lifting the cream satin skirt of her gown until it revealed the frills of the drawers at her knees, with their scarlet ribbons adding to the dramatic effect of cream and red. It was purity and decadence, and without warning Abbie began to enjoy watching Leon's face as her fingers edged slowly up the length of her own legs, stroking the matching pale silk stockings before fingering the frills of the drawers and seductively rucking up her gown with every small movement she made.

'You like, sir?' she said in a husky voice that seemed to fit the occasion and the mood she was in now.

Transforming herself into the role of a whore wasn't as difficult as one might expect, Abbie thought, especially when she could see that her gentleman was itching to feel those parted limbs and what lay between them for himself.

There was a lusty bulge beginning to strain against the cloth of his trousers now, she thought with satisfaction. He wouldn't be disappointed, and neither would she.

'I like the preview,' he said in answer to her question. 'But I'm impatient to see the rest of the goods.'

He suddenly pushed the skirt up around her chin, so that she felt the cool air on her moistness. Her gaze moved upwards to where the sight of her was reflected on the mirrored ceiling. She drew in her breath.

She had seen herself in mirrors before now, and in all kinds of positions, but dear Lord, this was a sight she had never thought to see in her life.

There she was on her back, with her legs opened wide, the cream gown pushed up nearly to her face, and the open-crotch drawers showing everything she had. Showing Leon Villiers – even as she thought it, she felt his finger worm its way into her, pushing into her with long, slow, strokes as she watched.

And then, when she wondered frantically how much longer this could continue without her revealing how much she wanted more of him, he withdrew, and began to slowly roll down each of her silk stockings in turn, kissing each portion of flesh as he went until her limbs were bare except for the drawers.

His lips moved into her, parting her and licking her, and her hands went to the nape of his neck, caressing it and kneading it and pulling him ever closer.

'Show me your skills,' she heard him order next.

'I'm not sure I understand –' she said faintly.

'Any whore worth her salt has a trick or two to show her client,' he told her. 'And I suspect your fancy is to play the Mother Superior.'

Although she guessed that this was his way of directing her, she still looked blank for a moment, but as he began to strip off his clothes, she did the same, until he surprised her by stopping her halfway.

'Not the drawers,' he said. 'I've a wish to see those lovely thighs bouncing above me in that silk garment while we fuck.'

Abbie gasped. She had never heard him use that word before, and nor did she recall having heard Sophie use it, but she knew instinctively what it meant, and that it was presumably the kind of language that was used between a prostitute and her client.

'If I'm to be Mother Superior, sir,' she murmured as Leon lay back on the bed, with his ramrod stalk throbbingly ready for her, 'do I take it that I'm to do the fucking?'

He laughed, pulling her down on to him so fast that he was inside her before she could properly position herself for penetration. But it hardly mattered, because she was so wet and slippery by now that he slid inside her up to the hilt.

'That's right, whore,' he said thickly. 'You're to do the fucking, and I'll do the watching.'

The silk drawers parted obligingly as she straddled him. Leon's fingers moved sensuously in her groin, and as she began to move on him, his hands moved upwards to fondle her breasts and pull gently on her nipples until they stood out straight and proud.

His swollen member filled her, and without conscious thought Abbie reached down and circled his flat male nipples with her tongue while she thrust down on him.

'God, but you have an instinct in you that's worth the touch of a thousand concubines,' he ground out. 'Ride me like the wind, whore.'

She wished he hadn't mentioned concubines, but the explosive sensations gathering inside her now were too momentous for her to care any more. He was suddenly thrusting with her, hard and strong, and her hands were

207

on his shoulders, pushing down on him, and she couldn't hold back the rushing pleasure she felt.

But she had already guessed that this wasn't to be a leisurely coupling. That wouldn't be what a gentleman expected from a whore. But for all that, it was quick and pulsating and exciting, and when she felt the surge of his seed inside her, she relaxed on him for a few throbbing moments until he rolled over, still inside her, and diminishing just a little.

'Are you all right?' he said eventually, when she lay with her eyes closed for several minutes.

Abbie slowly opened them, hearing the consideration in his voice. And surely this wasn't the way a gentleman treated a whore. He wouldn't care about her feelings. She nodded dumbly, and as she did so, he slowly bent his head and pressed his mouth to hers in a long, sweet kiss.

'If you wish, you may sleep here tonight,' she heard him say, and she knew this was an accolade never afforded to his other women. For a brief moment it made her feel humble and grateful – and in almost the same instant it infuriated her to think she could feel that way on account of the few crumbs he threw her.

'How generous of you – sir,' she murmured.

'Not generous,' he said, gathering her close to him. 'Just that I feel the need to have you in my arms tonight.'

She should rage against him and try to resurrect some semblance of the dignity she desired so much. But somehow she couldn't. As long as he needed her – even if it could in no way compare with her need for him – then for now, it would suffice. And who knew how soon it might change?

Abbie awoke slowly to the raucous screeching of the peacocks, and found herself still in his arms. They had made love more than once during the night, and she realised just how potent a young and virile man could be. It was early morning now, and at some time during the night Leon must have pulled the covers over them both, so that they were cocooned inside them. It was at once wonderful and intimate and poignantly comforting to her. It was how she imagined married people awoke every morning, still holding one another, still breathing the same air, still as close as if they shared the same skin.

She felt him stir, and his eyes looked into hers, dark and fathomless as ever. Abbie drew in her breath, wondering if he would have forgotten inviting her to stay, wondering if he would make love to her now, wondering if he could possibly know how much she loved him and wanted him for herself alone.

The futile ferocity of her own thoughts depressed her, for she knew how hopeless a wish it must be. He was a man who had loved many women, and one would surely never satisfy him, no matter how many variations and fantasies that woman was prepared to share with him.

She felt his hands move slowly over her bare shoulders, caressing the soft skin, before they moved around to the lush curves of her breasts. She could feel every part of his body pressing against hers, moulding her to him. Her heartbeats quickened, anticipating whatever was to come, but then she saw his expression change. His head jerked up, and the sensuous movements on her body were stilled.

Abbie became aware of a commotion in the courtyard below. It was so unusual to hear any kind of disturbance in this isolated place, where everything ran so smoothly, that it sent waves of alarm running through her.

'What is it?' she whispered.

'I don't know,' Leon said grimly. 'But I intend to find out. Wrap yourself in a robe and go back to your own room and wait for me there.'

'Should I dress?' she stuttered, feeling foolish for

asking, but hardly knowing what was required of her now.

'Of course.'

He was already tying a robe around himself and striding towards the door, and obviously had no time for small talk. The sweet mood of the morning had been shattered, and there was such a sense of danger in the air that Abbie could almost smell it, yet she had no idea what it could mean. The worst, the very worst, she found herself thinking frantically, was that somehow information about Leon Villiers' iniquitous way of life had been leaked to the authorities, and they were going to throw him into prison for debauchery and keeping a disorderly house.

As the wild suppositions raged through Abbie's head, she could almost smile at the thought. For never was a house more orderly and harmonious than this one. And never were servants more loyal. The thought gave her a small sliver of comfort as she did exactly as she was told and returned to her own room, to attend to her ablutions and toilet with shaking hands.

Chapter Thirteen

*A*bbie prowled about her room, feeling restless and uneasy. It seemed a long while since Leon had told her to come here and dress, and instinctively she had donned one of the more modest gowns in her closet and pinned up her hair with combs. Her mirror told her that she would easily pass for the young lady of the house, and she gave a wistful sigh at the thought. She might have filled that role at her uncle's house, but she could never be sure just what Leon had in mind for her here.

She jumped when Maya came into the room after a brief knock on her door, and she twisted round on her velvet-covered dressing-stool. Maya wore her neat housekeeper's garb once more and her eyes were guarded.

'Mr Villiers will come to speak with you in a few minutes, Miss. He requested that you be ready.'

'I am ready.'

She had been ready for what seemed like hours, but could only have been minutes. Like everything else in this house, time seemed to have no real dimension, she thought swiftly. Everything here was unreal, and the most unreal thing of all was her girlish dream that Leon might one day want her to the exclusion of all other women.

She gazed unseeingly at the Indian woman. Until this very moment she hadn't really put it into words in her head, but now that she had, the words wouldn't go away. She wanted to be Leon's woman, his only woman. They repeated themselves in her consciousness now, like a litany.

'So you are, miss,' Maya said hurriedly, obviously taking Abbie's stare to be a censure. 'Then please be patient for a few moments longer –'

'What's happening, Maya? I must know. Can't you warn me before I see Leon – Mr Villiers?'

The woman shook her head. 'It's not my place,' she murmured, and withdrew in her usual silent way, leaving Abbie fuming with frustration.

After all this time, and after everything that had happened to her, her natural spirit was fast starting to assert itself. And the strongest emotion in her mind now was anger at being treated this way.

She had given Leon everything he asked of her. In the beginning he had simply taken what he wanted, but that time was long past and now she gave herself freely, and it humiliated her to be treated like this, left in the dark with only a servant to bring her instructions.

He had no right to leave her here, letting her imagination roam wildly and fretting over all kinds of possibilities. All her instincts told her that something was badly wrong. Leon's own manner had forewarned her, and now the guarded, tense face of the normally bland Maya had underlined that suspicion.

With an impatient exclamation Abbie walked purposefully to her door and opened it. She had half-expected to find it locked in order to keep her confined, but it was not. She walked to the end of the corridor, past the endless rows of doors, to where a balcony led to the curving double staircase of the central part of the house. From here she could just hear the sounds of voices in the drawing room.

She strained her ears, but although she recognised the tone of Leon's voice, half-angry, half-amused, she couldn't quite catch the words he said. And then she caught her breath as another voice broke in. A louder, less cultured voice, and one that seemingly had little respect for a gentleman.

'The fact is, sir,' the disembodied voice said in a disagreeably pompous manner, 'we're obliged by the powers given to us to follow up every lead we're given. And since the young lady's been missing for over a month now with no trace of her, this is the first positive clue we've had. You understand our position, of course.'

Another voice added weight to the first. 'We're merely asking for your co-operation, sir. Of course, we could always get a warrant to search these premises, but I'm sure that won't be necessary –'

Abbie gasped, and she heard Leon's voice grow angrier now. But the thought of these men – constables, she presumed – searching this beautiful mansion and discovering all the secrets that Leon had managed to conceal so magnificently all this time was enough to terrify her. With the ludicrous thought that she was reacting like a mother-hen desperate to safeguard her chicks, she knew she would defend Leon to the death if need be – but then she heard him laugh.

'I think I've kept you waiting long enough, gentlemen. You caught me at an inopportune moment, and I have urgent business to attend to, so please be patient a while longer and we will continue this discussion. Meanwhile, my housekeeper will provide you with tea, or something stronger if it's not too early in the day for it. My wine cellar is very fine and well stocked with good French brandy.'

'That's very civil of you, sir,' Abbie heard one of the men say, and knew that Leon had got his reprieve for the moment at least. And since she guessed he would be coming for her now, she sped back to her room and waited for him, her heart beating so wildly it made her nauseous and her legs began to feel as if they would hardly hold her up. But she knew better than to let him know she had disobeyed his orders to stay in her room and been spying on him.

But if he made her confront the constables with him – as he surely must, if they were not to believe she had been abducted against her will – then –. Her mouth felt dry and her heart pounded. How could she not betray all that had been happening here? She was not versed in deceiving upholders of the law, and the very idea of it frightened her.

But not so much as giving Leon away, she thought grimly. All she prayed for was that her own awakening sensuality should not show in her face or her eyes, or her trembling mouth that Leon found so delightful and so very responsive to all that he asked of her.

She pushed away the images of the many times he had claimed that mouth and every other delicious part of her for himself. Seeking, exploring, stroking, licking, whether sensuously or in furious haste – everything he did was sheer pleasure to her now, and she wondered how much longer she could hide her love for him.

Her breath came more heavily now and she quivered deep inside her, longing for his touch as always – but now was not the time, she upbraided herself sternly. Now was definitely not the time, when she might be in real danger of being questioned mercilessly about her actions this past month, and even worse, when Leon might be in even more danger.

He came into her bedroom and stood leaning against the door for a moment. He was as commanding a figure as ever, and no outsider could detect the agitation that must be churning inside him. The only person who could see that was someone who loved him and recognised every nuance in his voice, every changing expression in his eyes, and the tightening of the mouth that had kissed her so many times, and in so many shudderingly blissful places.

'What is it?' she asked huskily when he didn't speak.

He strode across the room and caught both her hands in his, drawing her down on to the bed beside him. He let his fingers move to a stray tendril of hair that had escaped the silver combs, and the sweet, tender movement sent a shimmer of tears to her eyes.

'It seems that you have been observed riding White Dove,' he said carefully. 'Someone has passed on the information to your uncle, and the constables are here to find out if I am harbouring the missing Abigail Richmond.'

Abbie ran her tongue around her dry lips. So it was her worst nightmare come true. Once she might have thought of this as a kind of rescue. Now she could only think that all her wonderful new life could be at an end. If Leon was accused of harbouring her, or even worse, abducting her –

She shivered, knowing there would be no mercy for him. And she simply couldn't bear to think of him being locked away in a miserable prison cell for years on end. His was a truly free spirit, and she couldn't bear the thought of his incarceration.

'What can I do?' she said. 'You know you only have to ask. Should I stay hidden while you deny all knowledge of me? Is that the best course to take? They must surely believe the word of a gentleman.'

He raised her fingers to his lips, caressing them gently. He could be so tender when he chose to be, and his eyes were soft as they looked deep into hers now. Even though she was well aware that he could probably behave in any one of a hundred different ways in order to save his own neck, she didn't care. Nothing mattered but saving what they had, and letting the fantasy continue.

'I don't want you hidden away, Abbie,' he said, with a resurgence of the Master's arrogance in his voice. 'Any man in possession of such a beautiful prize would want to show it to the world.'

If she had felt so inclined, she could have said that she had been hidden away for all this time, so what was so different now! And she wasn't sure that he paid her the compliment he obviously thought he did by calling her a beautiful prize.

In her mind, possession wasn't love. It was domination. And while domination in his fantasy world was something she found acceptable to the point of delirious excitement, in real life there should be equal respect on both sides. She didn't know how to answer him, and she lowered her eyes so he wouldn't see the sudden hurt in them.

But he forced her to look at him. He cupped her chin in his hands and his thumbs softly caressed her mobile lips. She resisted the urge to capture and nibble them between her teeth, as she had often done before – that wouldn't be what he wanted now.

He looked so steadfastly into her eyes that she could see herself reflected there, and she caught her breath, wishing that what she saw in his eyes was love.

'Will you play a new game with me, Abbie?' he said quietly at last.

Her heart leapt in her chest and she felt her cheeks flush at his tone. There had been so many games, and each one had left her breathless with love for him. But it had never been Leon's way to be humble in asking her agreement. So why did he even need to ask now?

But then she knew. She could see it all in an instant. All the power was in her hands. If her Uncle Brindley had set the constables on to her, he obviously wasn't prepared to let her get away with running away from him.

She might be turned eighteen now and out of his control, but he could still make things very unpleasant for her – and even more so for anyone who had aided and abetted her in escaping from his plans for an arranged and unwanted marriage for her. He could ruin her reputation, and Leon's.

Abbie shivered, realising that she only had to say the word to these constables and she could denounce Leon Villiers for the hedonistic man that he was. She could tell them everything. She could tell of the practices in the eastern wing of the house, and the personal humiliations a young English girl had been subjected to at the hands of the women, and by Leon himself. She could take them to the *zenana* and his seraglio. And this house would be condemned and branded as little more than a personal brothel.

With all the attendant publicity and the scandal, Leon would be shamed and ruined. And she would have nothing. But even as the choices open to her flitted through her head, Abbie knew that it would never happen. She would never denounce him, ever.

'I think you know by now that I'll play whatever game you ask of me,' she said in a husky voice.

He pulled her into his arms and held her close, and she clung to him tightly, uncaring what he made of it.

'Then I must warn you that this is a rather more serious game than most,' he told her.

The constables would have been getting restless, had it not been for the decanter of fine old brandy that the housekeeper had generously put at their disposal, together with a dish of sweetmeats. Enjoying the unexpected repast, they hardly noticed that it was a good half hour before the drawing room door opened to admit the gentleman they now knew as Leon Villiers, and a lady companion. And what a lady!

The two men in their well-worn uniforms gaped at the vision walking into the room now, her hand easily linked through the gentleman's arm. As she met their startled gazes, her luscious mouth curved into a shy smile that lit up her glorious blue eyes. She wore a blue gown that emphasised those eyes, and in their now somewhat bemused state they could hardly keep their eyes off that stunning silvery hair.

'Gentlemen,' Leon said with confidence and pride, 'may I present my future wife – Miss Abigail Richmond.'

The constables tried not to choke on their brandy, their confused thoughts not quite capable of taking in this statement right away. There was surely something not quite right here, but they were too befuddled to decide instantly what it was. The close companionship of these two certainly didn't tally with the pompous old goat's vociferous demands to find the niece who must have been abducted – or worse – by some scurrilous villain. The first constable cleared his throat, but as he did so, Abbie stepped forward and spoke pleasantly.

'Please don't get up,' she said sweetly, immediately reminding the other two that they had been discourteous in not remembering to do so. 'I understand that you have been looking for me. Is that so?'

'It is, miss,' the second man growled, seemingly less inclined to be taken in by appearances than the first. 'Your uncle insists that you must have been abducted, and you understand that we have to follow up every complaint of that nature, especially when it involves minors.'

He paused as Abbie laughed easily.

'But I am not a minor, constable. Oh, I agree that I was a week or so short of my eighteenth birthday when I left my uncle's house, but since you've met the gentleman, I'm sure you won't find it hard to see why I felt obliged to do so. And I assure you I left quite voluntarily!'

The constables glanced at one another, not knowing how to handle the situation any more. It had seemed so cut and dried, and now there was a new complication. And the young woman seemed so self-assured.

'But we were told by your uncle that you were engaged to be married to another gentleman, miss –'

'My uncle has taken it on himself to exaggerate, then, since I agreed to no such marriage. Have either of you met Lord Eustace?' she asked. Both constables shook their heads at once. 'Well, let me ask you this. Would either of you want your innocent young daughter to marry a senile old man – especially when she was in love with somebody else?' Leon's arm tightened against hers, and she looked up at him with love in her eyes.

The constables shuffled in embarrassment and muttered uneasily to each other.

'So you see, you have had a wasted journey, and I'm sorry,' Abigail appealed to their better natures. 'But since my uncle would have dragged me back if he even guessed where I was, and forced me to go through with that awful marriage, it was necessary to keep my whereabouts a secret until my birthday had come and gone.'

They nodded slowly. Neither of them was the brightest of souls, and it all sounded reasonable enough. And the huge sapphire and diamond ring sparkling on the young lady's engagement finger was surely proof enough of the gentleman's intentions.

'In any case,' Leon spoke smoothly now. 'You've rather forestalled us. We had planned to go the The Grange this very afternoon to acquaint Mr Richmond of our forthcoming marriage. Since my fiancée is now of age, we don't need his approval or consent, but we both wish to let him know our plans out of common courtesy.'

'Then it seems that all is in order here, sir, and we can only wish you and the young lady much happiness for the future,' the first constable said a little clumsily.

'Thank you. But I would ask one more thing of you, gentlemen,' Leon went on. 'Would you do us the favour of not reporting back to Abigail's uncle for the time being? It would be a great disappointment to us if you were to tell him our news before we had a chance to tell him ourselves.'

'We'll not report to him until tomorrow then, sir. And of course, he'll then be able to verify that his niece is in safe hands, and the case will be closed.'

If there was the tiniest of barbed warnings in the constables statement, Leon ignored it. But what he had said was unavoidable, thought Abbie with a shudder. They would have to go back to The Grange to continue the charade, though she would rather face a dragon than her uncle's wrath.

But no one could have faulted Leon, Abbie thought admiringly. It was certainly a matchless performance, and she had more than lived up to it. Except that she was hardly playing a part, she was merely acting out her dearest fantasy of all.

When Leon had rung the bell for Maya to show the constables out of the house and they were alone again, she wilted against him.

'I'm sorry, Abbie. It seemed the only possible way to deal with the situation,' she heard him say.

It was so unexpected to hear him apologise that she found herself stammering a reply.

'You've no need to be sorry. I agreed to it, and it saved both our faces, didn't it?'

'We both know it saved me from far more than a loss of face. It seems I owe you my life as much as you owe me yours.'

Abbie held her breath. The words were so sweet, but

she daren't let herself imagine that they were sincerely meant. Not in the way she wanted them to mean, anyway, that he was hers for the rest of their lives. She swallowed, trying to make her voice more practical.

'My uncle will be incensed when you tell him our tale,' she said. 'I still fear him, Leon, and I'm sure he'll try to take some revenge on me for defying him –'

'He won't. You're under my protection now, Abbie. And the constables will verify all that we've said here today. There's nothing your uncle can do to harm you, but I suggest that I speak with him first if that meets with your approval.'

It met with her enormous relief. Besides, she didn't think she could bear to listen to Leon telling Uncle Brindley the white lie that they were to be married, when it broke her heart to know that they were not. Everything would simply continue here as before, and she would have all the pleasures and luxury he chose to give her. And she tried to smother the small voice in her head that insisted that it wasn't enough.

There was a great stir at The Grange when the small gig was seen arriving that afternoon. It was rare for Brindley Richmond to have visitors, save for the occasional elderly companions who came to play a game of bridge.

Sophie tore into the kitchen with her arms full of freshly pulled carrots, and dumped them on the kitchen table, ignoring Cook's complaints. Her eyes sparkled with excitement.

'You'll never guess who I've just seen –'

'I don't care if it's the queen herself. Get those dirty carrots off my table, my girl.'

'But it's Miss Abbie!' Sophie almost squealed. 'All done up like a lady she was, and with a handsome toff at her side.'

She had got Cook's attention now, but not in the way

she wanted. She dodged the cuffing that just missed her ear.

'You've been wool-gathering as usual,' Cook snapped. 'And that's not nearly enough carrots –'

'It was her, I tell you,' Sophie bellowed. 'But I might have known you wouldn't believe me! Anyway, I know I ain't finished outside yet, and I aim to have another look.'

She dodged Cook's second swipe and grabbed a trug from a shelf, marching indignantly out into the sunshine again. The kitchen garden was well away from the front of The Grange, but she could easily sneak a look at the imposing driveway and confirm in her own mind that the smart vehicle she'd seen arriving a short while ago was no figment of her imagination.

But she knew better than to dawdle, hopefully waiting for another glimpse of my lady. And what a fine lady, Sophie thought again. She'd been almost struck dumb at the sight of her in that shimmering blue gown and matching bonnet and gloves, with her gleaming hair all piled on top of her head now, instead of falling wildly over her shoulders in the way Sophie remembered.

She couldn't imagine why Abbie would ever come back, when she'd done so well in getting away from her uncle. But the biggest mystery of all was her companion. Sophie's tastes were for her lusty Tom, but she could quite see how a young lady would have her head turned by a handsome gent wearing elegant clothes, and with a darkly foreign look about him that would make any girl's toes curl. And not only that, she thought with a grin.

As she bent down to pull more carrots from the vegetable patch a gleam of blue caught her eye. Turning quickly as her name was called, she saw her fine young lady standing nearby. Seeing her now at such close quarters, Sophie was filled with unexpected embarrassment.

'Lord love us, Miss Abbie. I thought it was you I saw arriving a while back, but you've certainly changed in the time you've been away!'

'For the better, I hope,' Abbie said with a smile.

Sophie cocked her knowing head on one side.

'Oh aye, for the better, I'd say,' she said mischievously. 'And I'll warrant that the handsome gent I saw with you has summat to do with it.'

Now that Leon was taking over the task of informing her uncle of their fictitious news, Abbie felt easier in her mind and had opted for a stroll in the fresh air instead of accompanying him.

Sophie's tone and her eyes invited confidences, yet although Abbie laughed self-consciously, she suddenly saw the yawning distance between them. Sophie had freely told her everything she wanted to know about the art of making love. And once, Abbie might have been tempted to run gleefully into the garden and tell her that she too had a lover. Sharing secrets. Whispering confidences. But not now. Not when she had grown up and grown away from everything here in a way she could never have envisaged.

She could see that Sophie was waiting expectantly now, seating herself on a bench and clearly expecting Abbie to sit beside her. She did so after a moment's hesitation.

'So, come on, then, miss. Does he come up to scratch? Is he well hung and able to satisfy you like I told you?' she said in the lascivious voice Abbie remembered.

Abbie's face was flaming now, and she couldn't bear to have her feelings for Leon paraded in the way Sophie paraded hers for Tom. Nor would she tell this chit things that were private and personal and belonged to them alone.

'I'd rather not say –' she began awkwardly.

'What?' Sophie's eyes flashed. 'After all the things I

told you! Without my teachin', you'd never have known what a cock was, let alone what a man had to do with it!'

And then Sophie's words ran away with her.

'Anyway, I'm sorry for telling on you, but it was the Irishman's fault, not mine. He threatened to make trouble for me if I didn't say you'd been seen, but I never tried to get money out of your uncle, honest to God I didn't –'

'You told on me? Sophie, how could you?'

'I didn't want to, but it's all turned out for the best, ain't it? You've got a fine and lusty gent, by the looks of it, so are you going to tell me what he likes doing, or not?'

How crude she was. And after the shock of realising it had been Sophie who betrayed her, how shaming Abbie found it now to think she had once eagerly sought out such talk from this slut. The word slid into her head before she could stop it, but there was no denying it. Sophie was a slut and always had been.

'Things are different now,' she said.

'Oh yes? And does my lord and master do it differently then?' Sophie said nastily, not realising how near she was to a half-truth. The Master could pleasure her in so many different ways.

But seeing the defensive look on the other girl's, Abbie immediately backed down.

'Of course not,' she muttered, and knew her mistake when Sophie's eyes gleamed.

'So you do know what it's all about then! And did you follow all the advice that I gave you?'

Abbie almost laughed out loud. Sophie had told her the basics, but the real teacher, the wonderful, inventive teacher, had been Leon Villiers, the Master.

'I can see from your face that you did,' Sophie chuckled. 'And was it all that you expected?'

224

All that – and more than I could ever have dreamed about –

'I don't think I should talk about it –'

'Why the blue blazes not? We've all got the same equipment under our skirts, ain't we? And I always knew you was going to be a lust-bucket, given half a chance –'

'Because of this,' Abbie said, ignoring the taunt. She slowly drew off her glove to reveal the fabulous sapphire and diamond ring on her finger.

Sophie gaped at the sight of the costly jewel. 'Well, you struck lucky and no mistake, Miss Abbie,' she said at last. 'So when's the weddin' to be?'

Abbie stared down at the ring on her finger, her pleasure in its beauty replaced by sudden misery. For of course there was going to be no wedding. It was all a farce, a sham, a game, like everything else Leon Villiers played. Right at this minute, he was probably telling her uncle how much he was in love with her, and that now that she was eighteen this visit was just a formality to inform him of their plans and she could still denounce him and reveal everything.

Her head jerked up as she heard his voice close by.

'I've been looking for you, my love. Will you come into the house now? Your uncle wishes to speak with you.'

Leon was standing against the sunlight, and Abbie swallowed the quick lump that came to her throat. This situation was far too poignant for her, and she was aware that Sophie had jumped up from the bench, bobbing a curtsey at the gentleman and scattering carrots everywhere.

As Sophie ran the tip of her tongue around her lips, Abbie could almost read her wicked little mind. 'Lord love us, now that I see him up close, I wouldn't mind getting' me hands inside that gent's breeches meself –'
It was time to go.

* * *

Abbie stood up quickly, and took the hand Leon offered her, holding it tightly until they were out of Sophie's earshot, and realising anew how far she had come from this house and everything in it since knowing him.

'Don't be afraid,' he said quietly. 'Just follow my lead, and don't let him intimidate you.'

She nodded. But her heart was beating sickly, for he didn't know her uncle as she did. He could be tenacious in following through the idea that his ward was to be married. He would want to know that he hadn't been totally thwarted in his own plans for marrying her off to the highest bidder. At the thought she gripped Leon's hand more firmly.

'What have you told him?' she whispered. 'And what have you promised him?'

'Only what was necessary,' he said, and she had to be satisfied with that. But once inside the house where she had known such boredom and misery she felt as though a cloud had descended over her. She had always hated being here, and she hated it even more now.

Miss Phipps said 'Good afternoon', looking at her as though she was a scarlet woman, Abbie thought with faint amusement. For she was surely that. The most scarlet, debauched woman who ever lived, to enjoy playing such games with her lover as could never be imagined in this starched environment.

She held her chin higher as they reached the inner sanctum of her uncle's study, reminding herself that she was of age now, and he no longer had any control over her.

Brindley's eyes narrowed at the sight of her, and her apparent self-control seemed only to incense him. He pounded his fist on his desk, making her heart leap with fear.

'So, miss. You've decided to come home after your little escapade, have you?'

Leon swore beneath his breath, but Abbie's eyes

flashed at her uncle as she railed back at him, reminding herself again that he could do nothing to harm her now.

'No, uncle, I have not come home. I have come here with my fiancé to inform you of our plans, as you very well know by now. We didn't need to do so at all, but it seemed the honourable thing to do –'

'Honourable!' Brindley spluttered. 'To have some slut of a kitchen-maid inform me that my niece has been seen cavorting and horse-riding in some unknown person's grounds, and then you come here and tell me he's your fiancé –'

'I do tell you that. And whatever else you may have heard, it's the truth.'

She prayed he wouldn't sense any hint of desperation in the word. But then Leon spoke, and his voice was hard.

'All right, sir, you've had your say, and I'll not stand for any threats to Abigail. I'll repeat what I've already told you. She has been cared for by my housekeeper and servants since her accident, and has now consented to be my wife. And as a bride-price I'm offering you two of my best horses as compensation for any anxiety you've suffered since her disappearance. I trust it *has* worried you?'

'Of course,' the man scowled, but after what seemed an interminable scrutiny of them both, he gave a sneering smile. 'And how can I be sure that the girl has not been tampered with – sir?' he said. 'I'll remind you that a physician would soon ascertain whether or not she's still untouched –'

'How *dare* you,' Abbie screamed, crimson with fear and embarrassment now. 'You spoil everything, as usual! And you insult my future husband.'

Saying those words made her catch her breath, but they had to preserve the illusion at all costs. It was the most dangerous game they had ever played. One wrong word from this oaf could send the constables sniffing around again.

Brindley glared back at Abbie. Her defiance would make him eat humble pie in front of his contemporaries, especially Lord Eustace. Her closeness to Leon was forcing him towards defeat but he still tried to bluster it out.

'My niece's welfare is still my concern,' he said pompously, and far too late for it to be anything but an afterthought. 'So I'll need proper confirmation in due course that the wedding has taken place – but don't expect me to be present.'

'I wouldn't dream of expecting it, sir,' Leon said curtly and with barely-disguised sarcasm.

There was no offer of refreshment or hospitality and no further need to remain. All Abbie wanted now was to get away from The Grange and all its unhappy associations. But she was hot and mortified from all she had encountered here today – from Sophie's insinuations and her uncle's temper, from the fact that in publicly offering a bride-price for her Leon was as good as buying her.

'That odious man!' she raged, when they were in the gig once more and leaving the estate she never wanted to see again. 'He always made me feel less than human, and couldn't wait to be rid of me. I was always no more than an encumbrance to him, and he never wanted me.'

'Then forget him, and be glad that you have someone who does want you.'

'Have I?' she said, still shaking.

He gave a harsh laugh. 'If you don't know it by now, Abigail, then you're either deaf or blind, and I don't think you're either.'

She supposed it was some consolation to know that he wanted her – but in what capacity? Were they to go on forever playing games until he tired of her, and looked around for someone new to pleasure him? Although she knew very well he hadn't visited his seraglio in days now, it didn't mean he would abandon those lovely honey-skinned girls for ever.

And she wasn't sure if she could bear to share him with them any more. But if she didn't, then maybe she would be discarded as easily as an old glove.

She was plunged into deep depression, until she realised he had drawn the gig to a halt and was looking at her quizzically.

'This has been quite a day for you, hasn't it, my sweet? I'm thankful to have got you away from that ogre for good, but I wish I had some idea of what's going through that lovely head of yours now.'

Without thinking twice, she said what was uppermost in her mind. Out here in the open, in the warm summer sunshine, out of her uncle's clutches, and away from the heavy opulence of Leon's quasi-palace, she felt freer to speak as she felt.

'I was wondering how much you really want me, or if I'm just another toy for your amusement.'

He didn't speak for a moment, and when he did, it was with the voice of the arrogant Master.

'If there was some secluded place nearby, I would show you here and now just how much I want you.'

She hesitated for a moment, and then, 'I know such a place,' she whispered.

Chapter Fourteen

*A*bbie directed him through the shady undergrowth towards the secret cover of the copse surrounding the stream. In the weeks since she had left The Grange, the foliage had grown thicker, and the curve of the stream was completely hidden from anyone's view. Leon tethered the horse to a tree and left him grazing contentedly.

Just for a moment Abbie remembered with a shudder the Irishman who had camped here, and the way he had pressed himself against her, but she guessed he would be long gone by now. She had to forget too, that between them he and Sophie had been responsible for betraying her whereabouts, and it could all have ended in disaster.

In any case, those two were the last people she wanted to think about now. There was only herself and Leon, and she realised for the first time that she was taking the initiative in inviting him here to her secret place, and for one purpose only. Her brittle nerves gradually relaxed as they walked towards the stream and gazed down into the shimmering water, diamond-studded with sunlight.

And then, without warning, her breath caught on a

half-sob as the weight of this day threatened to overwhelm her again. This place had been her only sanctuary.

'I used to come here often,' she said in a choked voice. 'It was the only place I felt totally free with my own thoughts and dreams. I used to imagine a lover who would take me away from all the hypocrisy of my uncle's house –'

'And now you've found him,' Leon said, his arms encircling her and pulling her close, so that she could feel every hard sinew of his body inside the elegant garments he wore. 'What else did you dream of in your secret place?'

She made herself reply as coolly as she could, because to do otherwise would be to betray all her emotions.

'Oh, all the usual things a young girl dreams about. Being loved – being kissed – being so much a part of someone else that you couldn't tell where one of us began and the other one ended –'

Dear Lord, how juvenile she sounded, she thought painfully. Leon's world was peopled with sensual and beautiful women, skilled in the art of love, and he was a prince of seducers. And here was Abigail Richmond, talking and behaving like a naive young girl.

'Like this?' she heard him say, as his lips brushed her mouth, and his hands reached out to fondle her breasts through the confines of her demure gown.

'Or like this?' he said, and she felt his hand slide down her spine to reach the swell of her buttocks, rotating his fingers slowly and rucking up the soft fabric of the gown until he reached the smooth pearly mounds themselves.

'No one ever comes here, you say?' he murmured against her mouth now, and she felt the sweet wanton desire soar through her, sensing his urgency.

'I'm quite sure no one else at the house knows of its

231

existence,' Abbie said. 'I always felt safe and unobserved when I bathed in the stream –'

'Then we'll take advantage of its solitude together.'

Before she knew what he was about, he was unfastening her bodice, and the folds of the gown slid to her feet, swiftly followed by the petticoats and chemise that were so heavy and restrictive in the hot weather. Helped by her own willing hands, he had her naked in minutes. She swayed towards his seeking touch on every curve of her body as she felt the seductive heat of the sun on her bare skin.

But nothing was as seductive as the look in his eyes and the throb of his manhood against her, straining for release against his fine breeches now.

Leon looked her over slowly. All her senses shivered as he appraised her from top to toe, his fingers stroking every inch of her sun-warmed flesh as intently as if he were a blind man needing to imprint the shape and the feel of her on his mind for ever. Her skin tingled with pleasure and wild anticipation at his every touch. Her nipples stood out proudly as his fingers slowly circled them, wanting more.

'You may remove my boots, woman,' he said arrogantly, lying back on the mossy ground now. She knelt down, complying at once, massaging his feet before tossing his stockings aside as well.

'Do you have any more instructions – Sir? I confess I do feel rather at a disadvantage without my clothes.'

She knew she was being brazen, inviting him to disrobe completely too – as if there was any doubt that it was his intention. But he laughed as if her words delighted him, and pulled her hand down to the fastening of his breeches.

'Not yet,' she dared to tease him.

His eyebrows lifted. 'Oh? Does my lady dare to defy me?'

'My lady will do things in her own fashion,' she heard herself say, to her own astonishment.

Slowly, she pushed back the coat from his shoulders, and then untied the silk cravat with its fine pearl pin. Next, she unbuttoned his shirt, artlessly passing her hand over his bronzed skin with every movement, and finally tossing the elegant garments into the bushes as if they were rags.

She was filled with a new self-confidence in her skills in the art of seduction. She pressed her hands more possessively over the fine broad expanse of his chest, leaning over to kiss the little flat nipples and lick them into arousal.

She heard his indrawn breath, and knew how much he was enjoying this reversal of a man's role. She ran her hands slowly down the length of his arms, gently squeezing the hard muscles, and kissing the inside of his elbows, while his hands reached for her breasts. She was already very aroused. Her crotch was pleasurably moist, complemented by the sweet, quivering responses radiating through her core, and she had no doubt of Leon's own responses to her ministrations.

It occurred to her, for one brief moment, that none of the seraglio women would dare to take the initiative in pleasuring him, unless instructed or ordered by the Master himself. But in her secret place that now belonged to him, Abbie was the Mistress, and she would take what she wanted.

They had all the time in the world, and there was no need for haste. Her tantalising touch moved from Leon's arms to his taut, flat belly, and her tongue flicked in and out of his navel for a few seconds, while her fingers deftly unfastened the breeches and slid them down the length of his powerful legs. The evidence of his need for her was potent and throbbing, the love-head glistening and ready.

As he kicked his breeches and undergarments aside,

she lay over him, knowing that he was impatient now to penetrate her with that luscious instrument. She only had to straddle him, and he would be inside her in a moment. And she could no longer wait. The ache in her loins for him was too strong, too urgent.

Her heart pounded with a craven and lustful desire for him to be inside her, and she leaned backwards from him, opening wide and enveloping the swollen length of him. After the earlier trauma of this day, the exquisite feel of him filling her to the hilt was unbelievable.

But after she had made a few furious thrusts downwards on him, her head thrown back in ecstacy as she captured his swollen shaft in her heated cavern, he caught her wrists with his hands, his smile lascivious and mocking.

'Not yet, my sweet,' he said, taking her by surprise. 'I think we'll delay the ultimate pleasure, much as I'd love to stay inside that delightful place for ever. But first, I suggest we cool ourselves off in that delightful stream of yours, and then we'll do what nature intended. I'll wager you've never bathed naked before?'

Abbie's eyes glittered as she shook her head. Such a thought had never occurred to her. She had always observed modesty here, even when she was sure no one could see her. But then, she did so many things with Leon that she had never experienced before. He had awoken all her sensual instincts, making her feel new and alive. And she knew she would do anything he asked, be anything he desired. Hadn't she already proved that, time and again? Her face flamed, and her mouth was unable to resist curving into a smile.

'But I see that it appeals to you,' he said teasingly.

Leon rolled over her for a moment, withdrawing from her and swiftly bending to kiss the open orifice that had so recently held him. He pulled the silver combs from her hair to release the formal coiffure, so that the silky waves caressed her shoulders. He wound a tendril of it in his fingers, kissing its softness, and she could feel the beat of his heart, so close to hers. She could feel his warmth and his hardness and she wanted him so badly.

But she couldn't deny that each new experience he promised her had more than lived up to its expectations. So when he led her to the stream they stepped into it together, with their arms entwined.

The first touch of cool water on Abbie's heated skin made her gasp with shock. But she couldn't protest because by then Leon had turned her towards him, holding her close and kissing her mouth, and pulling her down with him beneath the shimmering, sun-blessed water.

For the briefest moment she had the strange sensation of drowning, even though she was still held tightly in the circle of his arms. And then she was coming to the surface, still gasping, and breathing in the fragrant summer air once more.

'You see that even the shock of plunging into cold water does nothing to dampen my desire for you, sweetness,' she heard him say with amusement. He thrust her hand downwards to where his erection was as potent as ever. Amazed, Abbie felt renewed desire run through her, as keen as a flame.

'So what do you suggest we do to relieve such an affliction – sir?' she said, looking into his eyes, as bold and brash as a servant-girl.

Without answering, he lifted her as if she was weight-less, and her legs automatically wrapped themselves around him as her arms clung to his neck. She felt his swollen member probing her, and she wriggled herself downwards, seeking to capture it, but the mood was suddenly broken. She gasped again, laughing, as he almost stumbled on the sandy floor of the stream.

'Leon, this is foolishness. It's an impossibility –'

'Nothing's impossible if you want it badly enough,

my sweet one,' he said arrogantly. 'Hold on to me tightly.'

She did as she was told, and somehow the balance was restored between them. Because she was opened so wide, his stallion-head entered her easily, filling her with an unexpected sensation. The inner walls of her pleasure-zone were throbbingly hot, while his rampant stalk was refreshingly cool and rock-solid. The thrill of fire and ice colliding was entirely different from anything she had felt before.

Leon kept his feet firmly apart to give him balance while he plunged into her, and she rocked with him, helping him, loving him until she felt she could stand it no longer.

'Leon, I'm falling –' she gasped.

They fell into the water together, laughing and breaking apart, splashing and cavorting like two children now. And it was all part of the pleasure.

'God, but I never knew a woman like you,' she heard him say, as he hauled her up from the depths. 'I never knew such a one existed, so sensual at every turn, but always ready to be my partner in whatever game I choose to play.'

'I never knew I was such a one, either,' she said, unable to resist giggling, because she was sure she must look a sight, her hair like rats' tails, and as naked as the day she was born, yet feeling no shame.

In fact, from the very first time the Master had invited her to look, to touch, to taste – which seemed so very long ago now – Abbie realised she had felt no shame with him. He could do with her as he wished, and she would follow him to the ends of the earth if need be. She had already proved that, in not betraying him to the constables or her uncle.

Unconsciously she gave a small shiver at the thought of how different it might have been if the constables had been astute enough to keep watch on the house before.

And they must always be careful, for if once the *zenana* was discovered –

'You're cold,' Leon said at once. 'And I think we've had enough bathing for today. There's a rug in the gig, and we'll wrap ourselves in it and dry off on the grass.'

She wasn't cold because of the stream, but she was happy enough to let him help her out of it, and to stand shaking her hair like a puppy and teasing him with her spray. She waited while he fetched the rug, marvelling at his wonderful physique, and the way he could still look so elegant and charismatic, even unclothed. And for the first time in her life she was glad of her own womanly shape, and that he found it so pleasing.

She was smiling when he returned with the tartan rug, and he smiled in return.

'You constantly surprise me, Abbie,' he said, to her astonishment. 'Right now you resemble a young wood nymph, quite unselfconscious of how beautiful you are. And once I've spread this rug on the ground, I intend to explore every little particle of you.'

A thrill ran through her at his words. So the game wasn't over yet, and the tantalising entries into her were just the *hors d'oeuvres*. The main event was still to come.

When the rug was spread out, they lay down together and Leon cocooned them both inside it, to dry off the surface dampness. She felt totally refreshed and invigorated, her skin softened and faintly scented by the crystal clear water.

It was sheer bliss to be so close to him like this, with their heartbeats so much in tune. Her eyes were closed against the strong rays of the sun for a few moments, and then she felt Leon slowly unwrapping them from their cocoon. She felt him gazing down at her, and she watched him beneath lazy, half-closed lids.

'You're so perfect in every way. I was right to call you White Dove, reflecting all that was pure and virginal.'

Abbie's heart stopped for a second, and then raced

on. She hadn't heard herself called by that name for some while now. Hearing it now on his lips filled her with sudden fear, as if all of this could be the prelude to his dismissal of her, since all that was pure and virginal about her had long since vanished. And she knew that his little empire had been in grave danger of being exposed, and all because of her.

She felt suddenly far too exposed herself, and without thinking she swiftly placed one hand over the soft regrowth of silvery hair at her groin. Leon removed her hand gently, looking deep into her eyes. He had such mesmeric eyes, she thought weakly, and perhaps she had never fully appreciated that fact until now.

'Why do you try to hide yourself from me? Don't you know that I no longer require coyness from you? Let me see you opening like a rose for me, Abbie.'

As if she had no more will of her own, she obeyed him, as she had been doing for so long now. Her legs were slightly parted, and she felt his hands slide beneath her, lifting her buttocks and thrusting her upwards so that her nether lips opened. The sensation of warm sun on her cooled inner flesh was potent and sensual, but before she had time to register it properly, something much warmer was deliciously probing its sensitive way inside her.

She leaned back on her elbows, watching Leon's dark head as he tongued her, alternating the thrusting strokes inside her moist walls by sliding his tongue slowly up and down the slippery sides of her fleshy lips. Its tip constantly tantalised her with its stroking movements, finally seeking and finding her pleasure-bud while she gasped in ecstacy.

The tip of his tongue circled her bud, then thrust against it, while his fingers dug into her buttocks. Her own hands kneaded his powerful back as he leaned over her. Then she felt his mouth open wider, and it seemed as if he captured the whole of her crotch inside it, as if he would devour her if he could. His lips nibbled her fleshy ones, while his teeth ground gently against her, and all the time that marvellous, questing tongue probed into her.

Without warning, Abbie could no longer resist the release of tension. The exquisite gathering inside her wouldn't be denied, and she felt her eyes dilate as she felt the explosive spasms begin. Her inner walls rippled involuntarily as she climaxed against Leon's tongue.

'I'm sorry,' she gasped wildly, as he removed his mouth after a few minutes.

'What on earth for?' he said. 'I was tasting the nectar of the gods, my darling girl.'

But he moved himself further up her body, and proceeded to do as he had promised, kissing every exposed part of her. He began at her eyelids, then every inch of her face and neck, before moving down to the firm, glorious swell of her breasts and the engorged pink nipples.

He took each one in his mouth, sucking and teasing, and slowly pampering each one with his tongue in the way he must know she felt so arousing. Abbie felt the throb in her crotch begin again as he did so. But he wasn't finished with her yet.

And it had been impossible for her simply to lie back and be attended to in this way, when she wanted to hold him so much. She had already reached out for him, and she caressed that huge, gleaming erection as lovingly as if she held a precious object in her hand. He was a stallion in every sense of the word, she thought faintly. And he was *hers*.

'Leon, I want to – to –' she whispered, as her thumb lightly grazed the moist tip of his glans. Somehow she couldn't say the words, but he wasn't prepared to let her off that easily.

'What is it you want to do? I won't know unless you tell me, and I won't let you do it until you say it.'

'I want to suck you,' she whispered again, her face flaming as she said it.

'And I want to fuck you,' Leon said. The harsh-sounding word sent a thrill of desire through her groin, and she knew that in one respect she was in complete accord with Sophie. There was something earthy and erotic in using forbidden words in that context.

'First suck, then fuck, since it's what we both want very much to do,' Leon went on, as if he could read her mind.

He rolled on to his back and Abbie ran her tongue around her lips in anticipation. As she leant over him, her hair fell across his stomach, teasing him with its softness.

She felt him catch hold of it, smoothing and stroking its silky sheen as she caught his straining shaft in her hand. For a few seconds she slowly teased its bulbous tip with her tongue, before plunging her mouth over it as if she would consume it whole.

She heard him gasp with pleasure, and his grip on her hair tightened for a moment, his fingers raking upwards into her scalp and sending pulsing waves of pleasure through her. She was already lost in sensation now, and the sheer delight of having him captive in her mouth was sending her near to delirium. She could feel how it delighted Leon to have her holding him in her mouth, alternately nuzzling him with her teeth and sucking him rhythmically.

The sun beat down on her bare buttocks. Leon swivelled her around so that she lay with her crotch over his face. A wild sense of abandonment swept through her now, as she felt that mobile tongue begin its work all over again, licking her and tasting her, and thrusting into her sweet inner recesses. Her responsive nerve-ends throbbed, and she clenched and unclenched her inner muscles as if she would keep him there for ever.

Her legs were spread wide over him now, and she felt

Leon's finger trace the sensitive crevice between her buttocks. She tensed slightly, and as if aware of her every nuance, he merely caressed the smooth, rounded orbs and continued with his tonguing where she wanted it most.

She let her fingers caress his testicles now, grazing them gently with her fingernails and felt their slight tightening at her touch.

Her fingers left his scrotum, to gently knead the crest of dark hair at the base of his root, and then to slide them upwards to where her mouth still sucked and teased and nibbled and tasted him.

'Enough!' she suddenly heard Leon's voice say, penetrating her bemused senses. 'I want my woman *now*.'

Once, in what seemed like another lifetime now, she had been so afraid of meeting this unknown Master and becoming his love-slave. Now, she found herself filled with impatient, inflamed passion at his commanding – no, demanding voice. She wanted nothing more than to be one with him in this special, secret place that now belonged to them alone.

Obediently she removed her mouth from his ramrod-hard penis and lay back on the rug. Without waiting for any invitation to do so she opened her legs wide and grasped his stallion-head, her fingers clutching it avariciously. All thought of modesty, of being anything less than his to command, had long since deserted her.

'No more than I want my man,' she said hoarsely.

He forged into her, and she arched upwards towards him, bucking and thrusting with him, as wildly as if she was truly possessed. And if she hadn't been so moistly ready for him, she was sure he would have split her in two, so rampant was his desire for her.

It was inconceivable that this coupling would be long-lasting, but the time it took was of no consequence to Abbie. She clung to him, her legs wound tightly around his back as she felt the hot gush of his seed. Her vulva responded with matching and spectacular spasms of pleasure, until they both lay, spent, but unwilling to break apart until inevitably nature dictated it so.

Neither of them spoke for long moments. They lay, still entwined, and Leon pulled the rug over them again, while Abbie felt the cool trace of tears on her cheeks. She dashed them away, not wanting Leon to think she had been anything less than satisfied, when such a word seemed so very inadequate for all the pleasure they had shared.

But she admitted to herself now that all this time, all this day, she had let herself believe in the fantasy they had created that morning – that the ring she wore on her finger was a true affirmation of his love, and that she was soon to be his wife. However, the brutal reality of it was that he had never told her that he loved her.

Late in the afternoon they returned to Villiers Manor and left the gig at the front of the house for the stable-lads to put away. By now they appeared once more as the epitome of fashionable and respectable society, and no one would have suspected them of being the unin-hibited lovers who had recently coupled naked by a stream.

As they entered the house, Maya came hurrying towards them, her normally expressionless face showing signs of anxiety.

'Is all well?' she murmured.

As if she were an older member of his family rather than the player of the various roles that Leon expected of her, he put a comforting arm around her shoulders for a brief moment. The gesture touched Abbie more than she could say.

'All is well, Maya, but we would both appreciate some tea in the drawing room.'

This was apparently all the information he was pre-pared to give, but it clearly satisfied her. She nodded briefly, her glance flicking over them both, before she departed to attend to the request.

When they were alone, neither of them spoke, and Abbie felt the first real awkwardness she had felt with Leon in a long time. A change in their relationship had been forced on them – and yet she had to admit that nothing had really changed at all. She couldn't relax, and her hands twisted together as she gazed unseeingly through the long windows towards the lovely gardens beyond the house.

When Leon finally spoke his voice startled her.

'Why don't you play something? Perhaps the music will calm you,' he said, patently aware of her brittle nerves.

She looked at him mutely. Nothing would calm her but knowing that he loved her as much as she loved him. But from his correct attitude towards her now, she doubted that such a luxury would ever be hers. She was still his plaything, and nothing more.

But she was also used to obeying him, and she walked unsteadily to the pianoforte and lifted the lid. Her fingers splayed out over the keys, and she went through a small repertoire of pieces without the remotest feeling of pleasure. Nor was there the slightest sense of sensuality as there had been when she had played for him before. She was thankful when Maya brought in the tray of tea and she could legitimately end the performance.

And oh yes, things had changed, she thought sadly. She was no longer at ease with him, and Leon himself seemed less than easy with her. Perhaps he was even cursing the day he had taken pity on a young woman who had been thrown from her mare, and thinking that not all the pleasure in the world was worth the anxiety she had brought him.

'I think I'd like to take a bath and lie down for a while,' she said, as soon as she decently could. 'I feel a little unwell after the encounter with my uncle –'

Lord, how feeble she sounded, she thought. But it was true. Her head throbbed, and her stomach was churning. And she couldn't bear to sit here making small talk with this man, with whom she had been so very intimate, and who was suddenly a stranger to her once more.

'I think that's a very good idea,' he said. 'I have some business to see to, and I shall see you again at dinner.'

She moved swiftly out of the room, wondering what possible business he had to attend to, or if it was more likely just an excuse. But he had no need of excuses. He was the Master here, lord of all he surveyed.

She went upstairs to her own room, and once there she wilted. The day had begun so traumatically and, until a short while ago, it had ended so spectacularly. She had felt, for the first time in her life, that she had held real power in her hands. Which she had, she reminded herself, for if she had denounced and betrayed Leon Villiers, he could well be heading for prison right now.

But now all her spirit seemed to be draining out of her once more, and she wondered just how long she could live with this see-saw of emotions.

'Stop being so spineless,' she muttered out loud. 'You've made your bed –'

At the words she bit her lip as her eyes strayed to the pristine bed in her room – The bed that Leon had never shared with her. But she had guessed long ago that it was beneath the Master's dignity to go to a woman's room to take his pleasures. The woman always had to go to him.

Almost angrily she began to shed her clothes, and she walked naked into her bathroom, more brazen than she had ever been before even in private. She hardly cared. He had made her into a wanton, and whatever became of her now she owed him for awakening her to her own sensuality in a way she could never have imagined.

The thought mollified her, but sensual thoughts were

furthest from her mind as she filled the bathtub with warm water and stepped into it. All she wanted was to refresh herself and then lie flat on her bed and let the tension in her neck and shoulders unwind.

She slept from sheer exhaustion, for when she opened her eyes again, the sun was lower in the sky, and from the gnawing emptiness in her stomach she knew it was time for dinner.

In a fit of petulance, she dressed in the dullest gown she could find in her closet and scraped her hair up in a more unbecoming style than of late. Let him think she was a puritan. She had had to face enough of his guises.

When she joined him in the drawing-room for *aperitifs* he looked her over thoughtfully for a moment.

'What's all this? Am I to dine with my grandmother or my maiden aunt this evening?'

Abbie flushed. Whatever else she might be, she was no longer anyone's maiden aunt!

'I'm sorry if my appearance doesn't please you –' she began stiffly.

'No, it bloody well doesn't please me,' he said, startling her by his language. 'I'm arrogant enough not to want anyone thinking I'd choose a nonentity for a wife.'

'But you didn't choose me, did you?' she was stung into replying. 'And we don't have to continue with this charade.'

'No, we don't,' he said calmly.

At once she knew how utterly foolish she had been, both in acting so childishly in her choice of dress, and in goading him into saying the very thing she wanted to hear the least.

Dinner was eaten in almost total silence. All the sweet rapport between them seemed to have vanished like a will o' the wisp. Abbie's spirits plummetted, sure that he was regretting ever setting eyes on her with all the trouble she had brought him. She remembered her uncle's snide words about wanting to be sure the marriage had taken place. Well, there was no likelihood of that, she thought!

As soon as was decently possible she would have to vacate this haven, unable to bear being here on sufferance. She would have to inform her uncle that she had made a mistake, and that she would be seeking employment somewhere.

It would be the worst humiliation to go to him with such news. But if she did not, he would undoubtedly send the constables to ferret around again, for his own satisfaction, and certainly not for any concern about her welfare.

She couldn't raise her pessimistic thoughts. She wouldn't let herself remember how wonderful it had been between herself and Leon. She couldn't swallow for the pain in her throat and her heart at knowing she was losing him, but she had to face the fact that he had never really been hers. It had all been a pretence, like the games he played.

He suddenly threw down his napkin with a gesture of annoyance. Abbie flinched, recognising that impatience. She knew him so well – she had felt she knew the very essence of that beautiful man – and yet she really didn't know him at all, except in one respect.

'It seems as if neither of us is interested in food this-evening,' he almost snapped. 'You may amuse yourself as you wish, Abigail, as I have to conclude my business.'

Just for a moment, as he passed her chair, he pressed his hand against the nape of her neck.

She longed to capture that hand, to turn his fingers towards her mouth and pull him down to her. But the moment passed, and he left the room, leaving her alone with tears blinding her eyes.

And then the silent Maya and her attendants came to clear the table, and Abbie went swiftly to the drawing-room, not wanting them to see her distress. For a while she let her fingers stray over the pianoforte keys, but even the music didn't calm her, and there were too many discordant notes echoing her turbulent emotions.

Finally she went upstairs to her room and undressed completely, scrubbing her skin with soap and water as if she would scrub away every touch she had ever received from Leon Villiers. And then her contrary senses made her long for that touch so much, and she pampered her tender skin with oils, trying to imagine that it was Leon's hands that caressed her.

She crawled into bed, and it had already grown dark when she heard her door handle turn. Her heart jolted, and then it raced crazily as she saw the figure silhouetted against the soft landing light.

'Leon –' she breathed.

He came to her bedside, as lithe as a gazelle, and her dazed senses took in the fact that he was once more the Master. His silky white robes were caught at the waist with a jewelled belt, and his skin was scented with aromatic oils.

Was she about to be taken to the golden chamber once more, where she had had her first initiation into love? Was this to be the last time?

'My business is finished,' he said quietly, 'and everyone has agreed to my terms.'

'What terms?' Abbie said hoarsely, not understanding.

'I have been to the *zenana*,' he went on. 'The women have been loyal to me for many years, and they had to understand why the time has come for change. But I'm confident that they'll be loyal again.'

Abbie felt a wild surge of hope. If he meant what she prayed that he did – but she couldn't ask. She could only lie mutely, her heart thudding like a drum.

Leon turned back the bedcovers, exposing her tense body inside the cambric nightgown, and his fingers moved to her breasts, squeezing them with an infinitely gentle caress.

247

'You've changed my life,' he said, almost accusingly. 'I should have heeded the ancient wisdom that once you find your soul-mate, there can never be another.'

There seemed to be an endless moment before Abbie managed to speak through her dry lips.

'And have you found yours?' she whispered.

'We both have. Haven't we?'

'Yes. Oh, yes!'

She realised that he was deftly removing her night-gown as he spoke, so that the cooler night air refreshed her skin. The skin that he loved to touch, and was doing so with such erotic expertise right now. And then it took no more than a moment for him to unfasten the jewelled belt and let the white robes fall to the floor before he slid into the bed beside her.

And for the first time, she realised, he had come to her. He was in her bed, instead of taking her to some-where of his choosing. It had to be somehow significant, but as yet she was too dazed to think why, or to care about anything except that he was here.

'So do we continue as before, my White Dove? Taking all our pleasures in whatever part of this house it pleases us to do so, and in whatever guise? The eastern ways have been part of my life, and I don't care to relinquish them completely.'

She jerked away from his seeking hands, even while she exulted in the fact that he wanted her so much. But from his words, it seemed as if he wanted those other women too, and she couldn't bear the thought of it.

'No! I can't share you, Leon,' she stammered, fright-ened at her own daring, but knowing that it had to be said, and somehow finding the strength for it.

'I'm not asking you to share me.'

She found herself parting for him as his hands moved downwards, stroking every inch of her yielding flesh, and her own hands were already reaching and grasping the potent part of him that thrilled her so much.

'What do you mean?' she whispered, closing her eyes in ecstasy as his probing fingers moved into her softness.

'Must I spell it out for you, my darling? I want you for my wife, and together we can have everything and more that a normal married couple have. We'll play the conventional couple in public, but the Master may have his White Dove whenever he desires it, and she can be my lady with the riding crop when it suits her. There's no reason for the games to cease just because you have a ring on your finger, my sweet.'

Almost delirious with happiness, Abbie took in all that he was saying, but the only words that mattered were those that she had never expected to hear. She savoured them over and over in her head.

'I want you for my wife.'

'Well? Do I have an answer?' Leon demanded. He was once more the arrogant Master as he half-lay over her, and she knew that glorious rampant desire of his was not going to be denied a moment longer.

But there was still something she had to know.

'You said we didn't have to continue with this charade, Leon,' she whispered. 'So why would you want to marry me?'

'For the best reason in the world. Because I love you, of course. So do I have to wait forever for an answer?'

'The answer's yes, yes, yes,' she said, just as if there had ever been any doubt. 'And you must know how much I love you too –'

His mouth covered hers in a long sweet kiss, stilling her voice. For one wild, wonderful moment she let herself envisage their future, a life consisting of a glorious montage of hedonistic delights that only two could share.

And then she stopped thinking at all, clinging to him as he slowly entered her, and gave herself up to pleasure.

Black Lace Booklist

Information is correct at time of printing. To avoid disappointment check availability before ordering. Go to www.blacklace-books.co.uk. All books are priced £6.99 unless another price is given.

BLACK LACE BOOKS WITH A CONTEMPORARY SETTING

☐ THE TOP OF HER GAME Emma Holly	ISBN 0 352 33337 5	£5.99
☐ IN THE FLESH Emma Holly	ISBN 0 352 34498 3	£5.99
☐ A PRIVATE VIEW Crystalle Valentino	ISBN 0 352 33308 1	£5.99
☐ SHAMELESS Stella Black	ISBN 0 352 33485 1	£5.99
☐ INTENSE BLUE Lyn Wood	ISBN 0 352 34496 7	£5.99
☐ THE NAKED TRUTH Natasha Rostova	ISBN 0 352 34497 5	£5.99
☐ ANIMAL PASSIONS Martine Marquand	ISBN 0 352 34499 1	£5.99
☐ A SPORTING CHANCE Susie Raymond	ISBN 0 352 33501 7	£5.99
☐ TAKING LIBERTIES Susie Raymond	ISBN 0 352 33357 X	£5.99
☐ A SCANDALOUS AFFAIR Holly Graham	ISBN 0 352 33523 8	£5.99
☐ THE NAKED FLAME Crystalle Valentino	ISBN 0 352 33528 9	£5.99
☐ ON THE EDGE Laura Hamilton	ISBN 0 352 33534 3	£5.99
☐ LURED BY LUST Tania Picarda	ISBN 0 352 33533 5	£5.99
☐ THE HOTTEST PLACE Tabitha Flyte	ISBN 0 352 33536 X	£5.99
☐ THE NINETY DAYS OF GENEVIEVE Lucinda Carrington	ISBN 0 352 33070 8	£5.99
☐ EARTHY DELIGHTS Tesni Morgan	ISBN 0 352 33548 3	£5.99
☐ MAN HUNT Cathleen Ross	ISBN 0 352 33583 1	
☐ MÉNAGE Emma Holly	ISBN 0 352 33231 X	
☐ DREAMING SPIRES Juliet Hastings	ISBN 0 352 33584 X	
☐ THE TRANSFORMATION Natasha Rostova	ISBN 0 352 33311 1	
☐ STELLA DOES HOLLYWOOD Stella Black	ISBN 0 352 33588 2	
☐ SIN.NET Helena Ravenscroft	ISBN 0 352 33598 X	
☐ HOTBED Portia Da Costa	ISBN 0 352 33614 5	
☐ TWO WEEKS IN TANGIER Annabel Lee	ISBN 0 352 33599 8	
☐ HIGHLAND FLING Jane Justine	ISBN 0 352 33616 1	
☐ PLAYING HARD Tina Troy	ISBN 0 352 33617 X	
☐ SYMPHONY X Jasmine Stone	ISBN 0 352 33629 3	

Please send me the books I have ticked above.

Name ....

Address ....

....

....

....

Post Code ....

Send to: Cash Sales, Black Lace Books, Thames Wharf Studios, Rainville Road, London W6 9HA.

US customers: for prices and details of how to order books for delivery by mail, call 1-800-343-4499.

Please enclose a cheque or postal order, made payable to Virgin Books Ltd, to the value of the books you have ordered plus postage and packing costs as follows:

UK and BFPO – £1.00 for the first book, 50p for each subsequent book.

Overseas (including Republic of Ireland) – £2.00 for the first book, £1.00 for each subsequent book.

If you would prefer to pay by VISA, ACCESS/MASTERCARD, DINERS CLUB, AMEX or SWITCH, please write your card number and expiry date here:

....

Signature ....

Please allow up to 28 days for delivery.